MW01707889

Tommy's Farm

# Tommy's Farm

## A NOVEL

BY DOUGLAS ORD

THE MERCURY PRESS

The publisher gratefully acknowledges the financial assistance of the Canada Council for the Arts and the Ontario Arts Council, and further acknowledges the financial support of the Government of Canada through the Book Publishing Industry Development Program for our publishing activities.

ACKNOWLEDGEMENT
The author thanks the Ontario Arts Council for a Works-in-Progress grant that assisted the completion of this novel.

Cover design by Gordon Robertson
Composition and page design by TASK
Printed and bound in Canada
Printed on acid-free paper

1 2 3 4 5 02 01 00 99 98

Canadian Cataloguing in Publication Data
Ord, Douglas, 1950-
Tommy's farm : a novel

ISBN 1-55128-061-2
I. Title.
PS8579.R386T65 1998 C813'.54 C98-932199-1
PR9199.3.O64T65 1998

The Mercury Press
Toronto, Canada M6P 2A7

# BROAD, WISE AND CAVILLING

## Barristers & Solicitors

Internal Memo
Re: File #37322

Jim—

If ever we've had a springboard from which to launch an insanity plea here it is. The guy has apparently been writing non-stop since remand, and is now completely convinced that he has "justified himself."

To make the obvious point: whatever thin gruel of argument is in this so-called "defense" we're going to have to develop ourselves. And just as obviously, we can't count at all on its representation of fact. But my own opinion is that the whole thing should go in as an exhibit. Especially if we can wangle a judge with a warped sense of humour.

Let me know what you think.

Chuck.

PS. Don't forget about Thursday's golf game.

PPS. Read any "Authoritative Hippie Books" lately?

Duty! Thou sublime and mighty name that dost embrace nothing charming or insinuating but requirest submission.

— Immanuel Kant, *Critique of Practical Reason*

The best I can make of the matter is this, replied Socrates. These Ideas exist in nature as fixed patterns. The other things are made in their image and are Imitations.

— Plato, *Parmenides*

## §1

Tommy and I were friends at university. Or we were sort of friends. We were in the same philosophy classes. And sometimes, after one class was over, we would walk together to the next one. Tommy would usually want to talk about Kant. I never could figure out why. But I didn't have anybody else to talk to in between my philosophy classes, or for that matter afterwards either. So I would let Tommy talk to me. About Kant.

But there were also certain occasions when Tommy came to class in what he called "an expanded mood." I didn't know then what he meant by this. But on such occasions, he did not so much talk about Kant as he walked beside me, as about his plans. For it was really his goal, he would say in this "expanded mood," to buy a farm with certain people who lived with him in a house off campus. He referred to this house, which he said was always "full of folks," as his "commune." And he referred to these "folks," of which the "commune" was always full, as "Hippies." "We're Hippies, man," he would say. And occasionally I would see him with them, these fellow Hippies, chasing a coloured disc called a frisbee. They wore brightly coloured T-shirts, that Tommy said were "tie-dyed." They wore blue jeans with patches, and work-boots that always seemed to look brand new. Some of them, including Tommy, wore glasses with wire rims. And all of them, male and female both, had hair that fell below their shoulders and streamed behind them. As they chased the frisbee.

What any of this had to do with Kant, and with categorical imperatives, and with transcendental amphibolies, and with dialectical antinomies, and with all the things that Tommy talked about when he was not in his "expanded mood," I was not quite sure. But I never mentioned this lest I offend him. I didn't want to offend him, because really I admired him, and his living in a commune full of Hippies, and his plan to move this commune to a farm. For these were things that, secretly, I would have liked to do as well. But in fact, I didn't even tell Tommy how much I admired him, in case he wonder whether I was trying through flattery to join his commune. And I certainly didn't tell him that I also admired...one other thing.

This was his girl friend. All of these events took place in the days before— in Imitation of a True Philosopher, such as Socrates— I had mastered my baser impulses in regard to girls. And women. Before that is I had resolved to give them up— girls, women, and impulses all alike— as unbefitting this vocation. But this being said...Tommy did have a beautiful girl friend. She had long blonde hair that cascaded like a shimmering waterfall down her back and below her waist. And she had a face that reminded me always, when I saw her in the distance, of the painting by Botticelli, the one of Venus on the oyster shell rising out of the ocean. Except I always saw her with her clothes on, the blue jeans and workboots and that sort of thing. So I can't say whether she might have looked like the Venus on the oyster shell in other ways too. Tommy might have known about this but I didn't ask him. Instead I just admired her. Though from a distance, because I was never introduced to her directly. By Tommy.

After I graduated, I didn't see Tommy again for many years. I got a job shelving books in a bookstore, because I believed that in the spirit of a true philosopher I should go forth into the world. Like Socrates. And this was the livelihood that my Degree in Philosophy entitled me to pursue. I also— with my parents' encouragement— got a room in a rooming house, that had a common kitchen. This allowed me to pretend that I too was living in a Commune. Even though I wasn't. And even though I mostly ate dinner— and lunch and breakfast— in company only with the dialogues of Socrates and his friends, as recorded by Plato. Which dialogues, however— besides offering better conversation than anyone I could think of— gave me endless opportunities to reflect on the meaning of my Vocation. And of what I came to consider its Core. Namely: the Theory of Transcendent and Eternal Ideas, and of their imperfect Imitation by the things of this world. As presented by Socrates.

But I had also never forgotten Tommy's plan. I even discovered, in the bookstore one day, a whole bin full of authoritative books on Hippies. Some of these had even been produced, I learned when I looked at them, in the very cities which stood in relation to the Origin of Hippies as Athens itself stood in relation to the Origin of Philosophy. And they had, for reasons beyond my comprehension, been remaindered. So they were very cheap. I bought as many as I could afford and read them at night, alongside Socrates. It was in this way, through careful study and comparison, that I learned a great deal more about Hippies. And in doing so arrived at two conclusions. The first was that if there can exist Ideas not only of perfect Justice and Friendship and Courage, but even of a perfect Couch — as Socrates claimed in the *Republic*— then surely there had to exist an Idea of something as important as Hippieness. And the second was that given their place of origin, the Authoritative Hippie Books, with their full-colour photographs and descriptions of Communes and Hippies, must point toward Knowledge of this. As well as of such Ideas as those of a Hippie Farm, and a Hippie Girl. Yet I was sure that such descriptions could be but pointers. Because somewhere, in a location unknown to me, the Truest of all True Imitations of the Idea of a Hippie Farm, and of a Hippie Girl, had their existence. As Tommy's Farm. And Tommy's Girl Friend. And it was these that I longed to see.

Then one afternoon, when I was standing on the little ladder in the bookstore and shelving books, I happened to look up toward the door. And there was Tommy, beside the magazine rack. I was so surprised I almost fell off the ladder. But luckily I grabbed hold of a row of books that were already shelved, so only a few books fell. I descended the ladder. Usually I am not so hasty in my dealings with people. But I didn't want to miss Tommy. Because at any moment he might turn, and slip out the door, and be gone again.

As I made my way toward him, I could see that his appearance had greatly changed. His hair was even longer than it had been in university. And he was wearing it in what I believe is called— for girls— a "pony-tail." He had also grown a little beard on his chin and upper lip. This seemed to stick out in all directions, and made him look— though not unflatteringly— like a goat. He was wearing a pair of old green overalls that were faded and dirty, and a pair of rubber boots that were streaked with mud. On his head was a cap, the kind that train engineers used to wear, with blue and white stripes that were also faded. But he was still wearing what looked to be the same little wire-rimmed glasses. When I got to him, he seemed to be staring at the magazine rack, and was pulling on his beard. Slowly. He still hadn't noticed me. But how could I fail to conclude, from these changes both in costume and facial hair, that he had indeed realized his goal, and was living on what I was sure could only be the Truest of all True Imitations, of the Idea of a Hippie Farm?

"Tommy?" I said at last, and after I'd been standing nearby him for at least a minute, marvelling, while he continued to examine the magazine rack. I didn't want to interrupt his concentration, and I'm certainly not so aggressive on most occasions. But I was getting concerned that Mr. Papadiguano, who owned the bookstore, might notice, and wonder what I was doing beside the magazine rack.

When Tommy turned and looked at me though, it was as if I had startled him, and his eyes behind the wire-rimmed glasses didn't see me. Then there was another moment during which they focused on me, but clearly didn't recognize me. Then at last...a change of expression crossed his face, and as the saying goes "ignited his eyeballs."

"Oh hi, man," Tommy said, with the sort of understatement that, from my reading, I'd learned was typical of Imitations of the Idea of Hippies when they moved to the country. "Long time no see. What are you doing here?"

"I work here," I answered, with perhaps just a jot of pride. Because while I didn't live on an Imitation of the Idea of a Hippie Farm, at least I worked in the store, among bins of Authoritative Hippie Books. Sometimes. But then I couldn't restrain myself, probably because I'd thought so often of asking him this question. "How is your Farm?" I said. "Did you go there with your fellow Hippies?" I had already concluded that he must have. But I didn't want to be rude. And neither— out of respect for his interest in Kant— did I want to remind him that his Farm, however True an Imitation, could never be The Farm itself, in its Transcendent Idea.

But Tommy didn't answer me right away. Instead, after a little pause, he just said, "Oh yeah, man. It's okay."

This clearly was more understatement. Nevertheless I was taken aback, that he wasn't more excited. But I didn't want to be rude about this either. "Are you still living there?" I asked instead.

"Yeah, man," he said. After another pause. "I still live there."

This was all getting confusing, in spite of what I had read about Hippie Understatement. I wanted to ask him more. But he was so unexcited that I was afraid to, lest he make excuses and take his leave, as people often do. Except there was also the likelihood he would make his excuses and take his leave anyway, whether I asked about the Farm or not. This seemed especially likely since he had not yet mentioned Kant. Which was the only other subject we had ever considered together.

I therefore made a great decision. And out of sheer Intuition, as Socrates would call it.

"I'd so like to see it," I said. "Is such a place not blissful?"

I had never spoken to Tommy with such forthrightness before. But I must commend myself that on this occasion, my Intuition was right. For at this very moment, Tommy began to look at me differently. He pulled on his beard again. And his eyes seemed to screw up a little, as though he were considering something. Then he said, as though it were the most natural thing in the world: "Yeah, well I'm driving back up tomorrow morning. If you want to come then."

Such Understatement! But for me this offer came as such a surprise, I reeled slightly backward. Fortunately I wasn't standing on the little ladder any longer. And so did not fall down. But Tommy had never, in the entire time we were in school together, even invited me to visit his commune. Or for that matter introduced me to his girl friend. And here he was, inviting me to visit his Farm. But I knew I'd have to make an arrangement with Mr. Papadiguano, because I was supposed to work the next two days. Then I had three days off.

"If I can make an arrangement with Mr. Papadiguano," I answered quickly before Tommy could change his mind, "I'd love to come." But then I remembered, even as I was turning to look for Mr. Papadiguano, that Tommy would be returning to the Farm to stay. While I would have to get back to the city. "But how will I get back?" I said. I was suddenly afraid that, as usual, I wasn't going to go anywhere. And would just spend the next two days in the bookstore.

"There's a bus route a couple of miles away," Tommy said. "I can drive you there. If you've got the fare."

I was so relieved. Quickly I rushed away in search of Mr. Papadiguano. Who proved to be in the office behind the bookshelves, and so had not seen me talking to Tommy. Or the pile of books that still lay around the little ladder. And looking out from beneath his bushy eyebrows, he was even more agreeable than I had hoped, perhaps because he knew about my passion for Hippie Books. I was able therefore to return to Tommy with his assent. As well as my own.

"How about the subway down the street tomorrow then, man," Tommy said. "About noon."

He had, I noticed, moved away in my absence from the magazine rack, and gone to the philosophy section. I thought that this too boded well for our renewed acquaintance.

Then, when I had agreed, he simply said, "Great to see you, man," and turned around, and was gone. So quickly that I had, when I went back to my ladder to pick up the books, to wonder whether any of this had really happened.

## §2

Tommy picked me up at noon outside the subway station. I'd been so excited the entire night I had hardly slept. Because at last I was going to visit an earthly Imitation of the Idea of a Hippie Farm. With its Imitations of the Ideas of Animals, and of Hippies, and of who could tell what else. But I admit I had also been thinking, a little during the night perhaps, that there might even be an Imitation of the Idea of a Hippie Girl for me too. Not as Beautiful or as True a one as Tommy's girl friend, maybe. But approximate. With long wavy hair. And a nice complexion. Such as were displayed by the girls in the photographs, in the Authoritative Hippie Books. I've since learned my lesson, that in Imitating the Idea of a Philosopher I should not permit such thoughts, not even let them enter my Mind. But at that time I couldn't help it.

Tommy arrived at the curbside in an old blue pick-up truck. When I went to the window to greet him, I could see that he was still wearing the overalls, the rubber boots, and the faded train engineer's cap. The window was rolled up, but he gestured toward the back. This confused me. Did he mean for me to sit there? But then he leaned across the seat and opened the door.

"Just put your bag in the back, man," he said. "There's not enough room up here."

So many lessons. And all at once too. I realized, as I walked around the truck, that I should myself have invested in a pair of dirty old overalls and some rubber boots and a faded train engineer's cap the night before. But instead I had idled away the precious hours, with dreams of

Approximations. Which meant I was wearing, instead of practical Hippie dress as revealed by Tommy...the bright yellow ski jacket that my parents had given me for Christmas. Yet where would I have found overalls so dirty or a cap so faded, except at the Salvation Army? And only then in the shredded rag box near the door. So I might have arrived wearing a work suit that was not just faded but shredded too. A fine sight! Especially when it might have occurred to Tommy that I was aspiring through appearance to Imitate more Truly the Idea of a Hippie than he did. And what would have been the point of starting the trip off this way?

Having decisively resolved this problem though, I still felt a slight embarrassment as I leaned into the back of the truck, and saw that it contained...garbage bags. Or, as Socrates might have put it: Imitations of the Idea of Garbage Bags. These were green and made of plastic, and there were four of them, not quite full. Around them lay wood chips and bits of hay. Imitations of the Idea of Country Things, the first that I had seen. I felt a quiver of excitement. Yet this was muted. For the bags did *not* Imitate the Idea of Country Things. This was because, though they were green, they were made of plastic. They must, I realized, be Imitating the Idea of Hippie Things, because Tommy was using them. I experienced Perplexity, as Socrates would put it. For if the Imitations of the Idea of Garbage Bags were being used as Imitations of the Idea of Hippie Things...then it seemed clear there must be a sense in which these— and who could tell what else?— might Imitate the Idea of a Hippie Thing, without Imitating the Idea of a Country Thing.

This was an insight worthy of Socrates. Yet I also felt some logical inadequacy, in the presence of such spectacular semantic juggling by Tommy. For I had simply arrived with my suitcase, which I'd been given by my parents for graduating. It should have been an Imitation of the Idea of a Garbage Bag, I saw this instantly. And this was even a problem I could have done something about, because the kitchen of the rooming house contained such Imitations. I could have taken one had I only known. But I hadn't known. So I was stuck with my suitcase, which was obviously most unlike the Idea of a Hippie Means of Storage.

I should, I appreciated as I set my suitcase beside the Imitations of the Idea of Garbage Bags, have given greater thought to this. But even as I resolved in future to be more conscientious, I was interrupted. By Tommy's voice.

"Hey man," it said, from— I assumed— inside the truck.

I looked up. His head was sticking out the window.

"If we sit here, man, we're going to get a ticket," he said. "Come on."

This meant I had to leave my meditation. But as I rushed to the door, I realized also that we were about to get underway, toward what would undoubtedly prove to be the Truest of all True Imitations of the Idea of a Hippie Farm. And this was remarkable.

"I'm ready," I shouted as I got into the truck and slammed the door.

"Great," Tommy answered. The truck chugged a little, and then moved away from the sidewalk into traffic.

We were on our way.

Once settled into my seat belt though, I experienced a problem. This was not new for me, in that it often concerned me as I stood on the little ladder— or on an Imitation of the Idea of a Little Ladder— shelving whatever they were. This time it was triggered by that business of the garbage bags. Or rather the Imitations of the Idea of Garbage Bags. Which is to say: if it was not simply a Hippie Farm that I was considering in terms of its being an Imitation of the Idea Thereof, and not only a Philosopher, or Hippieness, or even a Hippie Girl, but Garbage Bags too...then where would it stop? Was I, for example, at that moment sitting in an Imitation of the Idea of a Pick-up Truck? Looking through an Imitation of the Idea of a Windshield? At many Imitations of the Idea of Cars? Regarding which there was, at every instant, the danger of an Imitation of the Idea of a Collision? This was,

I Recollected, a problem which had challenged even Socrates. Only he had been asked by Parmenides whether there exist Ideas of Dirt, Mud, and Hair, of which physical dirt, mud, and hair are but Imitations. And what had Socrates answered? Why this had stumped him! He had experienced Insoluble Perplexity!

And here I was, experiencing this same Perplexity. But in regard to Garbage Bags! And Pick-up Trucks. And Cars. And Collisions. I experienced also, at this moment, a sense of the profound continuity, of Philosophical Tradition. As well as, I must admit, profound unease, as to the likelihood that the Imitation of the Idea of a Collision, which we might undergo at any moment, would still be painful. Or worse. What was I to make of this? Was Socrates, in his dialogue with Parmenides about dirt, mud, and hair, sitting in an Imitation of the Idea of a Pick-up Truck, hurtling through Imitations of the Idea of Traffic? He was not! He was sitting draped in his toga, with around him the Athenian marketplace, beneath a warm sun. Or beneath an Imitation of the Idea of a Warm Sun, who could tell? But certainly without the danger of Imitating the Idea of a Collision at any moment. That was certain.

But where did this leave me? I looked out the Windshield. Or out the Imitation of its Idea, this was so confusing. And what did I see? Happily, by this time, my Perplexity had been such that we, in whatever it was that Tommy was driving, were no longer in whatever sort of imitation of whatever it referred to the City was. We were, instead, hurtling past whatever it was that Suburbs were. But there were also, along the roadside, what must have been Imitations of the Idea of Trees. Yet I could not be sure. What if, as Things of Nature, they were simply trees? And if they were, what might this say about the Theory of True Ideas...and even about the nature of Transcendent Truth generally? If trees were simply trees, and not modelled each and every one after its own Idea...what might this imply also about the Idea of a Hippie Farm? Of which Tommy's was sure to be the Truest of all Imitations? What might it imply about the Idea of a Philosopher? Of which Socrates was the Truest of all Imitations?

When I was at work, these problems were resolved more simply, by Mr. Papadiguano shouting at me to renounce my Perplexity, and get back to shelving whatever they were. But I was not at work. There was no Mr. Papadiguano. There was only Tommy. Who was so clearly concentrating on avoiding Imitations of the Idea of a Collision, that I feared to interrupt him.

I had, therefore, to face the Problem myself.

But how?

My head began to spin. Or to seem to spin. Because I could not be sure as to exactly what it was that was spinning. Until, refocusing, I noticed once again...those entities outside the window. Called Trees. There now were a great deal more of them. That despite the appearance of hurtling past...I realized were anchored solidly. In the very Ground. And did the solidity of this Anchorage comfort me? It did. So much that I Recollected, in the face of the magnitude of this dilemma, the true purpose of my trip. Was I not on my way to the earthly Imitation of the Idea of a Hippie Farm? And ought not my ability to reflect on this to remain unhindered by philosophical problems of a perhaps unresolvable sort? Namely: the Imitation by *Everything*, of its own Idea? Did not both the Trees and their Anchorage provide a hint, instead, of what I was soon to see?

I observed them then with gratitude, these Trees. As their roots were anchored in the very Ground, so their branches— bare of leaves because it was November— thrust skyward, toward the Sun. Or...would have thrust skyward toward the Sun, had it been present. For it was, I suddenly noticed, obscured by clouds.

This was troubling. For I Recollected that, at the beginning of our journey, and before I had fallen into deep Perplexity as to whether there was available to my senses anything that was not an Imitation of its own Eternal Idea...there had been but few clouds, fluffy white in a deep blue sky. But such had been my meditation— in the style of Socrates, who his friends said could meditate for days without noticing anything— that I had myself failed to notice a change of weather. If this was what it was, and not merely an Imitation of the Idea of Weather. But then I recalled also that I had resolved to set this problem aside, until the time when— as such problems do for any philosopher— it thrust itself upon me again, so I could not resist it.

But this had not yet happened. I was then, I determined provisionally, dealing simply with Weather. And, as a subset of this Weather, with Cold Air. That I noticed now was swirling round my legs. And that was colder than it had been at the beginning of our trip. I shivered. Noticing also as I did that not only was the sky less blue than it had been when we started, and the clouds less white. They were instead getting greyer. And larger. And darker grey. Soon they filled the sky. Then it started to rain. Small drops, then larger drops, then a veritable sheet of water lashing the windshield. Through the window I watched the Trees along the road turn black. And glistening.

Beside me, Tommy responded to these changes with certain gestures. These I noticed as I watched the windshield fill with water. First he pulled a whitish knob on the dashboard. Gusts of hot air as well as cold swirled around my legs. Then, as the rain got heavy, he pulled another knob, beside the first one.

"Sorry about the windshield wiper, man," he said. "But the one on your side doesn't work."

I watched the windshield, whose translucent screen lay before my eyes. He was right. The wiper on my side remained inert. Even as the one on his side went into unflagging motion, clearing away the water. But this meant that once the rain got heavy, I could no longer see anything. Except water. This formed ceaselessly changing patterns, in shades of grey. Such was the intensity of the rain that soon even the window beside me— through which I had been able to watch the Trees— was being lashed criss-cross with streaks of water.

Thus then were the Trees too, even as I had resolved that they might be other than Imitations of their own Idea...blurred insofar as my own senses were concerned. A just rebuke! For would Socrates himself not have reminded me that here was an excellent metaphor, concerning the distortion wrought by the senses on the understanding of True Ideas? Even though, in this case, the distortion was possibly being wrought by an Imitation Windshield, with Imitation Water on it. But I was not deterred. For what else could I expect, from senses that necessarily distort the Truth of Ideas? Was the Imitation Windshield blurred with rain in this case not like the eyes themselves? Which give but a distorted impression to the brain cells inside the head? Assuming, of course, that there are such "things" as "brain cells." Inside the head. Really?

It was upon this important epistemological question that I was dwelling, when suddenly I was interrupted, yet another time, by Tommy's voice.

## §3

"Hey man," said the voice behind me.

I turned around.

"Do you think you could reach behind the seat there and pull out my coat?" Tommy said. "It's none too warm in here."

There had not been much conversation between us hitherto. This being because i) I had assumed he had to concentrate on avoiding collisions, or Imitations of the Idea Thereof. And ii), I did not want to violate any rules, concerning Hippie Understatement. And iii), I had enough to think about anyway. Nevertheless, I could not ignore this request. I therefore unhooked my seat belt, which for the sake of these proceedings I resolved to view *as* a seat belt. Behind the seat there was indeed a crumpled old canvas coat. This I extracted amid clouds of dust.

I brushed the coat off with my hand. It was pale green— the coat, I mean— with many rips and patches.

"I found that in the garbage," Tommy said, as I gave him the coat, "the year I worked as a garbageman after I got my philosophy degree."

There seemed a note of pride in his voice. Such as I had heard in my own, when I had told him I worked in the store.

"I was not aware you worked as a garbageman, Tommy," I said. This was the first real exchange of words since I got into the truck. But Tommy had, by this time, been driving long enough without disaster befalling us, as to suggest he might be able to talk at the same time. I sensed, therefore, that I might be in the presence of an opportunity. To converse at length with him, for the first time in years.

"Sure did," Tommy said, in such a way as to imply that he too might be ready for some good conversation. But first he had to put on the coat. He pulled it behind him, took a hand off the steering wheel, and thrust his entire arm into the sleeve. The truck veered left. My lower abdomen veered toward the floor. Then, when Tommy had got the first hand through, he put it back on the steering wheel, and went through the same sort of business again, with his other hand, in the other sleeve. But with the coat pulled across his back. He jerked around. The truck veered right. I heard the crunch of gravel underneath the tires. This was completely terrifying...until Tommy got both his hands back on the wheel, and the truck stopped veering.

By this time I was almost breathless.

Yet for all this breathlessness, still I did not want to lose the thread of conversation. Such as it had been. For these words held the potential for the first real exchange of views with Tommy since university. Even though they had been about being a garbageman. Still, I decided as I tightened my seat belt, this was certainly an improvement on Kant. So as soon as my heart rate settled down, I made up my mind. I would try to keep it going— the conversation, I mean— on this very subject of being a garbageman. Which was the only one that had arisen spontaneously between us. So far.

I knew, of course, that had Socrates been there, he would have found a way already, of turning even this humble beginning into an investigation of something important. Like Virtue. This was a hint of how far I had to go, toward adequately Imitating the Idea of a Philosopher, that I hadn't figured out how to do this. Still, I Intuited that, like Socrates, I now had before me a chance to make something lasting, a Dialogue even, out of mere conversation, that might have faded into oblivion otherwise. This made me eager. And all for the better too. For clearly if I mused too long, trying to figure out an angle by which we could make discoveries about Virtue, by talking about being a garbageman...I would probably lose the chance to talk about anything. This was because Tommy would have forgotten there had been a conversation of any kind, to begin with.

"What was it like to be a garbageman, Tommy?" I therefore asked. These were the first words that occurred to me. But they seemed to offer a good start. And just so he would know I was interested, I added: "I've always wondered what it was like to be a garbageman." This was an outright lie. But a strategic one. For I had at that point never wondered what it would be like to be a garbageman. The thought of picking up other people's garbage had always disgusted me. Yet I knew that I had better keep an open mind. Socrates would have. And at that moment I could almost feel his presence, inspiring me. Besides, I was now sure— Intuitively speaking— that picking up garbage could not be completely disgusting, because Tommy had done it. And what was more, he was wearing a cast-off coat, which he had kept instead of letting go to waste. This seemed to be a sign of great inner strength. And maybe— I realized in a kind of flash— of Virtue.

"Oh, it's okay," Tommy was saying meanwhile, even as I was realizing how this very exchange might be transformed into lasting

Dialogue, philosophically speaking. "You find a lot of interesting things in the garbage. It's amazing what people throw out. I used to come back to the depot with all kinds of stuff strapped to the truck. In fact, eventually they took me off garbage duty and put me on ditches. Because I brought so much stuff back on the truck."

I listened to this with great amazement. Not least because it was the longest speech I'd heard from Tommy in years. And what was more, it was not about Kant. Most of the speeches I had ever heard Tommy make had been about Kant, or— when he had been in his "expanded mood"— about his plan to buy a farm. But we were now on our way to the very Farm which the plan had become, and I did not want to spoil the surprise. And I certainly did not want to talk about Kant. Instead, I sensed I might now be on the verge of making some great discoveries myself, philosophically, concerning Virtue. So I could not let my being impressed with this speech deter me from my real objective.

"What did you do with the stuff you found?" I therefore asked, leaning toward him to obtain the best angle possible on where to go with my questioning. But I was getting a sense of its logic. Obviously, it was not the Idea of picking up other people's garbage that was disgusting, as I had thought. It was instead the State of Affairs that so much garbage was put to begin with beside the road. This had now been established, by Tommy himself, through Experience. Which had to carry more weight, in terms of Knowledge, than did my own initial Opinion or Doxa, as Socrates had put it. But the highest form of knowledge, or Gnosis, according to Socrates, was also Intuition. And wasn't my own Intuition telling me that this Knowledge derived by Tommy from Experience was accurate? That my opinion had given me a false Idea? And— most important of all — that this was a truly Virtuous Hippie Sentiment that he had expressed?

"Oh, Allie and I took it to a flea market," Tommy said meanwhile, as I was undergoing this truly philosophical Rapture of Discovery, almost. "We managed to sell a bit of it. Then we gave the rest to the Salvation Army."

Under ordinary circumstances, this mere mention of the "Salvation Army" might have served to confirm, as metaphor, the intensity of the experience I was undergoing, regarding the profound intrinsic Virtue in Hippie terms, of collecting garbage. Yet it did not. Why not? Because in the same group of phrases in which the proper name "Salvation Army" appeared, there also appeared— and I shudder to say this, given the outcome— another proper name. "Allie." The name of Tommy's girl friend. For this was the first time since I'd met him the previous day, and therefore the first time in years, that Tommy had mentioned her to me.

And the shame of it all! For I admit that when he did so, it was almost as if the Dialogue about the garbage— which was really starting to get off the ground— did not exist. Hadn't even begun. My realizations concerning Hippie Virtue became all scrambled. I even forgot about the Salvation Army. Instead, I felt a kind of tingle, that travelled up and down my spine like in some sort of animal experiment.

Socrates would have been ashamed of me.

But I couldn't help this. Or stop it once it had begun. The autonomic reactions of the body, which take place so far below the realm of Ideas, themselves make for such perplexity! Not to mention distraction. For suddenly, I seemed even to see her face. With the big blue eyes. And the full red mouth. And the little nose. All framed with that tumbling mass of golden hair. It was as though I had last seen her yesterday, so clear was the picture. Though slightly shrunken, on account of the distance from which I had always viewed her. But for a moment I even went limp, the bodily part of me I mean, just Recollecting. And also realizing that in a few hours time, I would see her up close. And maybe talk to her. Because Tommy would certainly have to introduce me to her at last. And hovering in the background too, of this Recollection...was the painting by Botticelli. Of the Venus on the oyster shell. I couldn't help this either. It was simply there.

How quickly then, how completely, my truly philosophical rapture concerning the Virtues of collecting garbage, had surrendered to this...potential rapture...of a carnal kind. Which required for its initiation not even the actual presence of a woman, but her mental image. A shrunken mental image too, based on two Recollections. Of a girl, on the one hand. And of a painting, on the other. Is it any wonder that Socrates took such care, almost always, to keep his Dialogues strictly masculine? In order that True Logic might prevail?

Yet this indignation, which I experienced mentally even as I was undergoing limpness physically, was useless, in helping me to recover my philosophical line of questioning. And there was more! For even as the tingles and the limpness were suffusing my body, and the images a certain lower part of my mind...I realized also that I could not let Tommy notice that this mention by him of his girl friend had so affected me. For he then might think I was taking an untoward interest and perhaps get jealous, in such a way as to jeopardize our *bonhomie*, such as it was. So I had, by whatever means, to maintain at least the sham of a Dialogue on an exalted level, in regard to the garbage. Socrates would certainly have been ashamed of this. But it was clear that, at this very moment, my friendship with Tommy might be on the verge of foundering. And because of a woman!

"Well, I think it's wonderful that you did all those things with the garbage," I therefore said, with emphasis. That was perhaps the product of my desperation. But I could by no means let Tommy get the idea that I had been thinking about other things. As I had been. This meant, however, that I had also to jettison any gradual lead-up, to a truly philosophical conclusion, such as Socrates might have provided. Because was there not the possibility that I might make some sort of slip, which would give away...what had really come into my mind? As soon as he had mentioned his girl friend? And this would be disastrous.

"If more people acted like you at such times," I therefore continued, with determination, "then the world would certainly be a MUCH MORE VIRTUOUS PLACE." I put great emphasis on these final words, shouting them almost, so that Tommy might infer they were the outcome of a complex process of reasoning. Even though, at that moment, I could no longer trust my mouth to disclose this methodically, in each of its careful steps.

Tommy looked at me sideways. It seemed as though he were scrutinizing me. I felt an urge to flee, even though I knew I couldn't. But from the look in his eyes, I could see as well, with a terrible sinking feeling, that he must have detected in my voice...that what I really had wanted to ask him about...was his girl friend.

"I mean it, Tommy," I therefore said. With even greater desperation. But by way of reassurance. "I think it's virtuous what you did with the garbage. VIRTUOUS. Really."

There was a pause. I was starting to panic. It occurred to me that he might even stop the truck, right then and there, and order me to get out. I glanced toward the window. Streaks of rain lashed the glass. I shivered.

But then Tommy said, "Yeah, man. I'm sure you do."

I looked away from the window, and back at him. But he had shifted his eyes to the road again.

After that we didn't talk. This I regretted. And for many reasons. There we had been, enjoying a philosophical Dialogue, concerning the Virtues of garbage. And of its collection. This was something that even Socrates had not considered. For the closest he ever got was that question of dirt, mud, and hair. And even then, he wasn't considering their potential, or rather the potential of their collection, as Virtues. But whether they existed at all. As Ideas. Of which perceived dirt, mud, and hair might be Imitations. So I could have been on the verge of a great discovery, philosophically speaking. And maybe— if I had had a chance to get the logic sorted out through Dialogue— a breakthrough even.

Though into what I didn't know. Nor would I probably ever know. Because the momentum had been interrupted. And on account of a woman. Because I was sure that by this time, Tommy's girl friend must be a woman. Of course...I had to wonder what she looked like now, as a woman I mean, and not as a girl...

But I did not allow an Image to form. For obvious reasons. Instead I sat up, and tried to keep my mind on Ideas. Which as Socrates said are always of more redeeming value than Images anyway. And neither could I afford to harbour ill-feelings concerning the failure of our Dialogue, that had perhaps robbed me of my place in philosophical history. For there would be other chances, for other Dialogues. I had a full two days at the Farm, with Tommy. As well as with the other Imitations of the Idea of Hippies. And who could tell what possibilities there might be?

But first I would have to get there, without being ordered by Tommy to leave the truck in the rain, on account of his jealousy. This gave me all the more reason to sit up straight. But as I did, I could not help but hear Tommy's words all over again. "Yeah, man. I'm sure you do." They seemed to echo, inside my Mind. They were so ambiguous. Were they sarcastic? I wasn't sure. They had almost sounded sarcastic. Which probably meant that, while he certainly wasn't going to come right out and say it, he knew, or at least suspected, that I hadn't wanted to ask him about the garbage really, but about his girl friend. Did he even suspect me of seeing her face, inside my Mind? I wasn't sure how he could suspect me of this. But I also knew that if he did, he could suspect me of seeing more than her face, the painting by Botticelli for instance too.

I fear the very thought of this made me tingle again. And go slightly limp.

Did he notice? I looked at him. He was still looking out the windshield. But had his expression changed? I wasn't sure. Would it be possible for me to ask him? How could I? Tommy, I wanted to say, are you still angry? Are you still thinking of stopping the truck, and telling me to get out? Are you plotting something? But how could I ask him any of these things...without giving away that I had been thinking about his girl friend after all? And so either confirm his suspicions. Or— just as bad— instil new ones, where there had not been any. For this was a possibility too, however remote. How could I know?

My heart, at this moment, began to beat violently. Was this because, by this time, the very thought of Tommy's farm, of arriving there, made me see in my mind again his girl friend's face? I felt further tingles, and overcome almost by limpness. What would I do? Not just at that moment, but when we arrived? My impulse was to grab Tommy's arm, to beseech him to forgive me for having wanted to talk about his girl friend, really, rather than about the garbage. Or Kant. Or for that matter anything else, even his farm. And not only for having wanted to talk about her, but for continuing to think about her uncontrollably once she was mentioned...

It is so understandable, now, as I remember this, why I made a resolution to give up women.

But I couldn't grab Tommy's arm. I might have caused a collision. And then where would we have been? This was a question even Socrates couldn't answer. So instead, in my desperation, I did the only thing I could do, in the absence of explanatory words, or gestures of conciliation. I moaned. I couldn't help myself. It just burst out.

Tommy turned and looked at me, or rather down at me, because I wasn't sitting upright any more, as had been my goal. I was instead curled around my seat belt.

"What's the matter, man?" Tommy said. "Are you sick?"

Now I really didn't know what to say. Even more than I hadn't known before, if this was possible. But how could I tell him I had moaned out of sheer concern, that we would not be able to resolve his jealousy, about my having wanted to ask him about his girl friend? Especially when there was still a chance... But if he hadn't been jealous, then obviously my asking about it might make him... Words failed me. So that all I could think of to say, or do...was agree with him.

"Yes," I said through my teeth, which were clenched. "I'm sick."

"Carsick?" Tommy said, looking down at me and then back at the road. "You mean you're carsick?"

What could I say? What other kind of sick could I be, that would not require him to find a turn-off, and drive to a hospital at desperate speed, perhaps even having a collision— or yet another Imitation of the Idea of a Collision, I was by this time most perplexed again— along the way? Only to find out, when we got there— assuming we got there— that there was nothing wrong. With me.

"Yes," I said again. "I'm carsick."

"Oh, Jesus," Tommy said. "Hold on then." He rolled down his window, and stuck his head out. Then he pulled the truck to the side of the road. Gravel crunched again, beneath the tires. But much more decisively it seemed.

The truck stopped.

"Okay, man," Tommy said. "There you are."

I knew suddenly, as by a flash of Insight, what he expected. Therefore I also knew what I had to do. I couldn't even stop to think, as I might have liked. Instead, I threw my left hand over my mouth, and pulled away. But my seat belt held me. I fumbled with it. It came undone. I pushed on the door handle with my free hand, and on the door, with my entire body.

Except the door wouldn't open.

"Gently, man," said Tommy's voice. "Gently. This is an old truck. Just pull the handle toward you. Gently."

I pulled the handle toward me. It moved. The door opened. I tumbled out. It was pouring rain. Cold rain. I lurched across the gravel. Getting wet. I knew what I had to do. And I also knew that if I didn't do it, then Tommy would wonder not only why I had said I was sick when I wasn't, but also why I had moaned when I wasn't sick. And if he wondered why I had moaned, without being sick, then he might also begin to question my mental processes. And if he questioned my mental processes, then he might also be reminded that he had been suspecting that I had wanted to ask him about his girl friend. Even if he hadn't been. And all of this, at least, he seemed to have forgotten. In the excitement.

These syllogisms presented themselves— I might add— with crystalline clarity to me, as I was making my way to the edge of the gravel shoulder, while getting rained on. And I think this was a mental achievement of considerable scale too, on my part, this construction of so clear a chain of syllogisms, not only while I was in constant motion and getting rained on, but also while I was preparing, mentally speaking, to pretend to throw up. Because this was, ultimately, what I knew I was expected to do. And what I knew I had to do, if I was not to set in motion in Tommy's mind that same crystal-clear chain of reasoning. Which I knew would be triggered, with all the impersonal relentlessness of Pure Logic, if I did not throw up. But I also realized, even as I stopped at the edge of the gravel, beside some long brown dripping wet grass, that if I did a really good job of throwing up...then Tommy might be so impressed that any suspicion that I had been thinking of asking him about his girl friend at all would be driven from his Mind, so to speak, forever.

This was great incentive. I leaned above the grass, and grabbed my stomach. I made loud noises, disgusting noises, the most disgusting noises that I could think of. I choked. I retched. I moaned. I coughed. I did all of these things, of course, mostly with an awareness of how they would sound to Tommy, in the truck. And also of how they would look. I wracked my chest. I wove back and forth, as though in agony. I made it sound, and even look from behind, I hoped, that my whole insides were coming up on that soggy grass, and not just the contents of my stomach. So vigourous were these exertions, that I even had to lean forward and put my hands on my knees. Lest I collapse. My back heaved. I spat globs of drool. My nose ran. Tears filled my eyes.

But then I realized, as I hunched there panting...that I had better stop. For what if I looked from behind as though I really were about to collapse? Then would not Tommy himself— with his truly Kantian sense of Duty— rush from the truck, to support me? This would be disastrous. Because then he would notice, even as he helped me up...that the only thing dripping from the grass...was water. This sobered me. I also realized, as I was leaning forward in the rain with my hands on my knees, that perhaps I had even been overacting. And that acting— according to Socrates— is not the business of a philosopher anyway. I felt ashamed. That once again, in the course of this trip which was less than three hours old, I had proved unworthy of Socrates. I stood up, and cleared my throat, the better to recover my dignity. I adjusted my coat. Then— unsteadily— I turned around.

I admit that I expected to see Tommy just behind me. Or at least stumbling across the gravel from the truck, to help me. But he wasn't. Instead the door to the truck, the door I had gotten out...was closed. This meant that Tommy himself had closed it. And it also meant that, probably, he hadn't heard me. Had he seen me? I felt a pang. Had my performance, then, been in vain? Might he still be slouched in the truck, suspecting me? But perhaps, I reasoned, as I walked slowly toward it in the pouring rain, it had all been too much for him. Perhaps, in spite of appearances, he had a weak stomach too, as I was supposed to have, and had been so upset by the sight and the sound of me...that he had had to close the door and look away. This possibility heartened me. Because if true, then it would certainly mean that with his own stomach starting to churn, Tommy would not be wasting energy still worrying about whether I had been thinking of asking him about his girl friend.

It was with some relief, then— as well as expectation— that I opened the truck door gently on my side. Tommy was leaning against the other door, with his head on his hand. He was looking toward me. His eyes behind the wire-rimmed glasses seemed tired.

"Feel better now?" he said.

"Yes," I said as I got in. "Thank you."

"Maybe you should brush your coat off outside, man," Tommy said, pushing himself away from the door. "It's soaking wet."

I looked at my ski jacket. He was right. But also, I realized, my hair was wet, and my trousers.

"Oh," I said. This was all that I could think of to say. I had expected more empathy, on Tommy's part. I felt a sinking feeling in my stomach, which was supposed to be empty. Had Tommy not been feeling sick, then, at all, from watching me pretend to be sick? Had he instead closed the door to keep the seat from getting wet?

"Oh," I said again. I was disappointed. Not only in Tommy. But in everything.

"Well, never mind if you don't want to bother," Tommy said. "I just figured you might dry out more quickly if you brushed it off." He leaned forward, and turned the key. The truck engine sputtered, then started again. "But then," he said, as he revved the engine until it was running smoothly, "if you went back outside, you'd just get wetter. Wouldn't you."

I realized, when he said this, that he hadn't been worried about the inside of the truck at all. He had been concerned about my health. This was excellent news. For did it not mean that he had ceased to suspect me? That my strategy had been a success? After all?

"Oh, no," I said quickly. "I'll just go back outside again and brush it off. I won't get wet." And with that, I opened the door again and leapt from the truck. Just to prove I understood his concern. And also out of sheer exhilaration at my achievement. Vigourously, I brushed water from the arms of my ski jacket, and from its front, and even from my hair. Even as all three were getting rained on again. The rain was cold. I shivered.

"Hey man," said Tommy's voice behind me. "Why don't you get back in? You'll catch pneumonia."

I brushed my sleeves a few more times, just so he would be absolutely clear that I appreciated his sentiments. Then I got back inside. My hands were freezing. So was the top of my head. I slammed the door.

"I'll try and turn up the heater," said Tommy. "To get you warm." He leaned forward and first pulled on, then jiggled, the knob on the dashboard. "How's it taste," he added. "Pretty disgusting, eh?"

For a moment, I didn't know what he meant. But then I remembered. I was supposed to have been sick to my stomach outside. Violently sick to my stomach. And that of course this would leave a taste. An awful taste.

"Yech," I said, putting great emphasis on this "Yech," in order to be convincing. "Awful."

"We'll stop at the next store we come to," Tommy said, as the truck began to move, "so you can pick up some chewing gum." He lowered the window, on his side, and leaned his head out. Then he swerved the wheel to the left, and the truck was back on the road again. Accelerating.

## §4

It took me a while to get warm again, and dry. But apart from this, I was much relieved. Because since Tommy wanted me to get some gum, then he obviously was convinced I had thrown up. While his very concern suggested he had forgotten— for the time being anyway— his suspicions. In fact, the excitement had been of such intensity, that even I was no longer thinking, in a way that might justify these suspicions, about his girl friend. I also felt a little guilty, of course, that I hadn't been carsick really, and was deceiving Tommy. But all in all, I decided, as I flapped my open coat to dry it, the ruse had been worthwhile. Since our friendship might have been on the verge of foundering. On account of a woman!

"There's a store," Tommy said suddenly, after we had been driving again for a while. And I was still flapping my coat.

For a moment, I didn't know what he was talking about. But then I Recollected. The gum. I was supposed to buy gum. To rid my mouth of what was supposed to be its disgusting taste. I looked up. But neither could I see anything through my side of the windshield, apart from blurs. That they were more colourful than usual, however, led me to infer that we were not surrounded by trees any more. And that I should trust Tommy's judgment, to the effect that among these blurs there would be...a store.

Tommy turned the steering wheel to the left. There was again the crunch of gravel. The truck came to rest. I had, this time, enough sense once I had done my coat up to take my mittens out and put them on. Then I remembered also that my ski jacket had a hood. I had, therefore, to take my mittens off again, to unroll this over my head.

"Are you ready to go, man?" I heard Tommy say.

"Decisively," I said, and opened the door. As I prepared to get out, I even had the sense to look where I was going. There was a large puddle. This did not surprise me. There are often large puddles, outside of whatever door I go through. I over-leapt it. The puddle, I mean. The thrill of such daring even compensated somewhat, as I entered the rain, for the fact that the store itself was about to prove disappointing.

As a student of Socrates, I had expected, of course, a store that would Imitate as closely as possible the Idea of a Store. But specifically, after three whole hours of driving, the Idea of a Country Store. One made of weathered brick, that is. With a small, tastefully proportioned window in the front. And with the proprietor's name painted on wood hung above the door. In the window, there should have been country knick-knacks. Leather harnesses, and tonics in bottles, and that sort of thing. Which would catch our attention.

But the store I saw before me failed dismally at Imitating this Idea. It had a neon sign that said, in bright red letters, "Joe's Convenience." It had a plate-glass window, behind which there were not country knick-knacks...but bags of potato chips. And it was made not of weathered brick...but of lime green plastic siding. This was so bright as to be almost fluorescent, even in the pouring rain. The entire store looked, then, like the corner mall in my parents' suburb. But worse.

I was disappointed. I wanted to ask Tommy, as we crossed the parking lot, why he had chosen to stop the truck at such a Poor Imitation of the Idea of a Corner Mall. Why, I wanted to ask, had he not found something at least a little closer to Imitating the Idea of a Country Store? Where, besides the harnesses and knick-knacks in the window, there would have been pickles in barrels, and candies in glass jars, and other such country dainties...

But I didn't ask him. Instead, as Tommy held the plate-glass door for me and I passed inside, I Recollected. I was not visiting this store to buy a pickle or candies. But to buy gum, to rid my mouth of its disgusting taste. Supposedly. But in fact to follow through on my ruse, and so quell Tommy's suspicions. Would a True Imitation of the Idea of a Country Store even have contained any gum? Or rather an Imitation of the Idea of Gum? The situation was getting complicated again. And not only on account of the unresolved conundrum, of what imitated What. For whether such a Store would contain Gum at all— Imitation or otherwise— was something I couldn't know. But this meant that I realized also, as I looked around the store's interior— Imitation or Otherwise— that I might have come close to making a big mistake. From this I had been rescued, though without his knowing it, by Tommy. For I was sure that if I had found myself in a True Imitation of the Idea of a Country Store, among pickles in barrels and candies in jars...then I would not have been able to control myself. And would have blurted out that I wanted a pickle. Or a candy. Or at any rate something highly inappropriate to the digestive processes of someone who had just thrown up. And then Tommy might start to wonder, all over again, whether I had thrown up at all...

Upon realizing this, then, I felt a rush of thanks toward Tommy. Precisely for his having provided this store. As a hedge against the seductiveness of Country Goodies. Or the Imitations of their Idea.

And yet...the store itself was so inappropriate to its location. Did its usefulness, then, imply that there could be times— such as this very one— when the True Imitation of an Idea was not to be preferred to the False Imitation? To the Simulacrum? As Socrates said it always should be?

"There you are, man," Tommy said beside me. Even as I was experiencing both this rush of gratitude and, paradoxically, this instant of profound Perplexity. "The gum's probably over by the counter."

I realized that, by an act of Will, I would need to thrust Perplexity aside. In order to get on with the business of buying Gum. But also, first, I had to show my gratitude to Tommy, for having rescued me from the perils of a True Imitation of the Idea of a Country Store. Which might have proved disastrous, in the form of pickles and candy. And I Intuited that I could do this, without his even suspecting that I was thanking him for more than his insight into where I could find the Gum.

"Oh, thank you," I therefore said to Tommy. Managing well, I thought, to put all of the emotion I was feeling into this simple phrase. I then walked directly to the counter, opting to show by actions as well as words that I did appreciate his efforts. And Tommy was, as usual, right. There it was, the gum I mean, laid out in in different packages, of different colours. This was impressive. Nevertheless, I again experienced Perplexity, in the presence of so much Difference. For which One was best? The closest to the Idea, if not of Gum in the absolute sense, at least of Gum-Most-Appropriate-To-Cleanse-The-Breath-Of-A-Person-Who-Was-Supposed-To-Have-Just-Thrown-Up. But-Really-Hadn't.

This proved a problem. For I have never been a chewer of gum. Yet I knew that under the circumstances, I was obliged not only to Choose— as some modern philosophers like to say— but also to buy...some gum. But how was I to make this Choice? There were green packages and red ones. And white ones, blue ones, purple ones, orange ones...

Fortunately at this moment Recollection came to my rescue. As Socrates, in the *Meno*, proved it always must. If we are patient. For I Recollected having seen and heard, at my parents' house...a television commercial. For something called "Spearmint Gum." Not that this brief episode had depicted its protagonists throwing up. Or even pretending to do so, as I had. And then stuffing their open mouths with Spearmint Gum. It had instead depicted them with wide smiles and shining teeth. Singing about how "fresh" their mouths were. After they had chewed Spearmint Gum.

*Mutatis mutandis*, then, this was clearly what I needed to find. I removed my mittens, inspecting as I did so the rows of coloured packages. And then I saw it. The small white oblong wafer, on which the words "Spearmint Gum" were inscribed in green. The only Gum which I could associate with the project of a "freshened mouth"! With a feeling of triumph, I seized a package. As, with my other hand, I reached into my trousers pocket and extracted...a dollar.

But as I did both these things...I also spontaneously raised my eyes. And what should I see, directly before me, on the other side of the counter...but a human figure. And not Tommy, either. A stranger. He was bald. Wearing a pale blue jacket. The front of the jacket was turned toward me. But the head was in profile. And staring fixedly, with eyes that looked to be pale blue also...past me.

So startled was I, that I very nearly dropped my gum.

This was, I instantly inferred, not the sort of Stranger who had proved such help to Socrates in sorting out the Difference between True and False Imitations, in the *Sophist.* Instead— and given his position behind the counter— he was probably the proprietor. And maybe even the Joe. Of "Joe's Convenience." But what was he looking at? To answer this question, all I needed do was follow the direction of his gaze with my own. And quickly learned that the object of this gaze was...Tommy. Who was still beside the door, having obviously decided not to join me in my rush for gum. He seemed to be looking...at the magazine rack, or at its highest level, which was also beside the door. He didn't seem to have taken down any magazines, because his hands were in the pockets of his coat.

But neither did he seem to have noticed...that he was being watched.

I considered the proprietor again. His eyes were twisted up and squinty as he looked at Tommy. But they also were sending out— and I could tell this on the basis of my reading of the Authoritative Hippie Books— "Bad Vibes." At Tommy.

This alarmed me. But I was unclear what to do. Tommy was still acting as though he didn't notice, gazing with great nonchalance toward the upper shelf of the magazine rack. I admired his *sang froid.* But my own first impulse was to warn him, that we both should leave the store. And quickly. For who could tell what effects such "Vibes" might exert, at a distance? I could not but fault, as I stood there, the Authoritative Hippie Books themselves. Which, while they had introduced me to the term "Bad Vibes," hadn't given me the slightest Idea how to counter them.

Almost, then, I rushed to the magazine rack, to warn Tommy. But I did not. Because I realized that were I to do this, then there would not have been any point to our having stopped to begin with, to buy gum. Because I wouldn't have bought it. I would have had to put it back in the box, so we could flee. And then Tommy— though he would surely appreciate my efforts— might feel obliged to go through the same procedure all over again, stopping at yet another store, for gum. And who could tell whether the proprietor of the next store wouldn't stare at Tommy too, or at both of us, in the same way? There was even the possibility— which crossed my mind fleetingly— that this might be how people did their shopping in the country. Staring at one another, and sending out "Bad Vibes." Which would also explain why Tommy was so nonchalant. Perhaps he was used to this.

I also admit, though, that it occurred to me, in the midst of this speculation, that maybe if Tommy had chosen a proper Imitation of the Idea of a Country Store..then we might not be going through this at all. Because the genial Imitation of the Idea of a Country-woman or a Country-man, who belonged behind the counter in such a store, with rosy cheeks and a checkered apron, would never stare in such a way. She, or he, would instead be, at this very instant, offering me...a pickle.

But then I remembered. A pickle wouldn't help. Because it might, were I to take it, jeopardize my status as someone who had just thrown up. It was gum I needed. And here at least— whatever the other limitations and dangers— I was in the presence not only of "Bad Vibes"...but of Gum. Which might, if I handled this situation carefully so as to rescue both myself and Tommy, help solve at least one of my problems. Of credibility.

All these thoughts, I should note, flashed through my mind, or brain, in quick succession as I was standing before the counter. Human neurology is fascinating in this respect, that so much activity on the level of neurons— my neurons, assuming these exist— could take place in such a short span of time. But all this activity, assuming it existed on the neurological level, did not bring me closer to deciding what to do, toward Tommy's rescue from the "Bad Vibes." Assuming he needed rescue. If I had known how "Bad Vibes" map onto the neurophysiology of the brain, my brain, Tommy's brain, even the proprietor's brain such as it was, then I might have known better how to thwart them. Or whether they needed thwarting. But I didn't. This was something the Authoritative Hippie Books didn't talk about. And neither did my philosophy books. With Socrates, this was excusable. Since he had not known the term "Bad Vibes." But regarding books of modern philosophy, there could be no excuse. Of course they would leave out the practical things. And as for the Authoritative Hippie Books...there was surely even less excuse!

What this meant, though, was that I was on my own. More modern philosophy! But what would I do? Fortunately, Socrates came to the rescue. Again. For at this moment I Recollected, I don't know why, that I was still holding onto my Spearmint Gum. And upon noticing the package, I also Recollected that this was why I was in the store: to buy this gum. And to buy the gum, I would have to get the attention of the proprietor, so he could take my money. I was impressed, again, not only with my Recollection, but with the clarity of my logic. This is the sort of capacity that has always convinced me that I was correct in choosing Philosophy. As my Vocation.

But to return to the Logic. It was clear, then, that what I could do was simply put the dollar on the counter, and take the gum, and leave. But apart from the fact that this would cost me my change, I was sure this would not be fair, to Tommy. Because then the proprietor would have continued looking at him, with all those "Vibes." Was Tommy absorbing the "Vibes," even though he appeared not to notice the proprietor? I wasn't sure. But I didn't want to take any chances. For who could tell what the effect of this might be, when we were back in the truck? Perhaps Tommy, for reasons he didn't understand, would suddenly feel confused. Or dizzy. And then what would happen? Why...we might drive off the road. Or worse even...off a bridge.

I knew then that, whatever the further cost might be to myself, I had to act. I had to get Convenience Joe's attention. And by means of the very Gum that I was holding in my hand! This would make him take his eyes off Tommy. And stop sending out the "Bad Vibes" at him.

Would he send them out at me instead?

This was a risk I would need to take.

I tried to speak. But my throat was dry.

"Ahem," I said. Or a sound to that effect.

Convenience Joe turned his squinty eyes and looked at me. Right on cue. So I had succeeded in Phase One, of my Rescue Plan. What was more— and no doubt fortunately— his eyes weren't nearly so squinty, or so focused with "Vibes" when he looked at me. Perhaps because he now had to look also at what I wanted to buy.

"Gum," he said, in a high-pitched voice, and stretched out his hand, palm up, toward me.

I put in it my dollar. Observing as I did so his face, which happily was focused on my hand. When seen from the front, he resembled a prune. What with all the creases and folds and droops beneath his eyes. These I hadn't noticed, when he had been facing away from me. And inspecting Tommy.

The irony in this being: that even as I noted these traits...this was exactly what he went back to doing, when he had the money. For even as his fingers punched the buttons on the cash register, he returned to staring at Tommy, and to sending out the same "Bad Vibes."

This made me wonder whether I had failed. And yet...I couldn't help but admire Tommy. For when I followed Squinty-Eyed, Prune-Faced Convenience Joe's gaze again...I could see that Tommy was not only still beside the magazine rack. He was even leaning against it, appearing to survey the magazines. Nonchalantly.

"Fifty, seventy five, one dollar," said Prune-Faced Squinty, as he put the change on the counter, still without taking his eyes off Tommy. As he did this, I had to wonder whether his face was so creased and drooping precisely from the strain of sending out such "Vibes." As well as from his age. Which must have been almost sixty.

I picked up my change. "Thank you," I said. As was appropriate, even in regard to the likes of Prune-Faced Squinty. But I was also resolved that— since I had my gum— I should now devote my efforts to saving Tommy. Decisively. From the renewed "Bad Vibes." Turning from the counter, I walked back to him. He still hadn't stirred. I continued to admire this. And all the more, for I realized too, at that moment, that he must have been demonstrating all along to Squinty and maybe even to me, how well he, as a True Imitation of the Idea of a Hippie, could resist "the Temptations of Consumer Society," which were scattered throughout the store. In the form of potato chips. Soda pop. Chocolate bars. I could see these around me, as I walked toward him. The Authoritative Hippie Books had a great deal to say about these— the Temptations of Consumer Society, I mean. And about how conscientious Hippies ought to be, at resisting them.

I decided, therefore, that Tommy was setting an excellent example, to me, and to Squinty too— if Squinty had been receptive— of how to resist these Temptations simply by standing there, Buddha-like almost, beside the magazine rack. Such simplicity! This example came at a good time too, for me, because I admit that, in the course of this walk, I had felt a twinge. On the part of my stomach. To the effect that I should perhaps buy, not a chocolate bar. Or potato chips. Or some other Temptation. But food. An apple perhaps. Or some cheese.

Except then I saw Tommy. Who was being so Virtuous, even in the midst of "Vibes," at resisting the Temptations that were all around him. So I was able to suppress this twinge. And a good thing, too. Because I also remembered, as I walked toward him, that if I had given in myself, and had bought even an apple or a piece of cheese...then Tommy might begin to wonder, yet again, if I had really puked. And this entire effort, which had included "Bad Vibes," would have been in vain.

"All set?" said Tommy, pushing himself away from the magazine rack, when I had reached him.

"Yes," I said. Holding up my Imitation of Gum's Idea. I wanted him to see, in case he hadn't noticed, that I too had resisted the

Temptations of Consumer Society. As well as my stomach's twinges. And had bought only what I was supposed to buy.

"Great," he said, with his usual understatement. Then, before I could even warn him about the "Vibes," he pushed open the door. And went out. Into the pouring rain.

I hesitated. Was it the case, then, given the speed of his departure, that Tommy himself had been aware of the "Bad Vibes" too? So that any warning by me would have been superfluous? I decided this was possible, even as I, too, following his lead, moved toward the door. Which he seemed to be holding open. And this made me feel relieved, as well as grateful. For it probably meant that Tommy, in ways I would not yet understand, had been fending off the "Vibes" all along. Perhaps through some sort of Hippie magic. So we would not in all likelihood go hurtling off any bridges after all.

And yet...as I was almost at the door, I could not resist taking one last, backward glance...at Squinty. At Convenience Joe. At Prune Face. Who, as the singular progenitor of all these epithets, had been the occasion of so much fruitful Meditation, as well as anxiety, on my part. I knew that probably I would never see him again, with his pale blue jacket and bald head and shrivelled face. Such moments always make me feel somewhat "poignant." So I looked. He was leaning on the counter, across it even, staring at us with his squinty eyes. Briefly I felt the poignancy. But then I realized that, having entered the same field of vision that Tommy was in, I too was now the target, of the "Vibes." That were obviously still coming out of Squinty's eyes. And even worse. Tommy was out the door. And so probably almost safe from the "Vibes." While I, though moving toward the door slowly, was still within range. And probably by this time the only target! And I also had no Idea, as Tommy certainly had, of how to protect myself, through Hippie magic. Or "Anti-Vibes."

I almost panicked. My very heart seemed to leap upward, from my chest. But fortunately I realized, before I gave in to impulse and began to run...that fleeing wouldn't help. Because then I would probably carry the "Bad Vibes" with me. With who could tell what results? But I had to act quickly, because I could sense them coming out of his eyes, and across the store...at me. How could I stop them? I knew I had only a split second, for a decision.

My response suggests that I must have been in contact with Intuition. Not to mention with Presence of Mind, of the sort that carried Socrates himself through great battles when he— like me— had not yet reached old age. And was obliged to fight in the Athenian army. For without thinking further, I too acted resolutely. I stuck my thumbs in my ears, left in left, and right in right. I opened my mouth, and stuck out my tongue, and shouted "YAH, YAH, YAH!" Loudly. And I must say I believe I succeeded in dispelling the "Vibes." Instantly. Squinty's gaze flew skyward, toward the ceiling. His mouth dropped open, and he raised his hands, in a gesture of surrender almost. I knew that by this gesture, I had thwarted any effect that the "Vibes" might have had on me. Obviously, my measures had had to be more drastic than Tommy's, on account of my inexperience. But they seemed to have done the job.

Quickly, then, I turned away from Squinty, who was still sending his "Bad Vibes" into the ceiling. I didn't want him to recover, and start sending them at me again. Ironically, of course, I had found myself in this situation, receiving the "Vibes," because I had felt "poignant" about Squinty. Silently, I reminded myself that I must be more careful in future, even ruthless. But was such ruthlessness, I had to wonder even as I turned away, compatible with Imitating the Idea of Hippieness? Was there perhaps some other...?

I did not get a chance to complete this mental question.

This was because I walked into the plate-glass door.

I suppose that Tommy, seeing me hesitate, must have let it close. He had, after all, been getting rained on. But this was a shock. Especially when I was expecting not to feel glass against my nose and face, but simply rain, on the top of my head. And to think there are some philosophers who claim that the world is no more than our Ideas! I even raised my own hands slightly— though not as high, I'm relieved to say, as Squinty's. I then fell down.

But even as I was sitting on my buttocks holding onto my nose...I realized that at any moment, Squinty himself would look away from the ceiling. And at me. Again. Perhaps he was already doing so. Then the "Bad Vibes" would recommence. Had Squinty tricked me then? And had my gesture, which had seemed so successful, been to no avail? I looked at my hand, which had been holding my nose. There wasn't any blood. I therefore decided that Squinty would only have tricked, or even trapped me, if I failed to escape. Having already rescued Tommy.

I gathered my feet beneath me, rose, and rushed for the door again. Which this time I saw, with the metal bar across its middle. I pushed this bar. The door opened. I fled outside. Still clutching my Spearmint Gum. Which, astonishingly, I hadn't dropped. The rain pelted my hood. I ran across the parking lot. I did not look back.

And I was sure that, as I did so, a slightly sore nose was a small price to pay, after all the "Bad Vibes" that had been sent in my direction, and in Tommy's, by Squinty.

I had, after all, escaped.

And so had Tommy.

## §5

"Did you see the way that motherfucker was looking at me?" said Tommy, when I was back in the truck.

"Yes," I said. I was rubbing my nose. It didn't seem to be broken. But my foot was soaking wet, from my having stepped in the puddle beneath the door. I was starting to wonder whether I'd absorbed more of the "Bad Vibes" than I'd thought. My impulse had been to raise this matter immediately with Tommy, of how he seemed to have resisted the "Vibes" himself. So I would know in future. But now he had raised it himself. Albeit indirectly.

"The bastard thought you were the front man," Tommy said, as he started the engine. "He figured that while you were up at the counter buying gum, I'd be swiping something."

I was stunned by this interpretation. It had never occurred to me that Squinty-Eyed Prune-Face might have been suspecting us of plotting a crime. This meant he had not been directing his "Vibes" at Tommy, and then at me, in a complete moral vacuum, so to speak. Why had this not occurred to me? Perhaps because I was not accustomed to being suspected of plotting crimes. Was Tommy more accustomed? And if so, was this because he did plot crimes? This confused me.

In answer to Tommy's claims, then, about both the strange sexual habits and the genealogy of Prune-Faced Squinty, whom he had called first a "motherfucker," and then a "bastard"...I was able only to muster the exclamation, "Ah!" Yet I hoped that this reply would sound sufficiently excited. For I also realized, in a kind of flash...that we might be on the verge of another Dialogue. And what was more, one that probably would not include reference to Tommy's girl friend, and so many risks to our *bonhomie*. Though I could not be sure. Because ordinarily, I would not have expected a Dialogue about the Virtues of garbage collecting to include such reference, or lead to such risks, either.

"Sure," Tommy said, in answer to my exclamation. "First thing you get used to out here, man, is that freaks aren't welcome. The locals see anybody with long hair, their first reaction is to want to call out the army. Or grab the nearest shotgun." The truck was out of the parking lot. He lowered his window and looked for oncoming cars. There mustn't have been any because he immediately accelerated across the road, and into the proper lane.

"Oh," I said, as Tommy rolled up his window. I was not contributing with great brilliance, yet, to our potential Dialogue. But I was by this time recovering not only from the effects of the door on my nose, and of the water on my foot, but of the acceleration, on my entire being.

"Don't worry," Tommy said, as he peered through the windshield. "You'll get used to it."

For a moment, I thought he was referring to the acceleration. But then I realized— from the sheer comradeliness of his tone— that he was actually referring to the situation he had just described. Did this mean he thought I might have possibilities too, as an Imitation of the Idea of a Country Hippie? I felt a quiver of excitement. Except... He hadn't used the word "Hippie." He had used the word "freaks." The quiver receded. I was almost sure that, given how he had used this word, and in conjunction with the term "long hair," it must mean something close to "Hippie." For those "in the know," so to speak. But this meant, then, that there was a sense in which I too was now "in the know," on the subject of Hippies. Or "Freaks."

This made the pain in my nose seem to go away. I realized, of course, that my being "in the know" might not actually make me a "Freak"— or an Imitation of the Idea Thereof— just yet. But it was a good start.

Yet...it was also troubling. Namely that somebody— a "Local" or "Locals," as Tommy called them— might get so upset about "Freaks" as to want to call out the army. Or get a shotgun. After merely seeing one. This made Imitating the Idea of a "Freak" sound dangerous. I felt another quiver. But of unease. For in view of what had just taken place with Prune-Faced-Squinty and the "Bad Vibes"...it was obvious that Imitating the Idea of a "Freak" *was* dangerous. But did this mean, as well, that insofar as Prune-Faced Squinty had been a "Local," and Tommy had been, and was, an Imitation of the Idea of a "Freak"...there had been a danger of Squinty's doing something a lot more serious than sending out "Bad Vibes"? Of his calling in the army, for instance? Or of his getting a shotgun? This was all beginning to sound quite terrifying.

But was it even possible for me to talk about this with Tommy? I wasn't sure. He had seemed so calm when we were in the store. And he seemed even more so now that we were back in the truck. To judge by his tone of voice, there seemed even to be a sense in which he enjoyed all this. Had he enjoyed the "Bad Vibes" too, then, that I had been so worried about? And since he had said that I would "get used to it"...did this not only mean that he thought of me, in some way, as a "Freak"? Or even as a "Fellow Freak"? But also that, eventually, I too could be expected to enjoy "Bad Vibes"? Or being chased by the army? Or shot at with shotguns? I squirmed in my seat belt. Perhaps, for all I knew, we were about to embark on a life of crime. Without my even being aware of it.

"This all sounds pretty dangerous," I finally said to Tommy. I couldn't help myself. I needed to find out what sort of risks I faced, when next I got out of the truck.

"What?" said Tommy, while continuing to look through the windshield.

I realized, when he said this, that I had been cogitating for some time. And so probably had let slip the chance for another Dialogue. But I was also starting to wonder why he hadn't warned me before we entered the store, about the danger. Given my lack of experience. As a "Freak."

"About the shotguns," I said. "And the army."

"What?" said Tommy. In a different tone. And turning to glance at me.

I sensed I'd made another blunder. Because Tommy, of course, was probably so used to living with all this danger, that he didn't think about it any more. This would also explain why he hadn't warned me. Once again I felt in awe, of his *sang froid*. But could I display such *sang froid*, as a "Freak"? I was beginning to think I actually preferred the Idea of Hippieness. Such as I had learned about from the Authoritative Hippie Books.

I did not, though, want to embarrass myself, by carrying this line of enquiry any further. Especially since, for the moment, there did not seem to be the prospect of further contact with Locals. And fortunately, even as I realized from the tone of Tommy's second "What?" that he seemed not to remember what he had said about the shotguns and the army... I Recollected also that I had a means of redemption. For my clumsy error.

"Would you like some gum?" I said. Holding up the package.

Tommy turned and looked at me again. It seemed he was scrutinizing me, from behind the wire-rimmed glasses. As had happened before. For a moment, I even wondered whether he was going to bring up that business of his girl friend again. So to speak.

But instead he just said "Sure." And turned toward the windshield.

I opened the Spearmint Gum, being careful to put the wrapping in my pocket. Lest I litter the cab. And so remind Tommy, when he saw the litter, of our other Dialogue, the one about being a garbageman. With who could tell what results. Then I pulled out a piece of gum. But as I did so, I couldn't help but remember, as by a kind of reflex...Prune-Faced Squinty. From whom I had bought this gum. And who had leaned across the counter, interrupting for an instant the sending out of "Vibes." And had pronounced its name. "Gum," he had said. And so did all of this mean, I wondered as I held up the slice of gum for Tommy, that Prune-Faced Squinty had had, at that very moment, a shotgun beneath the counter? Just waiting for a chance to aim it? And then discharge it? At Tommy. And maybe even...at me?

"Can you take off the paper please, man?" Tommy said. Even as I was Recollecting this, with the gum held up. "It's hard for me to do it while I'm holding the wheel."

I must admit that by this time it was hard for me, too, to peel the gum. This was because my hands had begun to shake. There I had been, so close to danger, and maybe even to death itself, for all I knew. And all I had been worried about were a few "Bad Vibes." The army was one thing. For they would only shoot, surely, on the orders of an officer. Who would ask for our surrender first. Before risking his men, in an outright assault. But this business of the shotguns was another matter. I tried to remember, as I put the tinfoil from the gum into my pocket, whether I had ever even seen a shotgun. A real one. I knew what they looked like, sort of, from having watched Bugs Bunny cartoons at my parents' house. With Elmer Fudd. Not that I had watched the cartoons *with* Elmer Fudd, with him sitting beside me, I mean. But rather that he had chased Bugs Bunny, through the cartoon forest...

And even as I Recollected this...I also realized, with a twinge of alarm, that this was exactly who Convenience-Joe-Prune-Faced-Squinty-Eyed most reminded me of.

Elmer Fudd.

The sheer power of this insight was such that, even as I handed Tommy the stripped-down piece of gum...I could not help saying, spontaneously, "Elmer Fudd."

Tommy turned and looked at me again. Then he noticed I was holding up the gum. He took it. But he also said "What?" as he popped the gum into his mouth, and turned to look at the road again.

I was surprised he had not said "Thank you." After so much effort on my part, at having bought, and then peeled, the gum. While under stress as well. Which stress should have been preoccupying me still, throughout this transaction. But I pride myself upon my observance of the rules of civilized etiquette. Except that then I remembered I was dealing, after all, with an Imitation of the Idea of a Hippie. Or "Freak." And that such Imitations— according to the Authoritative Hippie Books— were not keen on formalities, while yet being committed to Peace and Love. This seemed to challenge my assumptions on etiquette. I wasn't sure about the term "Freaks," though. But I made up my mind, as I was reflecting on this, that Hippies and "Freaks" did seem to be synonyms. At least for Tommy. And that I should declare this aspect of the question resolved. In order to stay focused on more important things. This meant, then, I decided, that the same rules, or lack thereof, regarding etiquette, must apply to Imitations of the Idea of a "Freak," as applied to Imitations of the Idea of a Hippie. I felt a twinge of satisfaction. It was nice to get something sorted out. For a change.

"Thanks for the gum, man," Tommy said. Even as I was feeling this twinge. "Now what were you saying? About Elmer..."

I immediately realized, that on account of my cogitations concerning the rules, or non-rules, of Hippie Etiquette...I had forgotten to answer Tommy. But I also realized, even as he said this, that my cogitations concerning Hippie, and also "Freak" Etiquette, had obviously been misguided from the start. Because he had just said "Thank you." This threw me into great Perplexity. So much so, that I believe I actually forgot to answer Tommy. Again.

"Elmer who?" said Tommy. Slightly raising his voice.

I looked at him. He was looking at me. But then he had to look back at the road. Lest, of course, the truck go off it.

"Fudd," I said. "Elmer Fudd." I realized, though, that I had made a mistake again. Probably no Imitations of the Idea of a Hippie, or "Freak," watched Bugs Bunny. Probably they had never watched Bugs Bunny. Probably Tommy had never watched Bugs Bunny. Bugs Bunny, after all, was a Temptation of Consumer Society, such as he had shown himself so adept at resisting. In the store. So undoubtedly I was appearing myself, to Tommy, at that very instant, as little better than a Tool, of that same Society. On account of my having revealed, so casually, that I had watched Bugs Bunny. Or at least Elmer Fudd. I thought this ironic, that I should now appear to Tommy as little better than a Tool of Consumer Society. When I had been so successful, only a little earlier, at resisting those same Temptations in the store. But now, obviously, I could no longer seem to Tommy like a "Fellow Freak"— or an Imitation of the Idea Thereof— at all. And this outcome was, I knew, a result of my having been overly spontaneous. As usual. Except that Hippies were supposed to be spontaneous. All of the Authoritative

Hippie Books were agreed on this. But were "Freaks" supposed to be spontaneous, in the same way? I was beginning to see why Socrates once said that Perplexity was the lot of those who Imitated Truly the Idea of a Philosopher. Even if not of those who Imitated Truly the Idea of a Hippie. Or "Freak."

"You mean from Bugs Bunny?" Tommy said. Even as I was experiencing this profound insight.

"What?" I said. I was so surprised, that he knew what I was talking about. And that what was more, there seemed to be no condescension in his voice. Such as might be merited by a Tool of Consumer Society. This was, therefore, all I could think of. To say.

"Bugs Bunny," said Tommy, turning and looking at me, and then looking back at the road. "You mean Elmer Fudd from Bugs Bunny cartoons."

"Yes," I said to Tommy. "Yes. That's exactly what I mean." I was so relieved, not only that he knew what I was referring to, but also that he wasn't being condescending. And that I might not even be as much of a Tool of Consumer Society as I had thought. My first urge in fact was to reach out and embrace him, as according to the Authoritative Hippie Books, seekers after the Idea of Hippieness do sometimes. Though of course I didn't.

"And what were you saying about him?" Tommy said. "About Elmer Fudd. I wasn't sure."

I tried to remember what I had been saying about Elmer Fudd. But I couldn't. My mind was blank. There had been so much Perplexity, and so much Excitement, and so many Discoveries since I had said it, that I couldn't remember. This was embarrassing. Not least because of the emphasis that Socrates himself put on Recollection, in the pursuit of Truth. But though I thought and thought...I couldn't Recollect what I had been saying about Elmer Fudd. Socrates would have been ashamed of me. Again.

Finally I was obliged to admit this failure, to Tommy.

"I don't know," I said.

"You don't know what?" said Tommy.

"What I was saying about Elmer Fudd," I said. "I don't Recollect."

"Oh," said Tommy, after a little pause. "I see." Then he looked at the windshield again, and kept his eyes fixed there, and was silent. As he chewed his gum.

This made me miserable, all over again. There we had been enjoying another Dialogue, and one that had shown signs of becoming philosophically interesting too. Even though, at that moment, I couldn't Recollect what it had been about. And then I had gone and wrecked it, for just that reason: namely, that I had forgotten what it was about. This disturbed me, not least because I knew that Socrates, in a similar situation, would not only Recollect what a Dialogue had been about, but would use it toward establishing the very Foundations of Western Philosophy. I felt most inadequate then, not only as an Imitation of the Idea of a Hippie, or "Freak"...but also as an Imitation of the Idea of a Philosopher. In fact, if anything I felt more inadequate as the latter than I did as the former. Because had Tommy not just proved to me conclusively that Imitations of the Idea of a Hippie, or "Freak," were familiar with Bugs Bunny after all? So that my own familiarity with Bugs Bunny did not disqualify me from being such an Imitation. This, at least, was a relief. But what about Socrates? And my problem of Recollection? Ought I to feel comfortable about not being disqualified from Imitating the Idea of a Hippie or "Freak"...when I seemed to be in the process of disqualifying myself from Imitating the Idea of a Philosopher? After the model of Socrates. Certainly, I could not. Feel comfortable, I mean.

But did Tommy experience this same confusion, between Imitating the Idea of a Hippie, or "Freak," and Imitating the Idea of a Philosopher? Not Imitating Truly of course, on account of his devotion to Kant. But Imitating Approximately, with a commitment to Kantian Duty that was showing at that very moment. For he continued to stare through the windshield, and drive the truck. Was it possible, then, that Imitating Approximately the Idea of a Philosopher, in the Kantian sense, was easier to reconcile with Imitating the Idea of a Hippie, or "Freak," than was Imitating Truly the Idea of a Philosopher, in the Socratic sense? I wasn't sure. Were the acts of simply staring through the windshield and driving the truck, in themselves, enough to make of Tommy an Approximate Imitation in the Kantian sense? Even though he didn't talk about Kant any more? But did he have to talk about Kant? Perhaps it was enough that he simply act Kant-like? By driving the truck. I was getting confused again. Not least because he wasn't talking about Imitating the Idea of a Hippie much either. Except for that business of "Freaks." And "Locals" with shotguns. And the army...

It was at this moment, of course, on account of the circumlocutions of my train of Logic, that I Recollected exactly, in a kind of flash, why I had thought of Elmer Fudd after all. It had been to do with the shotguns. And with Convenience-Eyed-Squinty-Pruned-Joe-Face. And with the army. And...with the dangers that pertained to Imitations of the Idea of "Freaks," and maybe even to me as Imitating the Idea of a "Fellow Freak"...from all of these.

The unpredictable meanderings, of electrochemical impulses, in the human brain! Or mind. Or in their Imitations. Such as mine.

Except that all the excitement of this sudden Recollection, for me, was tempered almost instantly by the realization that it was probably too late for me to bring up— so to speak— these matters with Tommy, again. I glanced at him. He was chewing his gum. Or the Imitation of the Idea Thereof. And staring out the "windshield." As his Duty obliged him to do. I had come at least to understand this. On account of Kant. But would he now want to be interrupted, in this Duty, by my explaining to him, patiently, why I had mentioned Elmer Fudd? What if, in executing Kantian Duty, he was also thinking Kantian Thoughts? Whatever these might be.

I experienced, in the course of these cogitations, not Perplexity—

with its honoured credentials, via Socrates, in the History of Philosophy— but outright Confusion. Here I had imagined that I could visit the Country, and would not have to worry. Except perhaps about how to become a True— rather than merely an Aspiring— Imitation of the Idea of a Country Hippie. But I was worrying. About Tommy. About Tommy's girl friend. About Prune-Faced Squint-Eyed. About the army. About shotguns. About Elmer Fudd...

And we hadn't even reached Tommy's Farm.

But would it not, I tried to tell myself for the sake of reassurance, be better there? At the very least, we would not be in an Imitation of the Idea of a Truck any more, in constant motion and therefore in danger, at every moment, of an Imitation of the Idea of a Real Collision. And there would surely not be any Locals either. Or Imitations of the Idea Thereof: I had not resolved— or even formulated— that one yet. But who might produce an Imitation of the Idea of a Shotgun, at any moment, and shoot us. Instead, there would be Tommy's Friends. All— like Tommy— True Imitations of the Idea of Country Hippies. Or "Freaks," I was no longer sure. But serving— as he had described them in his "expanded mood"— as his "extended family." Such vast horizons, elastically speaking! Though it was still the case, admittedly, that physical horizons were not so resilient. For what with the rain still pounding the windshield, and the thick grey sky, and the beating of the windshield wiper— thunk-thunk, thunk-thunk, thunk-thunk— it was getting difficult to imagine that the Truest of all True Imitations of the Idea of a Hippie Farm would be vastly different. In terms of weather. For the rain was not letting up, nor the clouds lifting. To be replaced, the closer we got, with skies honeyed with the orange of sunset. And with balmy breezes.

But still, I reasoned, at least there would be instant immersion, once we arrived, in a True Imitation of the Idea of Camaraderie and Friendship. Such as Socrates himself had tried and failed to define in the *Lysis*. And would this prospect not, therefore, offer me a further opportunity for philosophical breakthroughs, that had eluded Socrates? As well as the promised expansion of social horizons, even as the meteorological ones stayed dark and stormy? There would be freshly baked bread, such as Tommy had brought to philosophy class, and eaten in the seminar rooms. Perhaps there would be cider, made from tree-ripened apples, that had been grown in their very own orchard. And home-made jams. And canned tomatoes. And carrots and parsnips, stored in sand. I knew about all these things because frequently, in the bookstore, I examined the gardening section, as well as the Authoritative Hippie Books. Occasionally, I even took a book home with me at night, to meditate upon as I lay in bed, without bending the pages.

It was most consoling to Recollect all this, after such anxiety about Tommy's girl friend. And Prune-Squaced Finty. And the army. And such embarrassment, about Elmer Fudd. For in spite of all such tribulations, that we might experience in the course of getting to the Farm, these undoubtedly would be compensated for, by the Farm itself. And I could not help thinking too, I must admit, as I recovered from my embarrassment...of the True Imitations of the Idea of Hippie Girls. Who would greet me in peasant dresses. With long wavy hair. And smiling faces. And whole-wheat bread in their dainty hands. And who seemed veritably to dance through my mind...

## §6

I opened my eyes to the truck bouncing up and down. The light was greyer and I was leaning forward in my seat belt. The gum was still clasped in my hand.

"Are we there yet?" I heard my own voice say.

"Almost," said Tommy's voice beside me. "This is the dirt road we take to get in."

I realized, as he said this, that I must have sounded not like an

Imitation of the Idea of a Philosopher. Or even like an Imitation of the Idea of a Hippie. For these were the very words I had always addressed to my father, when I fell asleep in his car...and then woke up.

I sat up straight. And tried to look more mature.

"Ah," I said. "I see." But I did not see. Because, though the headlights were on, and the windshield hovered before me with a yellow glow, the glass itself was still translucent with rain. As well as coated on the inside with condensation. This was disappointing. The cab itself, along with Tommy, had also lost most of their colour in the dim light. I rubbed the window beside me with my sleeve. But beyond the glass there was only a flat grey darkness, like fog. Then a blotch of green appeared from this fog and passed within an inch of my window. While something else, a branch perhaps, scratched the door.

A shudder passed along my spine, because the sound was like that made by chalk, scraped across a chalkboard.

"Oh, it's not so bad as that," said Tommy, even as the branch scratched the door, and the truck itself went up, then down, especially sharply.

I was not aware I'd said anything to imply the road was "bad." Why, then, was Tommy implying that I had?

"I didn't mean to suggest there was something wrong with the road," I said quickly. The thought that Tommy might, even as we were about to reach the Farm, imagine I was being insulting... Why the Idea was preposterous. "I...I just meant when I said 'I see' that I couldn't see," I said. "On account of the fog." I gestured toward the windshield.

Tommy chuckled.

"You're always putting your foot in it, aren't you, man," he said. "I remembered while you were asleep how you used to get off some real winners in philosophy classes, too."

This was the first time Tommy had mentioned our having been in philosophy classes together. But I was not sure I liked what he seemed to have remembered best, about my presence. Yet I did not want to answer in such a way as might offend him further.

So I simply said, "Yes. I suppose I did."

"Well don't worry about it, man," Tommy said. He glanced out the window on his side. "Too bad it's raining so hard," he said. "If it wasn't, I could show you the fence line when we get to the land."

There seemed now to be pride in his voice, such as there had been when he told me about Imitating the Idea of a Garbageman. But still, I did not want to "put my foot in it" again, as Tommy had chosen to describe my comments in philosophy class. This remark had not been the most encouraging of greetings to waken up to. My impulse, in fact, was to lean forward in my seat belt, and go back to sleep.

Except I couldn't go back to sleep, or even pretend to, since we were almost at the Farm. And Tommy would certainly think me rude were I to curl back up, and ask him to waken me when we arrived.

But fortunately, even as I considered these matters, I was also realizing that we were indeed almost There. And that in a matter of minutes, I would be seeing Tommy's friends. And his girl friend. And also the other Imitations of the Idea of Hippie Girls, in their peasant dresses. Bearing loaves of freshly baked whole-wheat bread. This made me nervous. But not in a going limp way, as I had been before about Tommy's girl friend. More in a shaking-all-over way. Quickly putting the unchewed gum in my pocket, I with trembling hands began to adjust my coat. It also occurred to me that I ought to be accustoming my voice— after my nap— to renewed conversation. Lest I find myself through lack of practice speechless, in the presence of Tommy's friends. Or lest my voice shake, as much as my hands were shaking.

"It is remarkable," I therefore said, "to be out here in this..." I looked around me while I tucked in my shirt-tail. I was not sure, though, what we were out there in. Were there fields beyond the window? Or forests? Or merely fog? I hesitated. For I did not want Tommy to get the Idea that I was able, *a priori* as Kant would say, to make only those remarks that could be interpreted in terms of their having had a foot put in them. "To be out here in this truck," I therefore concluded. Just to be safe.

But I thought I heard Tommy sigh beside me.

Had I said something wrong again?

"It's so easy to forget what the country is like," I therefore added. By way of explanation.

"Well, you'll find out soon enough, won't you," Tommy said.

It actually seemed to me for a moment, as I reached beneath my hood to smooth my hair, that there might have been a note of menace in Tommy's voice as he said this. But was there? Or had I, in my intention to produce an enthusiastic comment...somehow put my foot in something? Again.

But suddenly, before I could think this matter through, the engine whined so loudly that— for an instant— I feared it had snapped its moorings, and broken backward into our little room. The truck lurched, and then sped forward. This happened so quickly, and so without warning, that I was thrown against the seat behind me.

"What's happening?" I managed to say as the entire truck tilted. It was as though we were in an airplane, taking off.

"Just a couple of little hills," Tommy shouted, as the angle at which the truck was tilted got even steeper. He pulled the steering wheel violently to the right. The truck swerved, and I was thrown against the door. Fortunately, both the lock and my seat belt held. Then he must have pulled the wheel just as violently to the left, because the truck twisted in the opposite direction. Had it not been for my seat belt, I would have been thrown into Tommy. I grabbed at the side of the seat. All around us the engine screamed, as though it were being tortured.

"Tommy?" I managed to shout, as I clung to the seat, "Is this how you always get into your farm?"

"Yup," Tommy shouted. As the truck, no longer lurching upward, began to tilt almost as drastically in the other direction.

I turned and clung to the back of my seat. As I did so I glanced at Tommy. His fingers in their gloves were clenched around the steering wheel.

"But it's the reason we could afford the place," he yelled. He was leaning forward, obviously trying to see through the windshield.

He twisted the wheel to the left again. The truck lurched upward. The engine whined. How long could this go on? I clung to the back of the seat. Then the truck tilted sideways. Much farther and it would surely tip over. I shifted my grip again, to keep from being thrown into Tommy. My heart was pounding. I actually wondered whether this might be the end. Would Mr. Papadiguano ever know what had happened to me? Would my parents?

But then, just as quickly, the truck seemed to right itself. We were descending slowly, with just the usual number of bumps and dips.

"Is...it over?" I couldn't help but say. My voice was shaking.

"Smooth sailing, man, from here on in," Tommy said. He was leaning forward, staring into the fog.

It was still not easy for me to let go my grip on the side of the seat. I looked at my chest. The fabric of my ski jacket was moving, in and out, in and out.

I tried, therefore, as I clung to the seat, to think positively. Matters could have been worse. I could have awakened in the middle of going up or down one of those hills. Then I would probably have inferred we were caught in an earthquake. And have lunged for the door. Without even asking Tommy. And what would the result have been then? I could, instead of still being warm and dry, have been a cold and soggy mass of tissue on the side of the road. Perhaps not even conscious.

"The fence line begins here somewhere," Tommy said beside me. Even as I was appreciating my good fortune.

I glanced at him. He was gesturing to the left with his head, which I could not see very well on account of the gloom.

Then he turned the wheel, slowly this time, to the left. I felt the truck pass onto a different surface. This passage made me aware that, since waking up, I had been hearing the crunch of gravel beneath the tires.

"I don't hear the crunch of gravel any more," I said. This seemed to herald a great change, a prelude to our Arrival.

"We're driving through the field now," Tommy said. "Thank Christ the track is packed down. A few years ago, in weather like this, we'd have been up to our axles in mud. And outside pushing."

The thought of being outside, in the darkness and pouring rain, standing in mud to our knees and pushing the truck, made me shiver. But I did not want to shiver too much, because we were indeed almost There. I leaned forward. I would, I decided, try to make out the lights of the house. Which— unless this was a very long field— I was sure must come into view soon.

But I couldn't see anything, apart from the narrow swath of silver light, that lay beyond the rivulets of rain on my part of the windshield. As inconspicuously as possible, I shifted a bit toward Tommy, so perhaps I would be able to see, through the part of the windshield that was clear of rain, the house.

But beyond the much clearer arc of the headlights, which lit a muddy track flanked by tall grass...I saw nothing. Only foggy darkness. I shifted back again in my seat. I felt dizzy. Where was the house? Where were the lights? Where were Tommy's friends? His girl friend? The other girls? With long hair and peasant dresses? Bearing whole-wheat bread?

I had an impulse, which with difficulty I fought back, to turn to Tommy and ask him all these questions. But I didn't. For was it not possible, I reasoned, that suddenly we would turn a corner, around some bushes maybe? And there would be the house? And the people? And the lights?

But we didn't turn any corners. The truck just kept moving slowly, over little dips and rises in the track, more or less straight ahead. And there wasn't any change that I could see in the pale yellow film of light that seemed to lie beyond the windshield, on my side.

Then, without warning, Tommy stopped the truck. He shut off the engine, but left the lights on. I still could not see anything beyond the windshield, though. Because now even his half, which had been cleared of water by the windshield wiper, filled quickly with droplets, and then with streams of rain.

"Well, here we are," said Tommy. "Home."

I didn't know what to do. Or say. Now that the engine wasn't humming, now that there was not the crunch of gravel under the tires or the thunking of the windshield wiper, or the swishing of branches against the truck...there was only the rain, its steady beating on the roof, and the deepening darkness, and the damp cold air. Which, now that Tommy had also turned off the heater, seemed to be getting much damper and colder. Quickly.

"It's...quiet," I said. This was all I could think of to say. But it seemed appropriate. For there was around us...a great quiet. Nor was it made less great by the pounding of the rain on the roof. I shivered again, without being able to stop myself.

"It's almost lonely," I said.

Tommy laughed his strange dry laugh again. "Quiet?" he said. "Lonely? Nah. It's the voice of Mother Nature. Talking to you, man." He laughed.

This was all starting to make me uneasy. For Tommy himself seemed to have changed. Could I even ask him, therefore, whether...

"Well," said Tommy quickly, and with a determination that interrupted my thoughts, "we'd better get in and get a fire on. Or it's going to be one long cold fucking night." He turned to me. "Coming man?" he said. Then with a sharp fast gesture of his left arm, he pushed open the door on his side, and was out. Into the almost darkness. And the pouring rain.

The door slammed behind him.

I sat for a moment trying to compose myself. Did this mean then...that it was true? And that my suspicions, which had been awakened so very recently— just after I myself had wakened up, in fact— were about to be realized? I sighed. Would there be no loaves of freshly baked whole-wheat bread? No girls with long flowing peasant dresses, and long flowing hair? Would there be anybody? I peered through the windshield, for any sign of a light that wasn't just the wide blurry arc of the headlights, beyond the slick of rain.

I didn't see one.

But did this mean, then, that this Truest of All True Imitations, of the Idea of a Hippie Farm...?

Perhaps, I reasoned, as my forehead began to feel very hot, they had gone to bed early, on so wet a night. And that in arriving, we would waken them...

The door opened on Tommy's side. I turned to see him climb in quickly, soaking wet.

"Jesus Christ," he said, and slammed the door behind him. His engineer's cap, his hair, his beard, were all dripping water, and his wire-rimmed glasses were streaked with rain. He took them off, looked around for something to wipe them on, and, not seeing anything, set them on the dashboard.

He looked at me. Even in the faint light, his eyes were intense and blue.

"I can't say I blame you for sitting here, man," he said. "I know you haven't got the foggiest fucking notion what to expect. And I suppose I should have filled you in a bit on the way up. God knows we had enough time."

"That's okay, Tommy," I said. But I was actually thinking, or feeling, or both, that he was right.

"Well anyway," he said, after looking at me for a couple of seconds, "the words just weren't there, man. I mean, I thought about it, but..."

He shrugged. "So I guess I'll fill you in when we get inside. And what I don't tell you, you'll see for yourself. But one thing I'd better mention first..." A look that I can only call "sheepish"— as distinct from the "goatishness" of his beard— flashed across his face. "I sure hope your suitcase is waterproof."

"My suitcase," I said. I had forgotten about my suitcase. Completely.

"Sorry about that, man," Tommy said. Brushing some of the water off his coat. "I should have thought. Everything I bring up here I stash in garbage bags. Because the weather can turn really shitty, really quickly. Especially at this time of year."

"Hmm," I said. The words did not seem to be there for me, either. But I could also not help Recollecting my meditation on these very garbage bags— or the Imitations of the Idea Thereof— in the back of the truck. Whose purpose I had never learned. Even during our Dialogue on the Virtues of collecting garbage. Because I had become so worried about his jealousy...

And this was when I realized. That possibly everything had been in vain. The worrying. The getting rained on while pretending to throw up. The pretending to throw up itself. The stopping for gum.

Everything.

Because...

"Look man," Tommy said beside me, even as I was undergoing this profound realization, that all had been, was, and probably would be Vanity, "I've got an idea. You don't know where anything is around here. No fault of yours."

I was glad, silently, that he had added the "No Fault" part.

"So maybe what we'd better do," Tommy went on, "is I'll get the stuff into the house, and get the lamp lit, and you can just sit tight here."

"Oh no, Tommy," I began to protest.

He laid a hand on my arm, just above the wrist.

"No," he said, looking at me with those intense blue eyes. "I've probably fucked you around enough already," he said, "by not telling you what to expect when you got here. I suppose you expected to see all the people I was living with when I was at school, right?" He paused. But before I could answer, he added in a more sober voice still: "And Allie. Right?"

I listened to all of this with growing amazement. What was I to think? Of course I had had such expectations. So had Tommy been misleading me? Or had he really not known how to tell me, about...whatever it was that had happened, to all the...people. And even, it seemed, to Allie. His girl friend. I shuddered, unable to stop myself. But the way he had asked me, about his girl friend Allie: did this mean he had known all along, or at least throughout the trip, that I had wanted to ask him about her, back at the beginning? But now I was completely confused. Did it matter whether he had known? Any more than it mattered that I had had tingles up and down my spine, and gone limp when he had mentioned her? Since it was now obvious that I wasn't going to see her, perhaps ever again, anyway? Involuntarily, I thought not of her actually, but of the Venus on the oyster shell. That she had looked like. And that made a clearer picture, a more complete one, than my somewhat shrunken memory...of the real Allie. Especially since I probably never was going to see her again.

Beside me, Tommy sighed. As he did, I realized I hadn't answered. I looked up. Had he perhaps been thinking, not about the Venus on the oyster shell, the memory of which I was more or less stuck with, but of the real Allie? His girl friend? Whom he could probably Recollect even more clearly than I could Recollect the Venus on the oyster shell. And with more animation.

"Well anyway," Tommy said, as I was trying to sort through, as best I could, these differences between the Recollection of an Image, and the Recollection of a Person, "I might as well tell you right now, to save you any more disappointments." He smiled faintly. It was now so dark that, except for his eyes, which seemed to shimmer, only half his face was lit, the half nearer the headlights. "There isn't anybody here any more except me. And you. And a little goat named Camilla." He frowned. "That one of the assholes who live up the road was supposed to come in and milk while I was away. But that I'd better go and see to because they probably didn't bother."

Tommy's voice softened when he mentioned the goat. As it hardened, when he mentioned "the assholes." I believe I even felt "touched" at this, at the softening part I mean. But a veritable cataract of questions seemed also to be pushing forward, inside my mind. Where had all the people gone? Where was Allie? Did Tommy look like a goat now because she had been replaced in his affections by...Camilla? Who were "the assholes" who lived up the road? And— though I could hardly expect Tommy to answer this question— what did all of this say, about my hopes of seeing, at last, an earthly Imitation of the Idea of a Hippie Farm? That I had been reading about. For all these years.

"Anyway," said Tommy quickly, as I was feeling this inner pressure, "you just sit tight. And I'll get that suitcase of yours into the house. Along with everything else."

And before I could protest again that I wanted to help him, Tommy was out the door and into the rain.

He left his glasses on the dashboard. I looked at them. And felt perplexed.

## §7

It took Tommy quite a while to get all "the stuff," as he had called it, up to the house. All this time I sat in the truck, and listened to the rain on the roof. I pushed my hands into my pockets, and withdrew my head inside the collar of my coat. Like a tortoise. But I could still feel around me this place that Tommy had referred to so sarcastically as "Home." Apart from the pounding of the rain it seemed very silent, and apart from the headlights' glow beyond the windshield, very dark.

Intermittently, thoughout this vigil, the truck would shake as behind me Tommy removed another of the garbage bags. But the truck also shook with each gust of wind. This got to be a game for me, to decide when the truck shook whether it was Tommy or a gust of wind. This game was boring. But it kept me from thinking too much about the things and the people I'd been expecting to see, and now would not. I played the game, and waited with my mind a blank, as Buddhist philosophers urge it should be, for the truck to shake. I also decided that I would have to read more of those Buddhist philosophers. Because it was to them, or at least to their methods, that I found myself turning in this time of disappointment. And not to Socrates.

Eventually Tommy came back not to the box of the truck, as I've learned such a thing is called, but to the cab, and opened the door. I turned to look at him. But as I did, I still didn't see any light through the open door, that might indicate where the house was. I found myself wondering, as he leaned in: Was there a house at all? Or perhaps he lived underground. In a sort of burrow.

"Okay, man," Tommy said, without getting in. "Are you still awake?" I nodded. He must have seen me in the glow of the headlights, because he went on, "That's great. Let's go. Your suitcase is up at the house, the light's on, and the stove's even lit."

I squinted past him, over his shoulder, into the darkness beyond the truck door.

"But Tommy," I said, "I don't see any light."

He leaned into the truck, looked around, evidently noticed his glasses on the dashboard, and put them on.

"Jesus," he said. "They're still not dry." He glanced over his shoulder through the open door, toward what I assumed must be the house— or the burrow. Then he looked back at me. "That's because

I lit the lamp in the kitchen," he said, "and the window faces the other way. Speaking of lights, though," and he leaned forward, "I'd better shut these things off, or we won't have any battery left. Then we'd be really stuck."

He pushed a knob on the dashboard, and the swath opened by the headlights disappeared. Instantly. We were plunged into utter darkness. This was terrifying. So that I had to struggle, in those first few seconds, not to scream. It was like the bottom of a coal mine. Or worse. But gradually I noticed, beyond Tommy's shoulder...a faint glow, tinted orange. And then, in the glow, Tommy's silhouette, or the silhouette of his head and shoulders, took shape. The silhouette moved.

"There. Look, man," said Tommy's voice, emerging from the blacker shadow of the silhouette. "If you just look over there behind me, you can see the light. Do you see it?"

"Yes," I said, trying to keep my voice steady. "I see a glow. Of some kind."

"That's the one," said Tommy's voice. "Now. I'm going to walk toward it, and you can follow. Okay?"

I nodded, then realized he would not be able to see my nod. "Okay," I said, in a voice I hoped wasn't shaking too much. But what I wanted to say was that all of this seemed spooky, what with the rain still pounding on the roof of the truck, and the pale orange glow that came from I knew not where, and his speaking out of this black silhouette, out of dense foggy darkness, so heavy with rain and cold, and the silence that lay around us. But I didn't say this. I only shivered.

"You'd better come out on this side," said Tommy's voice, from inside the silhouette. "Because if you get out over there you might slip in the mud. This way I can get a hold of you."

I also felt an impulse to ask why there was not a flashlight, so we could see the path. Or why he didn't just turn the truck lights on again. Or why he hadn't "lit the lamp," or whatever it was, in a room that was on this side, instead of on the other side of the house. Or burrow.

He'd had the benefit of the truck lights, when he'd been making his way to and from the burrow, with the garbage bags. Not to mention with my suitcase. So why shouldn't I?

"Man?" said Tommy's voice. "Are you coming?"

This was awful. Especially since, with his voice now coming from the silhouette, Tommy did not look so much like an Imitation of the Idea of a Hippie any longer. Or of a "Freak." Or even of a Philosopher. But like an Imitation of the Idea of... I didn't dare even complete this phrase, not even in my mind. But suddenly, it seemed as though Socrates might have been too optimistic, with his Ideas about Reincarnation. It was as though I...were being summoned. But not by Tommy. Did I dare resist? And were I to do so, would I not be casting aspersions on Tommy's hospitality, when we had been at his Farm for a mere half hour? And when I still hadn't even been inside the burrow? Or house? It was a house, I told myself silently, and not a burrow. Though I had still not seen any evidence. And as for Tommy himself, perhaps he was just confused. Or perhaps he was really worried, that if he did turn the headlights on again, then the "battery" would wear out. This was a level of technical language which, though I felt comfortable with terms such as "windshield" and "cab," was beyond me. For it has never been the business of a Philosopher to waste his time on mechanical things. But this meant I had to take Tommy's word, about the "battery." Even though he too had— at one time— aspired to be...a Philosopher...

"Man?" said Tommy's voice. Interrupting my thankfully reawakened reasoning processes. This legacy of Enlightenment. "Are you awake? Or what?"

"Awake," I said quickly. "I'm awake."

"Jesus, I was beginning to think you were dead or something," said Tommy's voice. "Anyway, do you want to slide along the seat here, man? And I'll get a grip on you."

This suggestion by Tommy that I might be dead, needless to say, alarmed me. Especially given recent associations. Concerning his own Imitative-ness. And his act of Summoning.

"I'm not dead," I felt obliged to say. "I'm alive. I'm right here."

"I know you're alive, man," said Tommy's voice, from the silhouette. "And I know you're right there. And maybe if you just come across the seat, so you're right here, and I can get a hold of you, we can get up to the house. I'm getting pretty fucking wet standing here, man."

"Oh," I said quickly, and shifted along the seat. Spontaneously, to be agreeable. I bumped into something soft, that must have been his hand. Instantly it grabbed my coat.

My first impulse was again to scream. And to pull away, in the other direction. I clenched my teeth. I even closed my eyes. But this didn't matter, because I couldn't see anything anyway. Except the silhouette. Which, even as the hand began to pull at me gently, I opened my eyes and saw again. I pulled away. I couldn't help it.

It was as though I were being pulled toward the burrow, that belonged to the True Imitation of the Idea of...

I was not sure what.

But neither did I want to Know.

"Man?" said Tommy's voice. From inside the silhouette. "What's the matter now?"

"I...I think I just forgot something over here," I said. Tugging away from the hand that had grabbed my coat. And was holding on.

"What?" said Tommy's voice. "But how are you going to see it, man? It's pitch black."

"I...I know," I answered. "That's why I think it would be nice if you just turned the lights back on for a minute. Just for a minute. So I can find it."

The hand, which had been tugging at me, released its grip. I moved as quickly as I could to the other side of the seat, to my side, where I had been before. I huddled there.

Then suddenly, the swath of light reappeared. Like magic.

I felt such relief at this, I collapsed somewhat, against the door.

"There you go, man," said Tommy's voice. "How's that."

I opened my eyes and looked at him. The engineer's cap. The glasses. The little beard. All wet, of course. But Tommy. Unmistakeably Tommy. And not...

"Thank you," I said, unable to control my emotion. "Thank you." But still I couldn't move. I was limp. Even limper than I had been when I thought of Tommy's girl friend.

"Is something wrong, man?" said Tommy. He was braced against the steering wheel. "Like I mean, my rear end is really getting soaked here."

"No, no," I said. "Nothing wrong." I tried to smile. I couldn't. I was like a rag doll, after all that groping.

It was only Tommy, I told myself silently.

And not the Imitation of the Idea of Something Really...

"You said you forgot something, man?" Tommy said.

Momentarily, I was confused. I could not remember what I had told him. So great was my relief. But I had told him something, to get away. So I simply nodded. "Yes," I said. "I forgot something."

"Well, do you want to pick it up please?" he said. "Or find it? I mean..." He sighed. Then he climbed through the door again, and sat down on the seat. He was dripping wet. "Jesus," he said. Yet again. "Well, I guess there's no sense in drowning while I wait, is there."

I marvelled, first, at the expostulation "Jesus," which had just come so easily from Tommy's mouth, now that he was lit by the headlights again. What a difference, archetypally speaking, a little flick of a light switch could make! I could also not but marvel that here we were, in the truck again. Together. I felt an impulse to turn to Tommy, and suggest that, now that we were back in the truck together, and now that he, courtesy of the headlights, had aligned himself with the angels again, so to speak...would it not be just as easy to close the door, on his side? And start the engine. And turn the truck around. And drive right back out the road?

But I caught myself. Had I not come to the country to see an Imitation of the Idea of a Hippie Farm? That in this case clearly did exist in unresolved relation to said Idea, which I had formed as a concept from my reading. But might the Authoritative Hippie Books themselves be wrong, in the concept they had conveyed to me? Might they themselves be but Simulacra, as Socrates would have put it, False Imitations of the True Idea, which they had failed to represent? Where then did the True Idea of a Hippie Farm lie? What criteria might I introduce, to separate the True Imitation of this Idea, from its Simulacrum...?

"Man?" said Tommy's voice beside me. So that I was roused from these speculations.

I looked at him. I was Perplexed.

"Man," said Tommy. "You're looking at me like somebody hit you over the head with a brick. I mean... Please...?"

This request was plaintive. I realized, however, with an inner glow of pleasure, just how much like Socrates, in his Perplexity, I must be looking in mine. For had his friends not said of Socrates that he could stand motionless for hours, in Perplexity? Though I could not be sure that he too had— in Tommy's words— looked like he had been "hit over the head with a brick."

"It's all right, Tommy," I said. "You can look like this, too. With a little study." I was referring, of course, to study of Socrates. And his Perplexity.

"You...said you...forgot something, man," Tommy said, leaning toward me, speaking slowly. "In the truck. Remember?"

There seemed to be an expression not of curiosity on his face, but...of desperation.

In fact, he seemed to have aged. In the past few minutes.

But it was at this moment that I did remember, that I had not forgotten something really, but had been engaged in another ruse. As when throwing up. Only this time, it had been to get away from the silhouette. This Recollection, which had been displaced during my Perplexity, now re-engulfed me.

"Yes," I said quickly. "Yes." I did not at this moment know what I was saying "Yes" about. But it seemed appropriate to be positive. Given recent experience. As well as Tommy's own frame of mind.

"Well...what?" said Tommy beside me.

"What?" I said. Not in the sense of not having heard him of course, but in the sense of...whatever it was he was asking about.

"What did you forget, man? Please?" said Tommy, sounding if anything more desperate. "If you can tell me, I can help you look."

I realized that I was not well placed after all, to assuage this desperation. This was because I lacked the slightest idea, of what I was supposed to have forgotten. I couldn't say this. But neither could I say that I had forgotten...whatever it was I was supposed to have forgotten. Even though this would have been the simplest route.

"Hmmm," I said, to stall for time. But my mind was blank, so to speak, in terms of things I could have forgotten in the truck. Perhaps this blankness, I realized as I was being blank, was an after-effect of my earlier intentional blankness, that had been inspired by the Buddhist philosophers. But if this was the case, I decided, it was certainly a strike against Buddhist philosophers. As alternatives to Socrates.

Would Tommy want to hear about this?

I decided that, probably, he would not. He was looking far too desperate as he leaned toward me, in the glow of the headlights.

So finally, under the circumstances, I had to say with a kind of smile, the best I could manage, "I don't remember."

I did not register the expression on Tommy's face when I said this. I had looked away from him toward the windshield. This meant, of course, that I was also smiling at the windshield.

"Oh," said Tommy's voice. "Then if you don't mind..."

I heard a click.

The lights went off, even as I was looking at the windshield.

All was dark again. Instantly.

"If we leave these things on any longer," said Tommy's voice, out of the darkness, "then we definitely won't have any battery left. Then we'll have to walk all the way out the fucking road. Some fun, man. I've done it."

I admit I was listening with only limited interest to these words. This was because I was registering that my ruse had failed. I was back where I had started. In the dark. I didn't even want to look in Tommy's direction, lest I see the silhouette again. I didn't want to do anything. Just sit. And listen to the sound of rain.

"Man?" said Tommy's voice. "Can we try again now? Please?"

"Yes," I said, into the darkness. I was disappointed that my powers of invention had failed so completely. This was, I decided, definitely a big point against those Buddhist philosophers, and their stupid "No-mind." That had led to blankness at a crucial moment. Silently, I recommitted myself to Socrates. I believe I even felt a little guilty, for having forsaken him. If only briefly.

"Can we go now, man?" said Tommy's voice.

Clearly, I was being Summoned. Again.

I closed my eyes. This was, I decided, not fair. It was not fair that Tommy had not bothered to light the lamp, or whatever it was, on the side of the house we were facing. But how to say this? I had to try. Because I knew I would not be able to stand being groped at by the black silhouette. Again.

"Do you think it would be possible..." I sort of muttered.

"What?" said Tommy.

"I can't see anything," I said. The words seemed to rise by themselves. From somewhere. At last.

But perhaps the more easily because with eyes closed...I could not see anything.

"Oh," said Tommy's voice. "I'll open the door."

I heard the handle of the door click, and the door itself unlatch. There was a burst of cold air.

"There," said Tommy's voice. "See the glow?"

I didn't look. Nor did I open my eyes. This was because I knew I would not only see the glow...but the silhouette.

"Yes, but what about a light?" I said. This came out of my mouth in a great rush.

"A...light?" said Tommy's voice.

"Yes," I said. With my eyes closed. "A light. So we can see."

"Hey man," said Tommy's voice. "It's not that bad between here and the door of the woodshed. Just a bit muddy. That's why I asked you to let me hold onto you. So you wouldn't fall."

"But why can't there be a light?" I said. Ignoring for the moment the full theological implications of his statement. "Why?" My pertinacity on this matter was proving remarkable.

I heard Tommy sigh.

"Because if you want to know the truth," said his voice, "it didn't occur to me to bring the light out and put it in the woodshed. Probably because I'm used to leaving it in the kitchen. And...I don't know. Partly because the headlights were on, I guess."

"But then you turned the headlights off," I said. I knew that in normal circumstances I would not be able to speak this way. And least of all to Tommy. But sitting as I was, with my eyes closed in total darkness, or almost total darkness, perhaps bestowed on me a kind of courage. Of the sort that even Socrates might recognize.

I heard Tommy sigh again. "Because if I'd left them on any longer," he said, "we wouldn't be able to get the truck started again. Just a minute." I heard a click. Then a slow chugging. Then the engine started. There was another click. And my eyelids were bathed in a reddish glow.

"There you are, man," said Tommy's voice. "I'm sorry. I should have left the engine running and kept the lights on. I just don't like to use the gas, that's all."

I opened my eyes. Before me were the windshield, the shifting droplets, the silver veil of rain. They were all quite heartening.

But it was also strange that I had been able to muster the courage to challenge Tommy about the headlights, only while I was sitting with my eyes closed in almost total darkness. In the midst of being heartened, therefore, I was also troubled. Why did I seem to be stronger with Tommy when I was in the dark? To the extent that he had even apologized to me. I didn't know. Except that now the headlights were on again... I felt confused. As usual.

How had I accomplished that?

"Man?" said Tommy's voice beside me. "Are you ready?"

I felt his weight shift on the seat, toward the door.

"Wait!" I said.

Tommy turned around to look at me. "Now what?" he said. His face was contorted, as though he were undergoing some anxiety.

"It's all right," I said. "You can switch the lights off. And the motor."

"What?" said Tommy.

"Yes," I said. "I'm fine now."

To prove this I shifted my eyes back toward the windshield.

"Are you?" said Tommy.

"Yes," I said. "Emphatically."

"All right," he said. "You're sure."

"Yes," I said.

"Fair enough," said Tommy. He leaned across the seat. First he turned the key, and the engine stopped. Then he pushed the button and the lights went off. Just like that.

"Okay man," said Tommy's voice. "Can we go now?"

I suddenly realized though, as I almost looked at him by reflex, that

I had not reckoned, in seeking the refuge of the darkness to maintain my courage...on the silhouette. Which had been my concern about the darkness before. This was what I had been able to avoid by keeping my eyes closed, during my period of assertiveness. Or at least by keeping them fixed in the direction of the windshield.

But now?

"I'll just go out my side," I said quickly, without even turning my head to look at Tommy. Or at the silhouette.

"What?" said Tommy's voice.

"I'll go out here," I said, feeling around for the handle of the door. "To save you the trouble." I found the handle and pulled it. The door unlatched, and I pushed it open.

"Hey man," said Tommy's voice behind me.

But I didn't answer. Instead I turned toward the door, and made to place my foot on the little ledge which, in vehicles, is usually beside the seat. But perhaps the ledge in Tommy's truck was narrower than the one which, at that moment, I Recollected from my parents' car. Because my foot, as I anticipated this ledge, missed it. Landing instead on empty air. And then continuing downward. Having committed my entire weight to this foot, I quickly followed. The foot hit mud and slithered. So, in quick succession, did my knee, thigh, hip, shoulder, and left arm. Fortunately my head did not. This was because it banged against the door, as everything else was going down.

"Man?" said Tommy's voice. It sounded far away.

The mud was cold. So too was the rain that now pounded not only on the roof of the cab, but on me. My head hurt within my hood.

"Man?" said Tommy's voice. Again.

I rolled around. The rain pelted on those parts of my clothing which were doused in mud. I could even hear it.

I realized, as I was rolling, that I had just taken my first step, onto Tommy's farm.

"Man, are you okay?" said Tommy's voice from somewhere above me.

"Yes," I answered, while rolling. I could not stand up. The mud was too slippery for me to get my footing. I did realize, though, that I was being granted a unique perspective on Tommy's farm. Especially since the lights came on again, almost immediately. I knew this because, even though I was not looking toward them, the general area ceased to be competely dark. There was a glow. I rolled around so I could see. And sure enough, there they were, the beams of light, cutting their swath through the rain and darkness. This was comforting. Except that I was still getting rained on. And my head hurt.

But suddenly, there were hands on my shoulders, and Tommy's voice, still above me but nearer, saying, "Hey man, okay. Come on. Let me help you," and other words to that effect. So that, with his assistance, I was able, moving first one knee and then the other, to rise slowly. By this means I found myself standing, at last, on the true earth of Tommy's farm. This should have been exciting, but was not. Even my glasses were smeared with mud, so I couldn't see. And when I moved my tongue, I also discovered mud, gritty mud, in my mouth. I spat it out.

"Man," said Tommy behind me, still holding my shoulders with both his hands, "maybe we'd better leave the lights on after all, til you get into the house."

About this I no longer had the will to quibble. I was weaving. My head, just behind my left ear, still hurt. But I couldn't touch it, because my mittens were wet and muddy. I was wet and muddy, and cold. And getting colder.

"Can you stand now, man?" said Tommy's voice behind me.

The truthful answer would have been that I didn't know. My knees were shaking. But they were far from alone in this, in that my entire body had begun to shake. Though whether from lack of balance, or from cold, or from both, I couldn't tell. But I also found myself marvelling, in a sort of haze, that it was likewise strange under the circumstances, Tommy's continuing to address me as "Man." For, given that I had just fallen into the mud, and was drenched and freezing, and had bumped my head, I thought dimly that it might be more...comforting, were he to use my name. And the more so since we were alone. There weren't any lights, apart from the glow of the headlights, in front of me. And there weren't any people, apart from us.

So why, then, was Tommy continuing to call me "Man"? I knew of course, from the Authoritative Hippie Books, that Hippies often called one another "Man." For that matter they sometimes even called women "Man," and children "Man." For all I knew, they called their dogs, cats, and cows "Man" too. Yet it seemed reasonable to think that even Hippies might, at some time, also resort to using the actual name of the addressee, whether that be man, woman, child, dog, cat, or cow. But had Tommy ever used my name, as the addressee, since the moment the two of us had met on the previous day? I tried to remember. I couldn't. It had been "Man" this, and "Man" that, *ad nauseam*. And for some reason, at that moment, even as I still felt Tommy's hands on my shoulders, this was upsetting. Could this imply that Tommy had actually forgotten my...

"Man?" said Tommy's voice. Behind me.

I was startled. Or perhaps delirious. From bumping my head. From the rain. The mud. Everything.

"What?" I said.

"Are you okay?" he said. "Can you stand?"

My impulse, unreasonably, was to pull away from him. And from his solicitude. And then to turn around, and tell him directly to his face that my name wasn't "Man."

But I didn't.

Because I suddenly Recollected.

Could this instead be the legacy of Kant?

For had I not heard it said— perhaps by Tommy himself in bygone days— that Kant had not only revealed to Man his uncertain place in the universe? But had as much as created the category Man in doing so.

Was this, then, a Hippie naming trait that Tommy was engaged in?

Or a philosophical one?

Or could this indeed be how he reconciled these?

Did I dare challenge such...success?

Ought I not instead to be proud...of my role in it?

Despite its indifference to transcendent Ideas?

Perplexity threatened to engulf me again.

I felt too weak to handle it.

"Yes," I said. "I can stand."

He took his hands off my shoulders.

I didn't fall. Though I felt myself weaving.

This at least was gratifying. That I could stand. On my own. As Man.

"I've got to turn the engine on," Tommy said. "On account of the battery. So I'll have to turn the lights off first. But just for a minute. I'll turn them right back on again. Promise. Okay?"

I was surprised that not once in the course of this disquisition had he used the word "Man." My impulse was to ask him whether there was something wrong, that he hadn't. But even as he had been speaking about the lights, I had been starting to shiver. Uncontrollably. So I would not have been able to frame the question verbally anyway. Because my teeth were chattering. I just said "Yes," without turning around. And even this emerged from my mouth as a kind of squeak.

Then the lights went off and I was left in darkness, freezing darkness, again. They went off so quickly that I even wondered how Tommy had done this. Except then I realized he had probably just climbed through the truck from my side, and pushed the button that controlled the lights.

The engine started. I smelled exhaust. The lights came back on.

The truck chugged beside me, like a living thing. The rain fell. I stared shivering through my mud-streaked glasses, toward the light beam. This was reassuring, to listen to the chugging truck, and to stare toward the light. Even though I knew that for a Hippie it shouldn't be. I felt vaguely as though I should turn to Tommy, who was perhaps still in the truck, and ask him to turn off the engine and the lights again. But this I could not do. Because, standing shivering in the pelting rain, and surrounded by darkness with my head still hurting...I liked the lights. I liked them. I even liked the sound of the engine. Its humming.

I felt Tommy's hand on my shoulder again.

"Come on, man," said his voice behind me. "Let's get into the house."

I let him guide me. The pressure of his hand. There had even been something reassuring, familiar, about his having called me "Man." That legacy of Enlightenment again, perhaps. We moved around the truck, through the very beams of light. The mud was slippery. But I didn't fall. Once, when I almost lost my balance, Tommy's hand grabbed the fabric of my coat, and rescued me.

I no longer feared him, as the silhouette.

Nor did I mind being addressed as "Man."

We went up a small slope.

Before me was a shadowy bulk. In the reflected light from the truck, and through my muddy glasses, I could just make out grey boards. A window sill. Walls.

"Doorway," said Tommy's voice, behind me.

I looked up. I could see little. Raising a soggy mitten I pulled my glasses down my nose. Ahead of me, as Tommy had said, was a doorway. Faintly lit. I saw a pale orange vertical crack.

"Step," said Tommy's voice. "Careful here, man. Don't trip."

I raised my right foot. It bumped, presumably, against a step. I mounted this step, first with one foot, then the other. I crossed the threshold of the doorway, into some kind of room which, apart from the strip of light at its other end, was dark. My boots made a scraping sound on the floor. But I also realized, as I heard them, that there was no longer the sound of rain on my hood and coat. It had receded to a steady drumming, from above.

"Okay, man," said Tommy's voice. "Here we are."

There was a little pause. I looked around the room as best I could. I couldn't see anything, apart from the thin vertical crack of orange light.

"The kitchen's that way," said Tommy's voice.

## §8

I was sitting beside the kitchen stove, on a wooden chair and wrapped in blankets. These were warm and dry, though they smelled as if they had come from a musty cupboard. Beneath them I was wearing dry clothes, and on my feet my bedroom slippers. All of these Tommy had found in my suitcase, which I had said he could open, and which had not soaked completely through. My head ached a little, and there was a bump behind my left ear. I felt this often to see if it was swelling. But it wasn't. So gradually I was able to conclude there was no permanent damage.

Tommy, meanwhile, had gone back to being Tommy. That is to say: he no longer displayed the archetypal aspects of the silhouette. On the contrary. He had, when we reached the stove, wiped the mud from my face with a rag. Then he had helped me out of my wet clothes, down to my underwear. As I stood there shivering, he had got the blankets. All of this he had done while still wearing his own coat, which was soaking wet, and his engineer's cap, which dripped. Such procedures would ordinarily have embarrassed me. But the time was exceptional. This was what I kept saying, silently, while Tommy helped me off with my clothes.

I admit I did not give much thought, during these events, as to how any of them might relate to the Theory of Ideas. I was far too cold. But eventually, as I began to revive, and had cleared from different apertures the mud missed by Tommy, I had an insight of great proportions. This was prompted by his making a cup of tea. "I'll make you some tea, man," he said, with his usual understatement, and as he set about hanging his wet coat, work suit and engineer's cap on a clothesline behind the stove. I was at that moment scraping the last bits of mud from my nostrils. And when I turned to look at him, I was initially confused in that, even as he hung up one work suit and engineer's cap, he had somehow found another of each, and put it on. But before I could become perplexed as to which of these was Imitating which, he turned to making the tea. This proved to be a complicated process. First, he poured some water from a plastic bucket into a sooty metal pot. He then set the pot on the stove. But he didn't leave it on one element, which he allowed to heat up. Instead he stood beside it, shifting it from one part of the stove's surface to another. And very soon, I realized why.

The stove itself was coated with white enamel. But on its top was what appeared to be a dark metal sheet, with circles cut into it. On the front of the stove, to the left, was a tall thin door. This too was enamelled, but was grey and sooty like the pot. After Tommy had poured the hot water over a teabag in a cup, which he gave to me, he opened this door. Behind it was another one, but smaller, and made of rusty metal with an open grate on the front. Through the grate I saw the flicker of flames. And that was when I understood. This was a Wood Stove, such as I had never seen before except in the Authoritative Hippie Books! And even as I was having this insight, Tommy opened the smaller door with a fork. Bending down he picked up a chunk of wood from beside the stove. So that beyond him, and through the door, I received a view of the flames themselves. They were licking around a log that had turned to embers, and was breaking into little pieces.

This was extraordinary! For I realized as I watched that I now was indisputably in the presence of a True Imitation of the Idea of a Hippie

Stove. Such as had been introduced to me, as Idea, by the Authoritative Hippie Books. Tommy pushed in the other log. Orange sparks swirled around. He then closed the smaller door, with a clang. The tall one he left open. This meant I could watch, through the grate, the glow of flames. With the blankets warming my body, and the tea my hands and stomach as I sipped it, I began to grasp the uniqueness of the moment. For in the terms provided by this very stove, as an Imitation of the Idea of a Hippie Stove...I had Arrived. At last. At one aspect anyway, of a True Imitation of the Idea of a Hippie Farm.

But even as I was undergoing this realization, Tommy himself said little. Instead, having given me the tea, he began to bustle around the room, not speaking, though I did seem to hear him sigh. First he sorted through the heaps of my soggy clothing, and hung them up beside his own. Then he sorted through the clothes in the suitcase, and hung the wet ones. Then with a frayed grey rope mop he cleaned up the puddles. Though not very well, because there didn't seem to be running water with which to rinse. Then, he put my shoes in a long box that extended the length of the stove about two feet above it, and that was attached to its back by a metal plate. Finally, when he had done all these things, he opened the garbage bags one by one, and removed from them various items, mostly in smaller bags. These he conveyed to counters and shelves that ran along one wall, and arranged them there. Much as I did every day— on neater shelves— with books.

Clearly, I did not want to interrupt this work. But as I watched, I realized that the light by which Tommy was doing it was not conveyed by fluorescent tubes, as at the bookstore. Instead— and apart from the fire's glow that flickered through the grate— it was produced by a lamp that had a clear glass chimney, and that Tommy had set on a table made of darkened wood. Within this chimney burned a yellow flame. It shone in such a way that— because of the fire also— the whole room was tinted orange, with many shadows. I could not recall having seen such a lamp, in the Authoritative Hippie Books. But it had produced, evidently, the orange glow from the kitchen window, and beneath the door. The shadows moved, as the flame in the chimney flickered. So there was a sense in which, as I switched between watching the flames in the stove and watching Tommy, the entire room seemed in motion. I found this motion, or this illusion of motion, soothing. Like being rocked.

The warmer I got, then, and the more soothed I felt, the more was I able to consider our new surroundings beyond the stove, while Tommy worked. But this was where— I must admit— the disappointment began. Again. We were in a large room, whose ceiling was so high the lamplight barely reached it. The walls, though, I could see more clearly. Apart from the shelves and counter, they were empty of adornment. And while there had once been paper on them, it was peeling off, and in places hung in ragged strips. Underneath, I could see chipped paint, that had also come off in patches, revealing still more layers of paint that were different colours. I couldn't tell what these colours were, because of the glow that tinted everything orange. Even the tall, curtainless windows, one in each of three walls, reflected orange, though with a pale grey sheen that seemed to come from their surface.

This bareness, this raggedness even, troubled me. As did also, when I looked at it, the laundry which dangled from several clotheslines beyond and above the stove. Especially Tommy's work suit, which— optimistic first impressions notwithstanding— I now began to recognize did not Imitate at all the clothing I associated with the Idea of Country Hippies. And not only on account of the Authoritative Hippie Books. But on account of how Tommy and his friends had themselves dressed, in university. The clotheslines completed the picture so to speak, in regard to the room. But did so in a way that— regardless of my insight also about the stove— I soon realized suggested not an Imitation of the Idea of a Hippie Farm at all. But rather...an old-fashioned immigrant kitchen, such as I had seen in black and white photographs, tinted brown. Except there weren't any immigrants. Any more than there seemed to be any Hippies. Imitations or otherwise. There was only...us.

Eventually, Tommy sat down in another wooden chair, beside the stove. He took his cap off and wiped his forehead, and then put it back on again, gathering the loose strands of hair that had fallen across his face.

"So," he said, and looked at me. "Feeling better?"

"Yes," I said. "Thank you."

Tommy nodded. "Great," he said. And then, settling his cap on his head, he turned away from me. He wiped his nose, and leaned forward in his chair, and rested his forearms on his thighs. Slowly, he nodded his head. "Great," he said again. And then was silent.

He seemed to be regarding the fire, as I had been, through the rusty door.

Clearly this was my chance, at last, to question Tommy. Especially since we were now surrounded by so many reminders, not of Hippie Farms...but of immigrant kitchens. My impulse, therefore, was to ask him directly: Where had everyone gone? Not the immigrants, of course. But the Hippies. Or at any rate the Imitations of the Idea of Hippies. In fact, now that I was warmer as well as drier, and the pain in my head had faded enough to reassure me I was not brain-damaged, the less was I preoccupied with my physical well-being. And the less also did the Imitation of the Idea of a Hippie Stove suffice as an adequate symbol, of the Idea of a Hippie Farm. Not least because it should have been doing far more, as such an Imitation, than warming us. For example: baking whole-wheat bread. Which bread should have been, at that moment, undergoing distribution. To us, as well as to the other Imitations, of the Idea of Country Hippies. And undergoing this distribution via the delicate yet workworn hands of Imitations of the Idea of Hippie Girls. Who had baked it.

And yet...it wasn't.

"Where, then," I wanted to say to Tommy, "are all the Imitations?

Where are your friends? Your girl friend? The home-baked bread? The peasant dresses?"

But I hesitated. Did I not hope that Tommy himself would supply this information? So that I, his guest, would not have to pry it out of him? And so soon after our arrival? Especially now that he did not have to drive any more. Or unload the truck. Or start the fire. Or change my clothes. Or empty the garbage bags. But I yearned in vain. Because Tommy, instead of speaking, continued to watch the fire through the grate, in silence. Even as the room itself, relieved of his bustling, settled into silence also, except for the crackling of the fire and the lashing of rain on the window glass. In the midst of this silence, it felt again as though we must be the only people for miles around. Which was how it had felt when we were outside, too. The difference being that we were now surrounded by an orange cocoon of light and warmth. Instead of by rain and darkness.

Yet the main effect of this difference on Tommy, seemed to be his transformation from a talkative silhouette...to the equivalent of a wordless statue. In many ways, this was an improvement. But it seemed even to be going beyond what I had read of Hippie Understatement. For I had never known Tommy to be so devoid of words. Had he not, in our philosophy classes, talked more than anyone else, including sometimes the professor? I wondered, as I sat across from him, whether perhaps it would help were I to reminisce a little, about that very time. By starting up a conversation, say, on Kant's Theory of the Beautiful in Nature, and the Sublime in Art. Not that I knew much about Kant's Theory of the Beautiful in Art and the Sublime in Nature. In fact, I couldn't remember which was which. But it occurred to me that this was a subject which might at least liven Tommy up.

Except that not only could I not remember whether it was Art which was supposed to be Beautiful, and Nature which was supposed to be Sublime, or vice versa. There was also nothing either Beautiful or Sublime, about the room we were in. Or from what I had seen of it, about the farm itself. It might prove difficult therefore, and quickly, to talk about either the Beautiful or the Sublime, in either Art or Nature, as I thought I could recall Kant doing...when we were surrounded by clothing which was dripping, and wallpaper which was peeling, and the rainy night beyond the peeling walls. All things considered, then, the room, as Art, and the night, as Nature, were neither Sublime nor Beautiful. They were Depressing. Did Kant have a Theory of the Depressing in regard to Art and Nature? I doubted this. But neither did I want to show my ignorance, by asking Tommy.

And besides, there was so much else I wanted to ask him. About the room where we were sitting, for instance. Never mind Kant. Apart from the Imitation of the Idea of a Hippie Stove, it left much to be desired, as an Imitation of the Idea of a Hippie Room. Such as I had been led, by the Authoritative Hippie Books, to believe such Rooms should look. Where were the posters? The "batiks"? The drying herbs? Where were the peace signs? The scented candles? The incense? Though perhaps the smell of burning wood made up for the lack of incense. I wasn't sure. Or perhaps this was not so much an "Imitation of the Idea of a Hippie Room"...as of a "Freak Room." But why was there such a difference? Why did the books tell me one thing, and often by means of pictures too, about Hippie Rooms? While this room, which belonged to Tommy, who I had thought was a Hippie, but who described himself now as a "Freak," was telling me something else? The warmer I got, the more Perplexed I got. And Tommy wasn't helping.

I resolved, therefore, that I should at least raise the question of Tommy's friends. For it was they who might have added the crucial plural to the very term "Hippies," as this could have pertained to the "Imitation of the Idea of a Hippie Farm." And had Tommy not even admitted, in the truck, that I had had every right to expect to see them? So did I not have a right to ask?

But I decided, nevertheless, that the best way to do this would be circumspectly. Lest he think I was prying.

"It's so warm and cozy here," I said finally, after we had been sitting in silence for at least fifteen minutes. "With the sound of the rain outside, it feels like we must be the only people for miles around."

"We are," said Tommy. Without looking away from the flames flickering through the grate.

"Oh," I said. But then, having said this, and having noted also Tommy's curt response, I could not but wonder whether I had been on the verge of a major *faux pas*. For did I not know enough about Imitations of the Idea of Hippies to be aware that, among them, impatience is viewed as a failing? This gave me pause. Was it not possible that this was how such Imitations of the Idea of Hippies, or "Freaks," in the country always talked? Or did not talk? "Going with the flow," as I had seen the phrase used in the Authoritative Hippie Books? And was it not also possible, then, that among Imitations of the Idea of Hippies or "Freaks" in general, people could "go-with-the-flow," and for that matter "come-with-the-flow," and maybe even "go-with-the-flow-for-good," without anyone's so much as noticing the difference? And certainly without their ever being so gauche as to talk about it. Was this then what had happened to Tommy's "Commune"? Had everyone else, including his girl friend, simply gone-with-the-flow-for-good?

This was a straightforward question which I wished I could ask, and receive in reply a straightforward answer, from Tommy. But I knew also that I could not so ask. For how often had I read, too, in the Authoritative Hippie Books, that this very desire, on my part, to do these things in a "straightforward" way, certainly did imply a failing? This was because, according to the Books, True Imitations of the Idea of Hippies have an aversion to anything "straight" on principle, and find it "a drag." I could not know what bearing this had on "Freaks." But as everything was so confusing anyway, I decided I should not let this deter me. So, not wishing to be viewed by Tommy as "a drag," on account of my preference for "straightforward" answers, and also as extremely gauche on account of my impatience...I resolved I had better be quiet after all. The way Imitations of the Idea of Country Hippies were supposed to be. And the way Tommy himself was being. As a shining example.

Accordingly, then, once Tommy had said "We are," and once I had answered "Oh," we went back to watching the fire through the stove-grate, in silence. This went on for perhaps another ten minutes, according to my also probably very un-Hippie calculations. But notwithstanding these calculations, I at least was able to pride myself on starting to Imitate, slowly but surely, what could only be the Idea of Hippie Patience.

But then suddenly, just as I was feeling that I might make a good Imitation, of the Idea of a Hippie, or "Freak," after all, if we stayed silent long enough...Tommy jumped from his chair, pounded himself on the forehead with the palm of one hand, and shouted, "SHIT. I FORGOT CAMILLA!" Then without another word, he rushed to the kitchen table, grabbed the lamp, and, shielding it with the same hand he had used to pound his forehead, ran out the door. I watched the orange glow, jiggling as it moved, get fainter, then disappear. So that apart from the flicker of the fire through the grate, I was left in darkness. By Tommy. Again.

This was, like the majority of things that had happened in the course of the evening, somewhat alarming. Although at least this time, on account of the stove, it wasn't completely dark. And neither was I getting rained on. What was more, there wasn't any silhouette either. Groping at me. So that, in my conscious effort to maintain my cultivation of the Idea of Hippie patience, I kept saying to myself, silently at first, and then in whispers, "It could be worse." While trying to remember that it had been worse, in the truck in the dark, and then outside the truck in the mud, just a little while before, in the pouring rain.

But this did not work for very long. Instead I began to notice the shadows that, in the flickering stovelight, were so much deeper than they had been in the lamplight. And that in Tommy's absence seemed to be dancing wildly, like demons almost, on the walls, with their peeling wallpaper and flaking paint. The clothes on the clothesline too, above the stove, began to look like phantoms. Ghosts. Spectres. Even my tea, when I tried to sip it, was cold. I began to wonder whether Tommy had been misleading me. Perhaps we were not the only people for miles around. Perhaps there were others, still, in that very house, just waiting til he had gone, to get me. Or what if there were ghosts? The Ghosts of Imitations of the Idea of Hippies Past, for instance. Who might be angry with Tommy. But who, because of his mastery of Hippie magic— of which I'd seen an excellent example in his handling of Convenience-Eyed-Joe's "Bad Vibes"— would be happy to settle for me. Instead. As Tommy's friend.

I set my cup of tea on the floor. I then turned my chair around, so it faced both the shapes above the stove...and the rest of the room. But even as I was doing this I had a flash of Recollection. Of where such flashes come from, of the neural paths they travel to reach awareness...I have no Idea. But I suddenly Recollected the name: Camilla. And with this name...an Association. Specifically: that this had been the very name shouted by Tommy, as he seized the lantern and rushed out the door. And far from being the name of a long-lost lover, for whom he had gone to search the moors of the Hippie Farm— assuming the Hippie Farm had moors— this was the name he had told me in the truck belonged to the little goat. Which— or whom— he had then described as his only companion. Now.

I sighed. Deeply. So Tommy, again, had merely been heeding the call of his Kantian Duty. Albeit with unseemly haste. Had I, then, in my concern, been silly? I wasn't sure. The shapes on the clothesline continued to dance. And there was, I realized, one way and one way only to convince myself that they were not what I feared they were. Rising, therefore, I gathered my blankets around my shoulders...and walked to the clothesline. This took some doing. But I resolved that...I would touch these shapes, their rough wet surfaces, and so be reassured that they were exactly what they were, and nothing more or less. Clothing. His and mine. In this they did not disappoint. How long I spent in touching them, in navigating with my fingers their gritty texture, I do not know. But I did feel comforted. Though troubled also, just a little, that I should be so comforted not by these objects' Imitation of an Idea...but by their being what they were, and no more than they were. A moment of weakness perhaps, that was hardly in keeping with Socrates.

I felt ashamed. But as I continued, nevertheless, to handle these surfaces, and be comforted, I noticed also, behind and to the left of the stove, a window. One of three. And realized: would looking through this window not provide a glimpse, less restricted than the one I had had whilst in the mud, of something whose Idea *was* important? Namely: the landscape, of Tommy's Farm? As some sort of Imitation, still, of the Idea of a Hippie Farm. But when I arrived, having first stepped over various logs that were beside the stove, I was— as could increasingly be expected— let down. Why this time? Because I could not see anything beyond it, except a black blur. Why was this? Because the window itself was covered, from top to bottom and from side to side...with stretched plastic. Stretched translucent plastic that, in the general lack of light, seemed pearly grey. And whose translucence reminded me most of my half of the windshield in the truck, that had not been cleaned by the windshield wiper. Holding my blankets with my left hand, I touched this plastic, with my right. It was taut, like a trampoline. I bounced my fingers on it, like little acrobats. But this was poor compensation.

Of course, I appreciated that directly before me was yet another metaphor such as Socrates might have used, for the distortion wrought by the senses on True Reality. I did not feel impressed by this. I had had enough of such metaphors already, in the course of one day. So that in spite of Socrates, I pushed my face into the plastic, to try to see what lay beyond. But this was useless. All I did was fog my glasses. So I next had to clean them with the blankets. This too was less than satisfactory, because these were bristly. I squinted, as I scrubbed the lenses. The plastic was secured by narrow strips of wood, that had been nailed into the frame of the window. My impulse, as I replaced my glasses on my nose, was to tear down these strips. And with them the plastic. Tear it down, yes, so I could get a glimpse, at last, of Tommy's Farm. A real glimpse. And one not clogged by mud and rain. Or distorted, by a piece of plastic.

Yet I knew I would be disappointed further, were I to do this. Why? Because what would I see? A window. And beyond the window, what? Darkness. Except, perhaps, for a tiny patch of grass or mud, that happened to be lit by the flames from the stove. Plus rain, lashing against the window, streaking it as it had streaked the windshield. Plus my own reflection. Which would be backlit poorly, and so would probably only remind me, when I saw it, of the silhouette that Tommy had become in the truck, when he had switched off the lights. This too made me shiver. Staring blankly at the sheet of plastic, I was even grateful for its existence. For what was it about this place, about Tommy's farm, that could so easily make both of us, me and Tommy, look...sinister?

But even as I was in the midst of these cogitations, the sheet of plastic became much brighter. And not from outside. I turned around. Tommy was standing by the counter, shaking water from his hands. Beside him was the lamp. He was wearing a yellow raincoat, and as I watched he began to wipe the rain off its sleeves.

"Sorry I disappeared like that, man," Tommy said, looking toward me. "But I remembered the goat."

"The goat?" I said, somewhat disingenuously, as though I did not know what he meant.

"I told you about her in the truck," Tommy said. "Our only other company here. Well, she has to be milked every day. And her udder was almost burst. Those assholes probably haven't been in here since I left. Or at least not since yesterday." He took off the raincoat. "Anyway," he said, "she's all right now."

This fury, on Tommy's part, left me speechless. He hung the raincoat on a hook near the door, then picked up the lamp and carried it to the table. After setting it down, he turned to the stove, and rubbed his hands together at the grate.

"You know," he said, staring toward the fire, "you'd think that when you ask people to do something, especially when I've done so much to make their lives easier here, they'd at least make an effort to reciprocate."

Still I was speechless, in the face of such evidence of an apparent lack— on this Not Quite Truest of All True Imitations of the Idea of a Hippie Farm— of what might be called "communal spirit." Though it also occurred to me, as I went back to the stove, that perhaps "the assholes"— whoever and wherever they were— had found it even easier than Tommy had, to forget to milk the goat. Especially if they had to drive in the same road in order to do it.

But I didn't say this.

Tommy, meanwhile, leaned across the stove, and lifted a lever that was attached to the steel plate on its top, above where the fire was burning. The entire plate rose. Orange flame flickered upward, with a quick little burst of smoke.

"Anyway," Tommy said, "looks like we need another log." He hooked the lever into a notch at the back of the stove. Then he picked up a log, that had been chopped in quarters, and threw it into the box, where the fire was. Sparks flew up. They lit Tommy's face, turning it a reddish orange and emphasizing his cheekbones and little beard. So that for a moment, he looked more than ever like a goat himself. But an insane one. Then, fortunately, he lowered the top of the stove again. The room went back to being mellow orange, from the lamp on the table, and from the fire that flickered through the grate.

The impression of Tommy's face had been brief. Yet it lingered.

"Well," he said, stretching his arms wide, and yawning, "I guess we should hit the sack. I don't know about you, man, but five-hour drives leave me wiped right out." He took off his hat and, holding it between the thumb and forefinger of one hand, scratched his head. "Let's see," he said. "There's really only one room upstairs that's heated." He stared toward the window, the one on whose plastic my fingers had played trampoline.

Then he walked to the counter, knelt, and began to rummage with both hands, in the darkness beneath.

I marvelled at how he could do this, and not be frightened.

## §9

It turned out that Tommy had been looking under the counter for a candle. Or at least this was what he emerged with, a few moments later.

"There we are, man," Tommy said, as he backed out on his hands and knees. He held up the candle, which was white. "This will give you some light upstairs." He snickered.

This made me wonder, with some unease, whether I was in for still more surprises. About which he knew more than I did.

Tommy stood up, and brushed off his work suit. He then turned and walked to the kitchen table. But even as he did so, the surprise arrived. And as a true surprise, since it was no more anticipated by him, than by me. For without giving any warning that it was about to do so...my stomach growled. Loudly. Nor was this only, from my perspective, surprising. It was also interesting, in a way that most of the surprises provided by Tommy had not been. For I, as a rational agent, had forgotten about my stomach, so intense had been the proceedings of the entire day, and the thoughts that had followed therefrom. But my stomach, evidently, had not forgotten: namely, that it had been without food, apart from a cup of tea, since early morning.

Upon hearing this sound, then, I was much relieved, especially given that not-so-distant episode with the laundry, when I had been satisfied in a most un-Socratic way with things as they seemed. For did this noise not imply, instead that, precisely as a rational agent, I might be closer than I had believed to Imitating Truly not so much the Idea of a Hippie...but That of a Philosopher? And for the following reason. How often was it said of Socrates, by his friends, that during his own periods of utmost Perplexity, which could last for hours and even days, he might forget to eat, and stand motionless against his staff, just thinking? So that while I had not exactly stood motionless for the entire day...I too had forgotten, in my Perplexity, to eat. And not only to eat, but to think about eating. Until my stomach itself, which was probably by this time really empty, reminded me.

Yet I could not but wonder, even as the growl repeated itself somewhat plaintively, whether Socrates' stomach did behave in this way. So that during days of Perplexity, he had also had to listen to, and maybe even be interrupted by, his stomach. Growling. Socrates' friends, of course, never mentioned this, perhaps lest it sound unseemly. Or perhaps, I reasoned, they hadn't needed to. Because Socrates, in keeping with his theory of the superiority of mind over body, had trained his stomach so it didn't growl. Upon my giving the matter second thought, this did seem the more likely possibility. And its implications were troubling. For my own stomach had just revealed indisputably that it was not trained in such a way. Could this mean, then, that, far from signalling that I was closer to my goal of Imitating Truly the Idea of a Philosopher...these noises meant I was further away? Because, though I had consciously forgotten that I hadn't eaten...my stomach was still protesting? Revealing thus that it was poorly trained. And might even prove untrainable.

"Hey man," I heard Tommy say, even as I was arriving at this dispiriting possibility. "Was that your stomach I just heard?"

This might, I realized, prove embarrassing. For what if he— despite his appearance as an Imitation of the Idea of a Hippie, or "Freak"— had trained his stomach? So that it was more like the stomach of that Truest of all True Imitations of the Idea of a Philosopher— namely Socrates— than mine was. Because it didn't growl.

"My stomach?" I said, as though I hadn't the slightest Idea what he was talking about.

"Yeah," said Tommy. "I just heard a really loud yowl. A couple of them. I thought it might be the cat. Except she hasn't been around for a couple of weeks. Probably gone off to get laid." He snickered again. "Did you hear anything?"

"Not a thing," I said.

"Well it didn't sound like her kind of yowl anyway," Tommy said. He looked at me again. "Are you sure your stomach didn't make a noise?"

This was becoming embarrassing. What was I to say? If I answered "Yes," then this would mean that, as an aspiring Imitation of the Idea of a Philosopher, I clearly had even less control over my stomach sounds than Tommy did over his. And he was not— to go by appearances— such an Aspirant at all any more, not even of the Kantian kind. Or was he? There was, after all, that business of "Man." As well as his steadfast execution of his Duties. Had Tommy then managed, somehow, to fuse his Imitation of the Idea of a Hippie, or "Freak," with continued Imitation of the Idea of a Kantian Philosopher, in a way that I did not understand? But that now meant he had full control over his stomach sounds? This was not only embarrassing, but confusing. I could even feel another bout of Perplexity coming on. But if it did come on, if I let it come on, might this mean I would lose control completely of my stomach? Would it then start to growl, and snarl and— as Tommy had put it— "yowl" uncontrollably? As a precautionary measure, I with both hands seized it through the blankets— or to be precise, seized the flesh that lay between it and the blankets. I squeezed. To ensure that it controlled itself.

"Hey man," said Tommy. "Is something wrong?"

"No," I said, as I squeezed. "Nothing's wrong."

"Then why are you...?" Tommy said. "Have you got a stomach ache?"

I squeezed still harder. Lest my stomach, becoming aware by circuitous means that it had now become a centre of attention, attempt to subvert me again. By yowling.

"No," I said emphatically. "I don't."

Tommy nodded, slowly, still holding the candle. "Then are you, like...hungry?" he said.

This was, I realized, becoming like Twenty Questions. Except that, by the Third Question, he was already getting awfully warm. For now that my stomach had, by its own methods, drawn attention to its dilemma, what I felt an impulse to answer was this: Yes. I'm hungry. I've eaten nothing since breakfast, except a cup of tea. Are you not hungry? Do you not have to eat? Except these questions, as they mentally formed themselves, seemed less a matter of potential dialogue Man-to-Man, so to speak...than of stomach-to-stomach. So would I not, were I to ask them, become little better than a mouthpiece? For my unruly stomach?

"Man?" said Tommy's voice. Even as I was being buffeted by this barrage of Perplexity. "Man, are you okay?"

I looked at him. He was leaning toward me, holding the unlit candle, with an expression of what I can only call Care on his face.

"I'm not hungry," I said. Enunciating each syllable. Lest he misunderstand. For this, I was sure, was the only possible way of convincing him that I did have a Truly Philosophical control over the Idea of my Stomach. As he did.

"Oh," said Tommy. "Okay. I wasn't sure. Because you were so

sick outside the truck and all. I thought maybe you'd want your stomach to rest. Overnight."

But what about you? I wanted to say. What about your stomach? You weren't sick. Neither was I, really. But you didn't even pretend to be sick...

"Man, your face is all contorted," Tommy said. "Maybe you should have some goat's milk. Now that I think of it, it might be good for your stomach, too. To calm it."

"Goat's milk?" I managed to say.

"Yeah. I put a jar of it down in the spring," he said. "After I milked Camilla. I thought we could wait til morning, when it was really cold. But if you'd like some now, I can get it."

Just this mention by Tommy, of a jar of goat's milk, set off, I fear, such a deluge of saliva inside my mouth, after the manner of an animal experiment even, that I could barely speak. Such is the contemptibility, sometimes, of the human body.

"No," I tried to say. "No. I don't want any." But all that was emitted from my mouth was a garble of noises mixed with spittle. As though— I realized with a kind of horror— my stomach were now conspiring...to control my speech.

Tommy seemed to be looking at me strangely.

"Man?" he said. "Are you sure you don't want something to eat? Or at least some milk?"

"No," I said clearly. If somewhat loudly. But imposing at last, by an act of sheer will, the order of language on this upwardly moving conspiracy. I was afraid, though, that there might yet be spittle, dribbling down my chin. Such had been the glandular reaction, ejaculation even, this is not too strong a word, inside my mouth. But I was resolved that I would master this. And not the glandular reaction only. Or the momentary takeover of my vocal cords. But also my stomach's own reaction, to its being empty. And, as well, the reactions of who-could-tell what other internal organs. That might be churning, and itching, and conspiring among themselves, to make their own demands. On me. An Aspiring Imitation, of the Idea of a Philosopher.

"No," I was able to say again. Feeling as I did so a certain triumph, that was highly satisfying, over the clamour of unruly organs. "I don't need anything. I'm fine." Then I reached up and wiped my chin, inconspicuously I hoped. Just in case.

"Oh," said Tommy. "Well, I hope I haven't offended you, man. It's just that I try not to eat at night myself, if I can help it. I haven't got a whole lot of bread. You know what I mean?"

I looked at him. Of course it was obvious that he did not have "a whole lot of bread." There didn't seem to be bread in the house at all. Whole-wheat or otherwise. Unless of course he was using Hippie Vernacular. In which case "bread" meant "money." This I knew from the Authoritative Hippie Books. And as I considered the matter, I decided that this must be what he meant. Or perhaps he meant both. No bread, in the form of bread. And no bread, in the form of money. Almost in spite of myself I could not but admire his own economy. Of language.

"Yes," I finally said, after this cogitation. "I know what you mean."

"I'm glad, man," Tommy said. "Then if you know what I mean, why don't we just find you your bed. Okay?"

But this realization, of the extent of his economy, only made me more concerned. For did it not imply that he retained control, not only over his stomach sounds...but also over glandular secretions, that might affect his speech? I was most impressed. Yet in a way— I realized— that had little to do with Tommy's Imitation of the Idea of a Hippie, or "Freak." But rather with his continued Imitation— unstated though it might be— of the Idea of a Philosopher. In his control of unruly organs. And it was, in fact, perhaps at that very moment when I began to grasp that it was more important, to me, to be seen— or heard— as Imitating Truly the Idea of a Philosopher...than it was to be seen as Imitating Truly the Idea of a Hippie, or "Freak." If there proved to be a conflict between them. But was there? Did Tommy himself not provide a living proof, that there might not need to be?

"If you're ready to go, man, then I am," said Tommy's voice. Interrupting this colloquy.

I looked at him. He had picked up the lamp from the table, with his free hand.

What was I to say? In the presence of Living Proof? Besides: "Yes. I'm ready."

"Great," said Tommy, and walked across the kitchen. The light went with him, brightening a part of the room that I had not before seen...and specifically, a small closed door.

I was reminded, as he did this, of *Alice in Wonderland*, and of the door through which the White Rabbit disappears. This was exciting. Not least because unlike Alice— who could not get through the door— I was actually being invited to follow, by Tommy. Into what sort of Wonderland? I therefore gathered up my blankets. Though without loosening the grip on my stomach flesh. Lest it again betray me.

As I reached him, Tommy raised the lamp. Standing just behind him, I could see a passageway leading upwards, and a narrow, slightly tilted staircase.

"Up here," Tommy said, and went through the doorway. The passage was instantly illuminated. While the kitchen, in which I was standing, got dark. This provided still greater incentive, for me to follow. The steps creaked beneath Tommy's boots. And as soon as I stepped on one, it creaked beneath my bedroom slippers. We therefore made a lot of noise. So I was able to relax, slightly, the hold on my stomach. Because even if it had growled at that moment, Tommy would not have heard. This was a relief somewhat, because then my stomach didn't hurt so much. And I was even able to use my left hand, to steady myself against the wall.

Yet I was once again to learn the lesson, that life is never simple! Especially those parts of it that involve transitions. For I noticed, as I ran my hand along the wall while climbing, that the plaster not only had many cracks, like little rivers seen from above, but had in places dropped away completely. So I could see, underneath, some sort of dirty grey wooden slats. Behind and between each one of these were holes. Black empty holes, which looked, at the very least, as though they would make a nice hiding place for rats. I took my hand off the wall, when I noticed these. They sent chills up and down my spine, so I even shivered. Certainly, Alice had never had to contend with the likes of them. Quickly, I moved away from the wall. Because at any moment, I reasoned, I might see a little snout, with twitching whiskers, poke out from between the slats, to nip me.

Except the stairway itself was so narrow, barely wider than I was, that the farther I moved from one side, to avoid a hole, the closer I got to the other, where there were still more holes. So by the time I was halfway up, I was forced to decide that the only course, really, to protect myself from rat bites, was to mount the stairs sideways, a step at a time. This I did. Until I realized, with a sinking feeling in the very stomach that I was holding, that this would not protect me, if a rat not content with poking its nose and whiskers between two slats, made a jump at me instead. And what was more, since I was facing sideways as I was going up, and not straight ahead, this meant I was unable to survey both walls, for holes through which rats could jump, but only one wall at a time. This alarmed me. Because it meant that even as I was surveying one wall, for holes and snouts and twitching whiskers, there might at that very moment be an entire ambush of rats, in the other wall, just waiting to launch themselves at my back as I passed.

I turned around, and surveyed the other wall. There were holes, a couple, that looked as though, actually, they had been punched through the plaster, by someone's fist. But there were not any snouts sticking through. Great relief. Then I looked at the first wall, just above the step where I was standing, trying to make myself as small as possible. Cracks. One hole. No snouts. Relief. Even as I did this, however, I realized that the best tactic to adopt would be to examine carefully the area on both walls that I was approaching, before I got there, facing only one wall, and going sideways. This, I knew, would not guarantee complete safety, from ambushes mounted by concealed and especially smart rats, that knew how to wait. But it was probably, under the circumstances, the best I could do.

This, therefore, was my approach. Standing as closely as I could to the centre of the step, and holding both my stomach and my blankets, I leaned as far forward as I could without falling over. By this means I examined the walls on either side, in front of me. Then having done this, and not seen any rats, I advanced sideways a single step. And having advanced this step, I craned my neck upwards, and looked around. The second time I did this, however, I realized the flaw in it. For by standing one way, while trying to crane my neck both ways, so as to examine both walls, I was getting a clearer view of the wall toward which I was facing, bodily, and a somewhat inhibited view of the other. This, of course, would be fine, if the rats who were waiting in ambush had confined themselves only to the wall toward which I was facing. But what if they hadn't? I realized, therefore, that to do this properly— and what other way is there, ever, to do anything?— I would have to advance one step sideways, crane my neck to examine the wall toward which I was facing, and then, having done this and seen no rats, turn around, on the same step. I could then, by craning my neck, examine the other wall to the same degree that I had examined the first wall. In this way, I was sure, I would not be giving the rats in either wall an undue advantage.

I was just getting into the rhythm of this, however, and with much success, having not been surprised by any rats, and having navigated a full three steps...when I was interrupted by Tommy.

"Man?" he said, from above me. "What's the matter?"

"What?" I said, stopping and looking up at him. This was difficult, on account of the fact that he was holding up the lamp. So I could not see his face very well.

"I said, what's the matter?" Tommy said. "What are you doing? Neck exercises or something?"

I realized, as he said this, that he clearly did not appreciate the need for precautions, on a staircase such as the one we were on, regarding rats. But on the other hand, I realized also that he just as clearly had mounted these steps many times, and had, by all appearances anyway, not been attacked by rats. Or had he? And what evidence had I that he had used these steps before? Or recently? I hadn't asked him any of these questions. Neither had he volunteered the answers. And besides: even if he hadn't been bitten, this did not imply, logically, that I couldn't be. It implied only that there was less probability, that I would be.

"Man?" said Tommy's voice.

I looked up. All I could see, this time, atop his body, was the dazzling light of the lamp. Which he had lifted. This made for an interesting and— I grasped instantly— comforting counterpoint to Tommy's earlier identity, archetypally speaking, as a black silhouette. In fact, it was so reassuring, this dazzling light, that must have been intensified by the narrow corridor, that I simply gazed at it, in a kind of wonder. For of what great transformations human beings are capable, archetypally speaking, sometimes! And how suddenly, how unpredictably, such transformations can erupt, into the everyday!

"Man?" said Tommy's voice, from behind the dazzling light. Again.

The use of the generic "Man" this time, from behind the light, was, of course, a profound experience. I felt I was being called. But from the light above this time, and not— as had been the case in the truck— the darkness beside me. Was this, I wondered as I stood, momentarily unable to move, or even answer, how Noah felt, when he was called? Or Moses, before the Burning Bush? But who was calling me? I gazed upward, at the shining light. Was Tommy himself aware of the transformation that, from my perspective, he had undergone? Never mind the Kantian version of "Man": this usage was positively Eschatological! Had Tommy then become a vehicle of some kind? A channel? A conduit?

But then, even as I was in the midst of this stupefaction, that was almost a rapture but not quite, I Recollected something. And this was that I must not be deluded. There was a clash of traditions going on, of which I must beware. For did I not aspire to Imitate Truly the Idea of a Philosopher, after the manner of Socrates? Rather than the Idea of a Prophet, or a Rescuer of all Mankind, after the manner of Moses, or Noah? With their dependence upon Divine Guidance, all the time. Had Socrates himself not said, at his trial, that his Inutition, his "Voice" as he described it, only dissuaded him from doing the wrong thing, and never guided him, as a kind of Light, toward the right thing? How then was I, as an aspiring Imitation of the Idea of a Philosopher, to respond to this? To this light that seemed to be radiating from Tommy's head, obscuring it, as though he himself were an angel sent from heaven, to guide me? Especially when there was no reference whatsoever to such figures, by Socrates. Nevertheless, philosophically speaking, St. Augustine had certainly believed in angels. While yet claiming inspiration from Socrates. Or at least from Plato. And it could not be denied that he too was a philosopher. Albeit in Christian register. Where then did this leave...?

"MAN, WILL YOU FUCKING WELL ANSWER ME?" shouted Tommy's voice. Interrupting this colloquy.

From on high, so to speak.

Such was the anger, and such the tone of command in this voice, that almost I dropped to my knees. In fear and trembling. I had, of course, been deep in Perplexity, Philosophical Perplexity, concerning the nature of Religion, and of Divine Revelation, and the relationship of both, to Intuition. And to Reason. And yet I was being called. Again. Generically. In such a way that my Perplexity was being interrupted. From above.

Was this, I had to wonder, how the Greeks themselves must have felt? With the arrival of the first Christian missionaries?

And yet...there had been that touch of obscenity tossed in. Perhaps for spice. But it did not contribute, either to the gravity or the profundity of the moment. This was disappointing. And what was more, when I looked up, I could see that Tommy had lowered the lamp somewhat. So I could see his face, his own face, leaning forward. And could not see his stomach. Which was now obscured. By the light.

"Yes?" I said. I did not know what else to say, amid such confusion. It even occurred to me that, given this new placement of the light, I was about to receive some new revelation. Concerning stomach sounds.

Tommy, meanwhile, did not answer right away. Instead he simply stared at me, squinting slightly.

"I thought we'd decided you were going to bed, man," he said, now placing a hand just above and in front of the lamp, to screen it.

This caused the light to be subdued considerably. So much so that the magic of the moment, such as it had been, subsided also. And I realized that I was alone on the staircase with Tommy, again. And not with any otherworldly presence, or angel, after all. I felt a pang, of what must have been still more disappointment. For how often is it that a person is vouchsafed a visitation, whether "real" in the sense of being a True Imitation of the Idea of a Visitation or not, that seems to come from a higher world? Not very often. Assuming, of course, that such a world does exist. And that speculations concerning it are themselves not delusions. But does it? Are they? It was clear that I had hit upon the moment to try to talk about Kant again, to Tommy. The phenomenal and the noumenal. In such a way too, I reasoned, recalling my earlier concern with his stomach sounds, or lack thereof, that I might be able to discover also whether he was himself still on the path to becoming a philosopher, a True Imitation of the Idea of a Real One.

"What about the phenomenal and the noumenal?" I therefore said. Looking up. At Tommy.

"What?" said Tommy, leaning forward and appearing to squint even more.

"The phenomenal and the noumenal," I repeated, disappointed that he, with his extensive knowledge of Kant, had not realized right away what I was getting at. "Kant," I therefore reminded him. "The phenomenal. The world of the senses. Of Reason. And the noumenal. The thing in itself. Intuition. Religion. Higher feeling." I even, at this moment, released what remained of my grip on my stomach. So as to gesture at him. I couldn't help it.

"What about them?" Tommy said. "I thought you wanted to go to bed."

What disappointment! That someone who had looked like an angel, on account of the bright light obscuring his head only moments before...could now sound so trite. And not only not like an angel. But not like a philosopher, either. Or at least not a philosopher of the true kind, such as Socrates. Who, according to Plato, had been ready to enter into Dialogue with anyone, at any time, and at any place. And to talk all night if necessary, in order to reach a higher plane, of Perplexity.

But then this, I reasoned, this reluctance on Tommy's part, to participate philosophically in Dialogue, was what must have come from studying those monologues of Kant's to begin with, instead of Socrates. But did it also come, I had to wonder, from his having decided...

"Man?" said Tommy's voice.

I looked up. He was staring at me, above the lamp. His expression was again one of Care.

"I can't cope much longer, man," Tommy said. "Either you come up those stairs, so I can show you your bed. Or I'm going to walk back down, and crash out in the kitchen. And you can find your own way up here."

I realized, at this moment, that Tommy's saying he couldn't "cope much longer" could only be a signal that— whether he was aware of this or not— he was indeed experiencing Perplexity himself. So there was hope. Which roused in me, understandably, the desire to explain to him the chain of reasoning, that had led to my perhaps surprising him, with Kant. Yet I did not want to drive him away, with too methodical an explanation to begin with. Far better to commence with a global survey, of the precipitating issues.

"The rats," I therefore said, counting each subject area off on my fingers. "And angels. Archetypes. Silhouettes." I paused. "Are you getting all this?" I said.

"What?" Tommy said.

"In the walls," I said. And held up finger number five.

Tommy nodded slowly.

In understanding, I assumed.

But instead, and before I could start on the other hand, he said: "Do you often go on like this?" The Perplexity had shifted to his face. "Is it, like, being in a new place or something?"

This transmutation of Perplexity from voice to face was, of course, an encouraging sign. And yet...even in the midst of this salutary development, I myself drew the logical inference from the first and last fingers I was holding up in front of me. To wit: that we were still standing motionless, in the stairway. And that at any moment, a rat might jump out at us. Perhaps they had even been accumulating, behind the walls. Except that Tommy himself was not in the stairway any more, really. He was standing beside an open door, at the summit. So that I alone was vulnerable, still, to a rat attack. I felt my skin getting very hot. I began to tremble.

"Man?" said Tommy's voice.

I had to ask him. At last. Even though he might infer that, in doing so, I was impugning his hospitality. While I was all too aware myself that this was hardly the way to get back to Kant. Yet I could not bear this burden of Unknowing any longer. I had to ask him.

"Are there..." I managed to say, in a kind of gasp, "Are there...rats? In these walls?" There. It was out. But my impulse was just to collapse. I braced myself. Though without, of course, touching either wall.

"Rats?" Tommy said. "Here?"

"Yes," I said. Still gasping slightly. "Rats. In the walls." I knew too, at this moment, that I had best unburden myself completely, of all fears at once. "And snakes," I therefore added. "Toads. That sort of thing."

"Snakes?" said Tommy. "Toads?"

I had to wonder, as he was saying these things, whether he knew he was sounding silly, repeating everything I said as a question. Or was he perhaps doing this on purpose, to mock me?

"Yes," I said more loudly. And emphatically, to let him know that I would not stand for being mocked. "Rats. In the walls. That might jump out at me." I leaned forward and stared at him. So that he might see how much in earnest I was.

"Oh," he said, finally. And as though the gravity of the situation was sinking in. For this I was grateful. "Rats. Toads. And snakes." I could see him shake his head, behind the lantern. "Well, you don't have to worry, man," he said. "I have never, in all the years I've been going up and down these stairs, encountered a rat. Or a toad. Or a snake. Not once."

This, of course, provided enormous relief for me. So much so that I felt again like collapsing. But I did not let on, lest Tommy begin to imagine that I was not up to country life. So instead I replied, with emphasis, "Good." And just to show that I trusted him— which I did, sort of— I gathered up all my strength, as well as all my blankets so I wouldn't trip...and ascended with determination up the rest of the stairs. This made for bursts of anxiety, as I passed each hole. But Tommy had vouched for them, that they were empty. And so they proved to be. Or at any rate: no snouts were emitted, as I passed. No whiskers twitched. And no teeth were sunk, into my leg or arm. Such relief! And so it was that, in this way, I arrived at the landing, at the top of the stairs.

Where still stood Tommy, politely waiting, with the lamp. And indeed, it was Tommy who was waiting, and not some visitation from another realm. This too was reassuring.

Somewhat.

## §10

"This is it," Tommy said when I got to the top of the stairs, and was standing beside him, panting. "The only other heated room in the mansion."

Then, before I could even gather breath to re-open our Dialogue, he ducked his head, and went through a low doorway. Once again, the light went with him. Quickly, therefore, I followed. He was just inside the room beyond. Which— apart from a much lower ceiling— immediately presented itself in the lamplight as an imitation of the one downstairs. The wallpaper was torn and peeling, and behind it were layers of chipping paint. And there was a single window which— like the ones downstairs— lacked curtains, and was covered with the same kind of plastic. Looking around, however, I did not notice any holes in the plaster. A small blessing. But neither did I notice any furniture, not even a table. Instead, the floor was strewn with cardboard boxes. A few of these were sitting upright. But most were tipped over, and spilling what looked to be old clothes. The floor itself was made of boards, whose paint— perhaps originally blue or grey— had also chipped.

Wonderland this certainly was not. And the extent of its failure as such was, I admit, enough to scuttle— for the moment anyway— my Dialogical resolve. Looking around, I did not see a bed either...though in one corner there did seem to be a mattress of sorts, that actually looked like a pile of rags. Or perhaps it was a pile of rags. That resembled a mattress. I squinted. I was facing the usual problem of reference again, of correspondence between words and things. Not to mention of things with their own Ideas. But the light was too dim for me to tell whether I was looking at a mattress that resembled a pile of rags, or a pile of rags that resembled a mattress. Or perhaps it was— and here I Recollected Tommy's words downstairs, when he had said we should "hit the sack"— precisely this: his "sack." Whatever it was, though, it appeared to be, above all, filthy. This being the category that instantly overwhelmed it. And that in overwhelming it, became the dominant defining presence of the entire room. Filth.

Socrates, I decided, might have found this room of use, in his Dialogue with Parmenides. In that by means of it, he might have replied in the affirmative, to Parmenides' question as to whether there exist Ideas of such visual phenomena as dirt, mud, and hair. For the room suggested, at the very least, a True Imitation of the Idea of Filth. Which Idea might subsume these other, and lesser, phenomena. But having found the room useful, Socrates would not have had to sleep in it. My stomach was beginning to knot up again. And not only because I had gone back to clutching the flesh around it with my fingers, perhaps for the sake of a familiar handhold. Was I expected, then— did Tommy expect me— to sleep in this...room? Or, to be more precise, in this True Imitation of the Idea of Filth?

I allowed my eyes to wander, as an alternative to considering this possibility. There was only one other feature that stood out. This was a thick black pipe near the room's centre, that ran from a hole in the floor to another hole in the ceiling.

"That's the pipe from downstairs," Tommy said, from behind me. He must have seen me look at it. "It's how the room stays warm. But it can get pretty hot at night. So you shouldn't touch it, man. Okay?"

I could only nod. I should have been getting used to the sort of surprises which were being offered by Tommy's Farm. Which itself was coming dangerously close to meriting relegation to that lesser league of things, so-called, that do not deserve to be thought of in terms of their degree of Imitation, of an Idea. For I could not quite bring myself to think about it any longer in terms of its Imitating Truly the Idea of a Hippie Farm. Or for that matter Imitating Anything, other than What It Was. More challenges, to the Theory of Ideas. But this room was even worse than the kitchen had been. For the kitchen had at least looked, with the clothes hung up, like an Imitation of the Idea of an Immigrant Kitchen, which might belong, then, to Hard-Working Immigrants. Or at least to Imitations of this Idea. Though it did not. But this room... This room looked as though whatever Imitation had been living in it had moved out quickly, leaving everything that he or she couldn't carry, and that was of no worth anyway, on the floor.

I had been under the impression, of course, from the Authoritative Hippie Books, that Imitations of the Idea of Hippies built beds that were picturesque. Lofts, they were called, with....

"Anyway, man," said Tommy's voice from behind me, "you can sleep in that bed over there." I assumed he was in the process of gesturing, toward the Imitation of the Idea of Filth that lay in the corner. For to what else could he have been referring? One of the cardboard boxes? I couldn't bring myself to turn around and look, for confirmation. There was only one pile of rags— or one "sack"— that didn't look like heaped-up clothing.

"I usually sleep up here myself..." he began to say.

"That's just fine, Tommy," I interjected quickly, as I turned to look at him. I did not intend to be rude. But... "You can sleep up here tonight too, if you want to."

"Don't worry about it, man," said Tommy. His replacement work suit itself now looked especially creased and dirty in the lamplight. "I can curl up on the floor beside the stove," he said. "That way I can keep the fire going."

I realized, as he said this, that he was probably resolved that, as the host, he should ask me to sleep in his sack. Or in his pile of rags. Or in his Imitation of the Idea of Filth, whatever it was. The room, as I turned to look at it again, reminded me more and more of a room I had looked at during my search for a place to live after graduation. It had been in another rooming house, which, when I had walked through it to reach the room, had been full of strange old men, with slicked back hair and bulbous noses and bad complexions. They had all been wearing cowboy boots. I shook my head. Why, my own rooming house, which at least was clean, had more in common with True Imitations of the Idea of a Hippie Farm, as I had read about them in the Authoritative Hippie Books, than this room did. I thought this a dreadful irony. Was this what I had gone through so much anxiety, never mind an almost mystical experience, to reach?

"Anyhow, man," said Tommy, walking across the room so I could see him again, "I'll leave this bit of candle for you here, in the middle of the floor. Just make sure you blow it out before you go to sleep. Okay?"

As he was speaking, I checked his feet, for cowboy boots. I could not resist the impulse, though I knew it was silly. Had I not, only moments before, seen the same old rubber boots beneath the work suit, as I mounted the stairs? It was these boots which now, as he crossed the floor, made a hollow sound, echoing against the wood. This was how I felt, too. Hollow. I watched Tommy kneel and lift the lid off the lamp. Vaguely, I wondered how he did this, without getting burned. The light dimmed as the glass came off. He held the candle against the yellow flame, turning it until it lit. I watched his face in the light, and the strands of loose hair that had not been pulled into his pony-tail. These stood out yellow also, in the light. Behind him, the shadows flickered.

So this, then, I reflected as I watched, was where Tommy slept. Every night. Here. In the pile of rags. Surrounded by cardboard boxes. And piles of clothes that looked like other rags. And an otherwise empty room.

Tommy, meanwhile, dripped some wax from the candle onto the floor, and then propped the candle itself in the puddle. Tommy, I wanted to say to him, where are all your friends? Your girl friend? Who had been, for me, the closest I had ever imagined to a True Imitation of the Idea of a Hippie Girl. What happened to them? Because it was now becoming obvious they could not simply have gone-with-the-flow-for-good, such that their being borne away by the current of the *Weltgeist*, so to speak, had not been noticed, by Tommy.

"Okay, man," Tommy said, standing up. He put the glass back on the lamp, and the room brightened up again. "There should be enough blankets on the bed." He then walked to one of the boxes, knelt, and pulled out what looked to be a couple of very large rags. He shook them, and clouds of dust swirled in the lamplight. "I'll just take these," he said, standing up.

"But...what will you sleep on?" I managed to say.

"There's a mat downstairs, man," he said, and chuckled. "It used to belong to the dog. Before she ran off with another man." He chuckled again. But before I could even begin to wonder what he meant by this...joke, he walked to the door, with the lamp in one hand and the large rags slung over one shoulder. He turned and looked at me. "You won't forget to blow out the candle, eh, man?" he said. "I wouldn't want to waken up to this glorious castle of mine all in flames now, would I."

"I won't forget," I said.

"Great," Tommy said. "Great, man. I'll see you in the morning, then." He went through the door. The light went with him. I watched the glow get fainter, until it disappeared. I also listened to the creaking of the stairs, as he descended. Then I heard his boots, on the kitchen floor.

I looked around the room again. It was much darker, because the light was gone, and there was just the piece of candle on the floor, flickering. I was alone, for the first time really, since our arrival at the farm. Because when I had been alone in the kitchen, earlier, Tommy might have come back at any moment. And did. But this time I felt alone. Really alone. It was as though there were circles of loneliness, radiating outward from me. I was alone, in the room. Tommy was alone, downstairs. And we were alone, in the house. Which was situated, apparently, miles away from anyone else, according to Tommy. He had said there were some "assholes." Somewhere. But it did not sound as though they would contribute much, to my understanding of the Idea of a Hippie Farm. And of what had happened to all the other Imitations— who seemed less True all the time— of the Idea of Hippies.

I forced myself to contemplate the room, its Filthiness. The boxes and clothes and rags were now much dimmer. To some extent this was a relief, in that I no longer noticed their specific filthiness, as a subset of the room's greater Filth. But I could not but wonder...what might...reside, amid such Filth. Tommy had said he hadn't seen any rats. Or toads. Or snakes. In the stairwell. And in the entire time he had been living in the house. Did this imply he had not seen any in this room, either? Given that he slept here every night, surely this implied he checked it regularly. Certainly, I would. But it was becoming clear to me that Tommy's standards, and my standards, were somewhat different. Was this because of Kant? I wasn't sure. Nor had Tommy's reply to my attempt to raise this question, in the stairwell, been satisfying.

I was at least, however, getting used to the dimness. So it was not quite so spooky any more. That is to say, I was able to suppress the first rising impulse to grab up my blankets, and pull them more tightly around me. So I could run back downstairs to Tommy's human society, the only one that was available. But in the midst of this impulse, I remembered that my hands were still gripped tightly around, not so much my blankets, as the flesh of my stomach, inside them. I released this. The blankets drooped. My stomach felt relieved. If empty.

I gathered up my blankets again, and walked across the room to the pile of rags. It looked like a large dark blotch, because I was standing in the faint light cast by the candle. I did not sit down. Instead I nudged it, the pile I mean, with the toe of my bedroom slipper. To see if anything was living inside it. Or perhaps anyone. This took some courage. But nothing moved. Just to be safe, though, and with mounting confidence, I walked along its length, kicking gently. As I did so, I wondered whether this was what Tommy had meant, when he spoke of "hitting the sack." Clouds of musty-smelling dust rose around me. But no rats sallied forth. Or snakes. Or toads. Or even large bugs.

By this means, then, I satisfied myself that, as species of higher living organism, I would at least be alone in the pile of rags. If not necessarily in the room. The question remained, though, as to whether I should also explore the entire room, kicking everything. The prospect was unappealing. And besides, my stomach had begun to hurt again, but in a different way, since the pressure of my fingers had evidently been obscuring the hunger pangs. It occurred to me, as the pangs began to percolate outward from the pure void of my stomach, that were I to go to sleep as successfully as my fingers had been pressing my stomach flesh, obscuring its hunger...then I would awaken all the sooner in the morning. So I could eat. Or— if Tommy proved as niggardly with the vittles in the morning as he had in the evening— at the very least drink some goat's milk.

This was great incentive to go to sleep. But it was also sufficient incentive, even in the form of hope, to trigger a glandular reflex again, so that my mouth began to fill with saliva, which I had to swallow. How unexpectedly the body asserts its prerogatives! All the more incentive, therefore, to go to sleep, because presumably I would then stop salivating, too. But how? To go to sleep, I mean. In the pile of rags? I shuddered. Fortunately, I still had my blankets around me. Which, though they too smelt musty, I was sure were not so musty, or so thick with dust— or with who could tell what else— as the ones on the floor. So having worked up sufficiently the resolve of desperation, on account of my stomach...I lay down. Or I did not so much lie down, as flop, all at once, on the pile. So as not to disrupt my blankets. Dust rose around me. There was a pillow of some sort, but I was able to pull up one of my blankets, so it was beneath my head. My hair, then, did not have to touch the bed. In fact, none of me, nakedly speaking, had to touch it, because I was wrapped in the blankets, and underneath the blankets, in my clothes. And even, on my feet, my bedroom slippers.

Except that then, being supine on the pile of rags, I realized I had not blown out the candle. In the rooming house, there was a small lamp beside the bed, and on its base a switch. By this means I could turn the light off when in bed. I missed this switch. The paradoxical simplicity of the gesture by which— whatever its complex ties to the electricity grid— I simply turned it off at night. I missed this. Even at Tommy's farm.

I did not, however, reflect on the implications, both philosophically and in terms of Hippieness, of such a longing. There were other concerns. How, I wondered, as I lay on the pile of rags and stared at the candle, would I get up again? With my blankets wrapped so tightly around me? This was all very tiring, and I would have preferred to drop off, from the sheer exertion of thought, right then. So to make matters simple, and to avoid disrupting my blankets, I rolled. Off the pile of rags. My hip, and then my shoulder, made faint thuds as they hit the floor. I rolled across it, holding my blankets. Fortunately, this expanse of floor contained only the odd bit of clothing over which I rolled. I reached the candle, manoeuvering the angle of my approach so my head, and not my waist or feet, was beside it when I arrived. The little flame was directly before me. I was about to blow it out.

But then I remembered that, were I to do so, I would need to get back to the pile of rags, still rolling, in darkness. This did not appeal. What should I do?

It was in this state of Perplexity, before the candle, and staring at the yellow flame, that I must have fallen asleep. With the problem still unresolved. I dreamt vaguely of being chased by black silhouettes. In the distance there was someone with a yellow head. I ran toward this figure. Only to have him, when I was almost there, lift this head off his shoulders and throw it at me. As with Ichabod Crane. It flared up, like a brilliant sun, the closer it got. I woke. The candle, in my mental absence, had melted down to nothing, or to a puddle, and the wick, or what was left of it, was lying in this puddle, burning fiercely. Still wrapped in my blankets I rolled away, in order that I too not incandesce. I then surveyed the small conflagration from a distance of one full roll. The room seemed white in its glow. Having recovered some composure, I rolled toward it again, the full roll, and blew. To no avail. I drew a deep breath and then blew harder, drawing inspiration from Recollecting how I had done precisely this, with great success, at birthday parties. My own birthday parties. I blew. And blew. And blew.

The flame first flickered, and then went out.

Darkness.

I rolled back toward the pile of rags. Or in what I imagined was its direction. I was disinclined to unwrap my blankets. I watched, as I rolled, the rectangle of the window, which was only slightly less black than everything else. I could not but speculate. Had I not wakened up, might there have been a fire? Might the candle, or its puddle, have dropped through the floorboards, burning? Might they have landed even on Tommy's head, underneath? And then, of course, the entire house might have burned, to the ground. Not a great loss, architecturally speaking. But would I have been able, myself, to escape outside?

This gave me pause. Though I didn't pause, in my rolling. I bumped, with my shoulder, against what could only have been the pile of rags. Rolled onto it. Pulled my blankets around me. Lay there staring on my back. In silence.

And eventually, I must suppose...slept.

## §11

The first thing I noticed, when I opened my eyes in the morning, was the pile of magazines. That was lying beside the pile of rags. On which I was lying, wrapped in blankets. The magazines were partly covered with another rag. This I had perhaps disturbed in my nocturnal thrashings. But as soon as I saw these magazines, and realized what they were...I could not but wonder whether Tommy, in giving me his sack to sleep in, had not made a big *faux pas*. For if this was indeed where he slept every night...then clearly all my hopes, of finding on his farm Imitations of the Idea of Hippie Girls, in peasant dresses and baking bread, had been misplaced.

I sat up and rubbed my eyes, the more clearly to see what I thought I had seen. But fortunately, my doing so made for another distraction, that I could not ignore. Namely: an urge that welled up stinging in my abdomen, and signalled the unease of whatever fleshly organs they are against which urine pushes. I was, therefore, obliged first to wonder what Tommy himself did, in the morning, when he had to pee. Was there a bathroom? I hadn't seen one. And in the absence of electrical power, I couldn't imagine there being one. What then did he do? Had he as much control over his urinary tract, as over his stomach sounds? This would be impressive. But I did not. And there was no sense pretending I did, as I had been able to do with my stomach sounds, by clenching my stomach flesh. For my bladder was not so easily clenched.

I stumbled to my feet, then, on the pile of rags, pulling my blankets around me, and quickly glancing at that portion of the topmost magazine which was visible. On its cover was displayed— quite clearly as I had kept my glasses on— a photographic Imitation, in colour, of a young woman's face. Along with other parts, usually hidden, of her surface anatomy. I focused on the urge to pee. In order that this urge might quiet a further one, which now began to mount with the force of genetic blindness. Namely: to pick up this magazine. And to consider more closely this Imitation, this Degraded and perhaps even False Imitation, as Socrates would have called it. In that it was but a two-dimensional Image of an Imitation, of the Idea of a Beautiful Girl...

From this temptation, I was rescued by the urge to pee. Looking around the room, I saw behind the stovepipe a large can, which looked to be lidless. Shuffling toward it I picked it up. It sloshed. A vile odour filled my nostrils. Leading me to conclude that this can must serve, for Tommy, the very purpose it could serve for me.

I parted first the blankets, then my zipper, then the fly on my underwear. The morning air was cool on my own exposed anatomy. The stream made a clanging sound. The odour mounted as the can's contents swirled with the force of spray. The pee steamed. I nearly retched. But even as I swallowed bile, I remembered...the magazines. I felt a stirring as the pee trickled to droplets. A thickening, even.

Setting the can down, I with determination put my noodle back where it belonged. First inside my trousers, then inside my underwear. I closed the zipper, and pulled the blankets around me.

I was again faced with Choice, as those modern philosophers like to belabour. I could take this opportunity to go downstairs. And ask of Tommy where the can might be emptied. Yet I did not do this. Instead I stood, more or less inert, except for twitches on the part of my noodle. I felt another kind of stirring. This time of anger. For relieved of the pressure that the pee had exerted, I began to appreciate the oddness of this situation. This was supposed to be an Imitation of the Idea of a Hippie Farm. Was it not? Should such an Imitation contain such magazines? Such False Imitations, of the Idea of...Exquisitely Beautiful Young Women? Beneath a pile of rags?

I shook my head. Then gathering up my blankets, I walked to the window. There was grey daylight coming through the plastic. Now, especially, would be my chance to look through this window, and see

Tommy's Farm. For the first time. And in such a way— did I dare to hope— as to dispel the pull...to go back to the pile of rags, and fling myself, blankets and all, upon it.

I squinted through the piece of plastic. But all I could see were grey, brownish, and dark green shapes. More distortion, such as the senses— according to Socrates— wreak on everything. I could, however, by that time have done with a great deal less. Distortion, I mean. The grey, I decided, was where the sky should have been. And the brown and dark green where the land should have been. I looked at the window frame. Strips of wood and little nails secured the plastic. My impulse— again— was to tear these off. Then the plastic would fall, and I would be able to look out in daylight at Tommy's Farm. With only that degree of distortion wrought by a pane of glass. For this, at least, this looking through a pane of glass, at clearly defined trees and grasses and sky, might allay the stirrings, the thick...hungry...warmth...in my noodle...

But did I dare, as Tommy's guest, to do this? I clenched my teeth. Recollecting as I did so, and without being able to stop myself, an event of my youth. I'd been invited to babysit. And had found, after the babies or whatever they were had gone to bed...a pile of magazines. Just such as these. My noodle was thickening again, I could feel it doing so, with its own brand of Recollection...

But this had been before I discovered Philosophy. And had learned about the value of Chasteness, in those who seek to Imitate the Idea of a Philosopher. Why, had Socrates himself not said that the highest form of Love itself is Chaste?

And between Men?

But had Socrates ever seen such magazines? I closed my eyes. Surely, the best course would be for me to turn around and walk down the stairs, to the kitchen. There, I dared hope again, to engage Tommy, if he was awake, in some bracing philosophical Dialogue...

But what if he was not awake? I opened my eyes, and gazed at the blotches beyond the piece of plastic. Why, then, I could set off myself, upon my own exploration of Tommy's farm. Not so ambitious a one that I would risk getting lost in the forest. Assuming there was a forest. More an exercise in orientation, around the barnyard. Assuming there was a barnyard. Or what about the fields? Were there fields? I tried to look through the plastic. But the blotches were as blurred as ever...

I bit my lip. Hard. My face was suffused with pain. Why had Tommy done this? Why had he left such magazines there, beside his sack? For clearly they belonged to him. There was no one else, he had told me, for miles around. But why Tommy? Who in our earlier acquaintance had been blessed with the most beautiful girl friend in the university. Which girl friend had served, for me, as a Model. For the Truest of All True Imitations, of the Idea of a Hippie Girl. What had happened? And why had he left these magazines for me to find? But I realized, even as I mentally asked this question, that it, at least, had a simple answer. He had not left them for me to find. Because he had not planned, when he left his farm, that he would return with someone. Whom he would then install. In his pile of rags.

But did this imply, then, that he kept these magazines beside this pile all the time? And that instead of waking to the sounds of birds, and to the country sunshine, and to sweeping vistas across his farm, and to his fellow seekers after the Idea of Hippieness...he awoke instead...to them? To the False Imitations in the form of Photographs? That were especially False because they represented Girls...as though they were always smiling? Always...naked?

And if the answers to all these questions were Yes...then what did he do?

I did not want to think about this.

But even as I decided not to...I had a further insight. Had I not first seen Tommy, in the bookstore, beside the magazine rack? And what had he been doing, too, while being watched by Squinty-Pruned Joe-Face Eyed? Why...examining the magazine rack, and the upper shelf at that, in the store. So was it possible that both these times, Tommy had been looking, not for magazines on organic gardening, or even for journals of philosophy...but for precisely the kind of magazines that now lay piled, beside the pile of rags?

That he should have come to this. Yet had he not been lucky, in Mr. Papadiguano's store? And not only in finding me. For if he had been looking for such magazines there, he had been disappointed. Mr. Papadiguano did not permit them. He told us that they were immoral. And I, who worked there, felt relief in this. Because it meant that, as someone who had to stock this very rack, I would not myself be subject to such Temptations. While at work.

But this did not make me less disappointed in Tommy. For it meant that, all the time I had been watching him beside both magazine racks, and thinking him so successful in the latter case at renouncing the Temptations of Consumer Society...he had probably been waiting for just the moment when he was *not* being watched. So he could seize and open and flip through and ogle, drooling, precisely the Falsest of False Imitations, that were contained in these magazines. For could these Imitations, of the Idea of a Real Girl, carry on a conversation? They could not. Could they move? They could not. Could they even look back? They could not.

For they were False.

And yet...were they in this sense any more False...than were the photographic Images in the Authoritative Hippie Books? Especially the ones that depicted Imitations of the Idea of Hippie Girls, in peasant dresses and baking whole-wheat bread? These terms of comparison sobered me. Had I actually seen such Imitations, on Tommy's Farm? Encountered them? Talked to them? I had not. Nor had I seen any— in the moving, looking and talking-back-to-someone format— since university. And as for these other Images...could I really judge Tommy too harshly? For I too knew a little of this...Temptation. I too had faced it, even in my moments of greatest focus, on Philosophy. And sometimes, it seemed, especially in such moments. And thus subjected, I would rise from my book, and resolve that this was indeed the time to shop for milk. Then, before I bought the milk, in some convenience store not unlike Joe's, I would make a point, while the proprietor was occupied with someone else...

But why go on? In me, an aspiring Imitation of the Idea of a Philosopher, who had renounced more lively Imitations of the Idea of Women as a distraction, such indulgence might be excused. Occasionally. And besides, I also reasoned as I gazed at the blurs beyond the plastic, contemplation of such magazines, though amid the surroundings of a store, most often followed, did it not, upon disinterested Contemplation of Philosophy. And following so closely upon such Contemplation it also bespoke— did it not?— a certain appreciation, detached and purely aesthetic, of the Female Form. Or of the Imitation thereof. And also of a kind of Beauty, which, when given proper proportion, inspired even the ancient Greeks— of whom Socrates was one— to heights of rapture. Of the purely contemplative kind.

And, in fact, when I began to consider the entire matter from this perspective, I had to wonder at my indignation. For had not many philosophers throughout the centuries owned to similar appreciation of the Female Form? Of, that is, the Idea of Female Beauty? As exemplary of Beauty and Proportion generally. And did such philosophers not also commend the...Aesthetic Imitation of this Idea? Especially— as with classical statuary— in the absence of clothes? In order that all the perfect proportions, mathematically and timelessly speaking, might be revealed. In a way that even Socrates and Plato, with their love of mathematical harmonies, might appreciate. Perhaps had appreciated. Maybe. At some time.

Perhaps, then, I reasoned, this was why Tommy himself kept such magazines beside his bed. So that he might be reminded, too, upon wakening each morning, and as a residual Imitation of the Idea of a Kantian Philosopher, of the mathematical perfection that is possible through Harmony, in the Idea of the Female Form. And in its Not

Entirely False Imitations. For insofar as strictly visual Form was concerned, were these Photographs themselves not...Approximate Imitations? If not of Individuals perhaps, then of a Universal. Much as the photographs in the Authoritative Hippie Books depicted— through individuals— the universal Ideas of Hippieness. And of a Hippie Girl. For what is an Individual, after all, besides itself an Imitation...of a Universal? Were the pictures then to this extent True Imitations of the Universal Idea of Female Beauty? By means of the contemporary medium of photography. That might even, in its revealing capacity, present this form in ways analogous to how the tools and marble of the great Greek sculptor Praxiteles did. Creating something as fixed, and inalterable, as an Idea. Yet Visible.

This line of thought I found fruitful. As well as exciting. In philosophical terms. For was it not possible that my own interest in such magazines was itself a function of my disinterested Love of Aesthetic Form? Of Mathematical Perfection? Of Ideal Proportion? And of True Imitations, of all of these? As inspired by Socrates. Was it really such a bad thing, then, that Tommy himself kept such magazines by his bed? Perhaps they even served for him— and with his own philosophical preference— as aids to what I Recollected Kant himself said about "aesthetic judgment": that it involves "pleasure without interest." Yet might they not also, without his knowing it— be enhancing his grasp of Socrates? And of the Theory of True Ideas? And of their Imitations? Would it be a bad thing either, then, if I were myself to further my appreciation of Ideal Forms— and of their Imitations— by contemplating...the magazines, too? But with detachment. Complete detachment. And with an eye, only, for their Aesthetic— not to mention their Philosophical— merits. As Imitations of the Idea of Harmonious Proportion. Such as even Socrates referred to. Some place.

This opportunity being recognized, then, I turned around and walked to the pile of rags. Just as decisively as I had walked to the window when, in a state of confused thinking, as we philosophers like to say, I'd imagined that the magazines, which Tommy had so kindly assembled, served only a salacious purpose. It was such a relief, to disabuse myself of so low a notion. And not only in regard to the magazines. But in regard to Tommy. And there they were. I saw them, as I approached the bed. And did I not Intuit, the closer I got to them, what purely Aesthetic wonders might lie between their covers? I even let go my blankets and rubbed my hands together, in purely disinterested Aesthetic pleasure, as I looked down at them. And would they not be so much more pleasing-without-interest, than were the blotches of plastic-covered landscape that I had been looking at through the window? It even occurred to me that there had to be irony, in the fact that the only landscape I had so far seen, at this supposed Imitation of the Idea of a Hippie Farm, had not only looked like a badly done abstract painting. It had also come plastic-wrapped. I chuckled, at my little joke.

But this joke being made, I resolved I had best get down to purely detached Contemplative business. I had not looked closely at the topmost magazine, as I approached. So as not to initiate, prematurely, an intensity of detached Contemplation that would be interrupted by my getting settled. I squatted in the pile of rags. It did not seem so offensive, and I barely even noticed the smell. Instead I pulled my blankets around me, and leaned toward the Object of my Philosophical Investigation.

I regret to say, though, that all of this fine resolve notwithstanding, such detachment as I had been able to muster dissolved instantly, upon my first long glimpse... I had to swallow. I couldn't help it. And I began to feel stirrings again, right away. The Proportions, mathematically speaking, of the young woman whose Photographic Imitation graced the topmost magazine's cover were certainly...Ideal. But... This did not stop my noodle from swelling inside my trousers. I could feel it getting thick again, as by an entirely sub-contemplative reflex that I couldn't stop. And least of all by grabbing hold of it, as I had with my stomach. Quickly I flipped through the magazine, without removing it from the pile. Within it were displayed still further Photographic Imitations, that revealed even more, anatomically speaking, of the young woman on the cover. Or of her Imitation. Or of the Image of her Imitation...

I was getting confused again. I closed the magazine, and withdrew my hand. My throat was dry. But my underwear, oddly enough, was not. I sensed a certain...seepage, from inside out. So it was clear that, were I even to open the magazine again, or fix my eyes with contemplative intensity upon its cover...my noodle would register its objection, irrefutably and even irrecoverably, to these claims about my detachment. With who could tell what consequences. For might not my very Masculinity— which according to certain ancient philosophers resides mystically in certain bodily fluids— thereby be menaced...?

I grabbed a blanket, the nearest one that wasn't wrapped around me, and flung it over the magazines. Then I stood up, with great resolution, and pulled my own blankets tightly around me. But this didn't help. Sub-cerebral processes, regarding whose epistemological status I did not dare speculate, were underway. Suddenly, it seemed as though the entirety of my Being were focused...down there. Where my noodle was twitching. I could feel the pressure building inside it. I had seen too much...

Vigourously I propelled my legs, up-down, up-down, up-down. Intense calisthenics, that might distribute the pressure. This was difficult, the calisthenics I mean, on account of my blankets. But I persevered, even as I became aware that I was making a certain thudding, as my bedroom slippers struck the floor. A necessary risk. Would it not be humiliating for me to waken up, on my very first morning on an Imitation of the Idea of a Hippie Farm, which happened to be devoid of Imitations of the Idea of Hippies... At any rate would it not be humiliating... Was this not something I had long dreamt of doing? Fantasizing about it at night, when I wasn't fantasizing about other things...?

I stopped jumping up and down. For this was not, as discipline, sufficiently extreme to dispel the building pressure.

Keeping my grip on the blankets with my left hand, I seized hold of my treacherous noodle through the blankets with my right. I squeezed. But harder than I had squeezed my stomach. Much harder. The sensation was excruciating. But worthwhile. I twisted, as well as squeezed. What are referred to in novels as "bursts of searing pain" convulsed my lower body. But still this was not enough, to dispel the pressure. I grabbed hold of my right testicle, between the thumb and forefinger of my hand. And scrunched. This took great resolution. I almost swooned. But I consoled myself that these were perhaps the sorts of exercises, in meditation, to which subscribed the Desert Fathers. The pain this time caused bile to rise. I opened my mouth, in a silent scream. Then I fell to the floor. But I dragged myself back to my feet. Taking a deep breath, I mustered all my strength...and punched it. This time the pain was such that I fell backwards onto the pile of rags. Dust rose around me. I sneezed. But as I was sneezing, I noticed that the pressure, down there, had given way to a throbbing ache. The hot itch was gone. And I no longer felt as though the bottom were about to drop out of my very Being, in an ecstasy of surrender.

I was back to normal.

Panting, I got to my feet. So I had beaten it back, my noodle I mean and its desires that, had I allowed them to be fulfilled, would certainly have compromised my first awakening to early morning on the... ...on a... ...on... Whatever it was I was on, I felt composed. On account of my triumph. Of conscious will. Over blind desire. In the conservation of masculine Substance. And, by implication, of my commitment to Imitating the Idea of a Philosopher. Truly.

But what of Tommy himself, I had to wonder, as I both savoured this triumph and endured the pain in my testicle and around my noodle. I glanced toward the magazines, that were still covered with the blanket.

Was it possible that he too struggled with them? As I had? And might this struggle provide for him— as it had for me— an exercise in discipline? In self-denial? To be enacted every morning? Was he, then, himself like the Desert Fathers, too? An aspiring anchorite engaged in exercises of self-mortification every day, made all the more challenging by the very presence of the magazines?

If this was so, then I could only admire him. For it made even his success at subduing his stomach sounds seem easy by comparison. But was this the case? I didn't know. Nor could I ask. For what if he did not engage, every morning, in self-mortification, using the magazines as instruments after the manner, perhaps, of St. Ignatius of Loyola's Jesuitical Code, or Descartes' Rules for the Direction of the Mind? What if, for example, I were to ask for details about the routine of his morning discipline, as he woke up to the magazines and then, perhaps, flogged his noodle with barbed wire to subdue it? Only to learn, from him, that he did not flog his noodle, with barbed wire or anything else, in the presence of the magazines. But instead gave in to it, to its own inside-out pressures, without inhibition, according to his noodle's lamentable willingness to be seduced, by the basest illusions. Thus becoming, not just a "Tool of Consumer Society" as I had feared becoming in June-Squaced Printy-Feyed Convenience O's store...but its very slave?

Could this be possible? And if it was, then was I not being optimistic, in anticipating a frank response? Might he not be embarrassed? Angry even? That I had learned his secret? Tommy, I imagined myself saying, do you or do you not use these magazines, toward a rigourous discipline of self-mortification? Or do you instead give in to them completely? Not as stimuli to Contemplation of Higher Forms. But as Temptations of Consumer Society, toward the squandering of your Masculine Substance?

So intense was the mental pressure of these questions, that I felt dizzy. The room seemed to spin. I sat down again on the pile of rags.

Beside the pile of magazines. Which fortunately was still covered up. I employed my hand, not to extract a magazine from beneath the rag, but instead as a cup, to support my head. Which at that moment needed support. Yet this only enabled me, for unclear reasons, to feel the full effects of my nostalgia for the Innocence of— literally— the day before. In all its melancholy. I blinked back tears. I had had such hopes, harboured over years, for this Imitation of the Idea of a Hippie Farm. And such expectations, also harboured over years, regarding Tommy. And his friends. And— yes— I was obliged to admit this, about his girl friend. Whom I would have been willing even from a distance to see again, in all her glory. For she, certainly, as the Truest of all True Imitations of the Idea of a Hippie Girl, had been so Beautiful...that not only had she outshone, as such and within my own Recollection, the photographic images in the Authoritative Hippie Books, of other Imitations of the Idea of Hippie Girls. She could certainly have outshone also, in any competition, the girls on the covers, and on the inside pages of the magazines. That lay beside me. Beneath the rags...

It was at this moment that there occurred to me an unworthy thought. But such are unworthy thoughts that, once they have occurred, they cannot be un-occurred. My unworthy thought was this: did Tommy keep the magazines beside his pile of rags for just this reason? Because his girl friend Allie, or Photographic Images thereof, did grace the covers of some of them? Or all of them? And might even grace the pages inside? Might she be absent only temporarily? And this was how Tommy kept himself reminded? Of her?

Had she then, in other words, gone from being a Model for the Truest of All True Imitations of the Idea of a Hippie Girl...to being...a Model...of a different kind?

I removed my head from the palm of my hand. I knew that this was an unworthy thought not only in regard to Tommy. But also in regard to Allie herself. Whom I had never met. But regarding whom I had enormous respect. As a person, I mean. But then, I reasoned, while it might be unworthy of Allie, certainly, for me even to imagine that she would stoop to displaying her exquisite features, both facial and otherwise, on the pages of such magazines for all to behold...would it really be so unworthy of Tommy if, unbeknownst to him, she had done precisely this? Behaved unworthily that is, perhaps after a domestic spat? Which seemed still to be going on, insofar as it had made, apparently, for her absence. But was it possible, then, that Tommy kept the magazines beside the bed as aids to Recollection? Regarding precisely...her?

I knew then, of course, that the only way I would be able to resolve this question, that had so many implications regarding Tommy's character, and his girl friend Allie's character, too...would be to look at the magazines. Or at least at one of them. To see if it contained a picture of Allie. Because, I reasoned, if I looked at one of the magazines, the top one say, and it didn't contain a picture of Allie, then that would mean, certainly, that Tommy was looking at the magazines, not because they contained pictures of Allie and so served as aids to Recollection in regard to her...but because they contained Photographic Imitations of the Idea of Pretty Girls generally. With their bodily surfaces and...who could tell what other things, exposed. I could feel myself getting warm again, down there. Despite the bruising. Such are blind genetics.

But I pressed on with my Logic, in the interests of Truth. Would, however, the possibility that the topmost magazine did not contain pictures of Allie...imply that other magazines, in the same pile, also did not? Logically speaking, no. Did this make a difference? I was no longer sure. My empty stomach was, perhaps, intruding on my reasoning processes. The question, however— and this much I could remember— was whether I should look at one magazine, to see if Allie was inside it, or rather if pictures of Allie were inside it, or for that matter on the cover. Or whether I should look at all of the magazines, for the same reason. Or at none of them, for different reasons. The different reasons, in this case concerning the capacity of my own constitution to endure, undisturbed, and at such close quarters, another bout of precisely the same sort of stimulation that I had successfully fought back a little while before. And that I had not anticipated would figure in my visit. To Tommy's Farm.

In the end, however, I am almost ashamed to say, I did not come to any decision of any kind, at least, by myself. Perhaps this was fortunate. What happened instead was that I was interrupted, in my inner colloquy, its pros and cons, by a voice. Not one such as Socrates claimed he always heard, decisively dissuading me from further action. But rather— and on this occasion far more prosaically— Tommy's. Calling me. From the foot of the stairs.

"Hey man?" it said. "I've got breakfast ready. How about it?"

## §12

The flight down the stairs was so precipitate that I almost stumbled over my blankets. Which upon my arrival in the kitchen panting, Tommy suggested I get rid of, before sitting down. He also handed me my Desert Boots, which were completely dry from having spent the night in the long box above the stove.

"Take a seat, man," Tommy said, and gestured to a place at the kitchen table which had been set with a bowl and spoon.

I did as he suggested, and replaced my bedroom slippers with my Desert Boots. Which given the exertions upstairs seemed more appropriate footwear than ever before. On account of the Desert Fathers. Though I did not say this to Tommy. I then considered the bowl before me. It was of white porcelain, with many small cracks. Inside it was food which was also mostly white, with a sprinkling of small brown spots.

"It's muesli, man," Tommy said, as he sat down also to his own bowl across the table. "Goat's milk. Raisins. And rolled oats. Simple. But it should give your stomach a pretty good rest."

I considered this bowl of muesli. My mouth was awash with saliva. Glandular secretions from the upper zones overcoming, happily, and in the presence of a new set of stimuli, those from the lower.

"Well, go ahead then, man," Tommy said. "Dig in." And with a certain flourish he picked up the spoon that was beside his bowl.

I did not, at that moment, want to consider further the implications of my discovery upstairs. Nor could I be so bold as to ask Tommy himself, to resolve the conundra that it raised. I therefore picked up my own spoon. Anticipating as I did so that this, at least would be a good way to banish— through the sheer sub-cerebral simplicity of ingestion, mastication and digestion— the disappointments I had thus far experienced.

But is it ever possible for those who seek to Imitate the Idea of a Philosopher to assume that any state of affairs will be so simple? Logically speaking, it should not be. But beyond the logic...I should by that time have come to expect that there would be complications, regarding practically everything, at Tommy's Farm.

Which complication was in this case introduced by the simple act of my lifting the spoon. As I did so, at the very instant when I was about to plunge it into the bowl of muesli...I noticed something that, in sheer visual impact, was enough to displace all lingering impressions, even from the pile of rags. And this was the following: the spoon itself contained, in its concavity, a green-brown encrustation. This did not fill the concavity, or even cover its entire surface. But regardless of its size and undistinguished shape, it was disgusting. This is to say that, as soon as I saw it, I stopped being excited about the prospect of eating, and became disgusted instead. Human emotions— unlike Reason— are so changeable. This being why they are so unwelcome in matters of great importance. Such as eating a bowl of muesli, after an involuntary fast of over twenty four hours. With an encrusted spoon.

Thus did I face another quandary. I swallowed. But copious amounts of saliva only. For how, I wondered as I looked at the spoon, and my stomach seemed to plead to be filled at last, could I possibly eat my muesli with it, and not feel like throwing up? Really throwing up. Not that there would be much to throw up with, a bit of stale bile perhaps. But still, the sensation would be unpleasant. While the action itself would be extremely rude.

And yet: would it not be just as rude for me to draw Tommy's attention to the fact that he had given me, not a clean spoon, but an encrusted one? Might it not perhaps suggest to him also that I had been less than happy, with his pile of rags? And besides— to drag out the usual objection— was it not possible that, on what was left of this Imitation of the Idea of a Hippie Farm, that lacked practically any Imitations of the Idea of Hippies...this might be how the only remaining one ate all the time? For all I could tell, Tommy himself was eating with an encrusted spoon, at that very moment, and not complaining. I tried to Recollect, as I held my own spoon, whether I had seen anything about encrustations, in the Authoritative Hippie Books. That might reveal to me what role such a phenomenon might play, for Tommy. But I could not.

As I was reflecting in just this way, though, and with increasing perplexity, I happened to notice that Tommy himself was looking at me.

"Is something the matter, man?" he said. "I'd have thought you'd be pretty hungry."

The quandary was thus intensified. For how could I tell him that I was reluctant to eat my muesli, to whose preparation he had devoted such effort, on account of the greenish gunk on my spoon? For if his spoon, the spoon that he was using, did not have an encrustation, then my pointing out my own to him would put him, instantly, in the role of a clumsy host. Who had given me, his guest, the spoon with the encrustation, and had kept the clean, or the cleaner one, for himself. But if his spoon did have an encrustation, and he was using it, then my pointing out my own encrustation might entail my abuse of whatever remained, on the Hippie Farm, of Hippie Rules. And these seemed by this time abused enough, that they did not need further to be so by my breaking them. Out of ignorance.

And yet...was there not one possibility that would incriminate neither myself nor Tommy? This was that his own spoon contained an encrustation, of which he was not aware. Then...

"Man?" said Tommy's voice. Interrupting this inner colloquy that actually seemed on the way to being resolved. "Are you sure you're...all right?"

"Just fine," I simply said. Reluctant to interrupt the process by which I might solve the riddle of the encrustation.

"You're sure?" Tommy said. "You're not...eating anything man."

I realized, at this moment, that my very care in addressing this riddle might be working against me. For though I had not so much as asked him about my own actual, and his potential, encrustation, he might as my host already be anxious somewhat, because I wasn't eating the food he had prepared. Did I want to contribute to such anxiety, in Tommy? And after he had gone to the trouble of making me muesli? I did not. I therefore had, out of sheer altruism, to trade the integrity of logical process...for the simplicity of action. To his benefit. If not to mine.

"Of course I'm fine, Tommy," I therefore said, with enthusiasm. "Mmmm. This looks delicious." And with these words said, I veritably plunged my encrusted spoon into the bowl of muesli, bracing myself for what I knew would be the disgusting feeling against my tongue. I picked up a spoonful, aware as I did so that the milk with its lactic acid might already be corroding the encrustation, turning green, acquiring who could tell what vile taste. But in the interest of Friendship, and with as much determination as I'd used to plunge the spoon into the muesli...I likewise plunged it into my mouth. Full and dripping.

Even as I did so, however— and as my stomach was convulsing in anticipation of receiving whatever scum of malodourous goo was already seeping off the encrustation— I realized there might yet be a way of avoiding contact between the encrustation itself and my tongue. Which, I feared, might lead to an abdominal contraction so intense that whatever bile and acid were left in my stomach might erupt into my bowl of muesli. As well as— who could tell?— across the table and onto Tommy himself. And what would be the point of my altruism were this to happen? I would avoid it. And the means by which I would avoid it were these. Were I actually to flip the spoon over, as it entered my mouth, it would in the manner of a dump truck release its load of muesli onto my tongue. And would do so without its concavity, which contained the encrustation, ever needing to touch me.

This, with the decisiveness of desperation, I therefore did. Kerplunk. Though with my mouth still open, in order that there be no danger at all of the encrustation's scraping my tongue. And while I still felt revulsion, because the muesli which had touched the encrustation itself touched my tongue, still I was able to control this. So I could even say, as I dumped the muesli, "Mmm, mmm," several times. But as my mouth was open, this "Mmm, mmm" sounded somewhat choked. In fact, it did not sound like "Mmm, mmm" at all. As more like "Gnggh, gnggh." Notwithstanding my intention to produce "Mmm, mmm." To let Tommy know that I really was enjoying his meal.

Except that Tommy continued to look at me as though I were doing something strange, and not appropriately altruistic at all. More Perplexity. Even as, with a supreme effort at overcoming physical resistance...I chewed. Up-down, up-down, up-down. As in my calisthenics. Then I gulped. Almost, my throat contracted— and not only out of muscular revulsion, but also because my mouth was still partly open. In resistance, to the very process of chewing. But even as the muesli slid downward, semi-chewed and I hoped not too drenched in sludge, I sensed that Tommy might not yet be fully convinced. Of my commitment. So having initiated another downward movement with my spoon, even as I noticed he was looking at me strangely, I followed through. Thrusting the spoon into the bowl of muesli, I filled it. And having so filled it, I conveyed it, toward my mouth.

But just as it was about to arrive, I recalled something that made me stop it. This was that the encrustation, which had been dry when I was given the spoon...would now be wet. On account of its lengthy contact with the soggy muesli. Depending upon what sort of material had initially formed the encrustation then, it was possible that the green-brown substance in the spoon's concavity was beginning to dissolve, and actually to mix with the muesli. In greenish, and maybe even slimy, streaks. Which streaks I was about to dump, truck style, onto my waiting tongue.

This I could not do. And while Tommy was still looking at me strangely. Fortunately, at this moment, Recollection came again to my rescue, as it had done already in the course of my visit. And as Socrates said it always should. For I Recollected that I had once seen a picture, in one of the Authoritative Hippie Books, of Hippies actually drinking bean soup, out of bowls. The caption had advised me of this. Even if it had not exactly said: "Hippies Drinking Bean Soup Out Of Bowls."

But this was an amazing insight! As well as a timely one. For I realized instantly that if True Imitations of the Idea of Hippies could, in an Authoritative Hippie Book, drink their bean soup from bowls, then this was plausibly an acceptable Hippie Practice regarding muesli also. And perhaps one even more acceptable than eating with an encrusted spoon. Because the latter I had never seen represented in one of the Books.

Without further hesitation, then, I made my choice. I set the spoon on the table. Though without emptying it of its cargo of muesli, because this might already be fouled by the encrustation, and so belonged neither in my mouth nor in the bowl. Which bowl I then picked up and put to my mouth. I began to eat. Or not quite to eat, but to slurp, somewhat loudly perhaps, because this was only way I could get the muesli to my mouth. Without actually raking it in, with my finger. For it had not the thin consistency of soup. But I was sure that, this small difference notwithstanding, I must still be acting in appropriate Hippie fashion. Because, as Socrates urged, the Idea must precede its Imitation. And where better to acquire Ideas, concerning Hippies, than from Authoritative Hippie Books?

I now was also able to taste the muesli. Which, because I had been so concerned about swallowing before, and not touching the encrustation with my tongue, I had not yet savoured. I therefore made further noises of appreciation, as I slurped. "Mmm," I said. "Mmm. Mmm." And this time, the "Mmm. Mmm. Mmm." even came out sounding like "Mmm. Mmm. Mmm." And not like "Gnggh. Gnggh. Gnggh."

Eating the muesli in this way also had the advantage that— because my bowl was in front of my face— I did not have to deal with the fact that Tommy had been and might still be looking at me. Strangely. I even hoped, as I was slurping, that my performance might be so convincing that when I lowered the bowl, he might be regarding me with admiration, for this display of Sound Hippie Etiquette. But for this reason, to give him time to stop looking at me strangely, and to go back to eating his own bowl of muesli if not to start gazing at me with admiration, I did not lower my bowl for some time. But just kept on slurping. I admit I even wondered, as I slurped, whether Tommy might be so inspired, that by the time I did get around to lowering my bowl, I would be greeted not by the sight of his face, looking at me strangely, but by the sight of his bowl. And specifically of its bottom, up around his face. Because he would be slurping too.

But alas, I was in for more disappointment. Because when finally I lowered the bowl, having kept it over my face for as long as I could, even going so far as to lick out the inside completely...what should I encounter still, but Tommy's eyes? Looking at me strangely. From behind his glasses. His own bowl was still on the table. And his spoon was even in it. So I could not have learned from it whether it contained an encrustation of its own or not. In fact, I saw from his bowl that he probably hadn't taken a single bite, or at least not more than one, since I had lifted my own bowl and begun to slurp. This was alarming. Had I, then, in ways unbeknownst to me, done the Wrong Thing? Was it somehow acceptable, in Hippie terms, to drink bean soup from the bowl? But not to drink, or slurp muesli? But who then decided these things? Did Tommy have an Even More Authoritative Hippie Book? That he consulted?

All of these questions flashed through my mind, or brain, in quick succession, as soon as I had lowered my bowl. But I didn't ask Tommy any of them. This was because, still looking at me strangely, he said first: "You know, man..."

I looked at him. I sensed that perhaps he was on the verge, of making some revelation.

But instead, he just shook his head slowly, set his elbow on the table, and set his cheek in the palm of his hand. He closed his eyes.

"Yes, Tommy?" I said. I was beginning to be concerned that I had made a real *faux pas*. In Hippie terms.

"It's okay," Tommy said. Still with his eyes closed.

I sensed he perhaps needed reassurance. That I had been sincere about the muesli.

"The muesli was wonderful, Tommy," I said. My impulse, in fact, was to ask if I could have some more. Because while it had partially filled my empty stomach, I could sense there was still some room.

"I'm sure it was, man," said Tommy. Still with his eyes closed, and his head resting on his hand. "I'm sure it was."

This was beginning to distress me. It seemed that, far from doing something altruistic by eating with my encrusted spoon, and right by slurping my muesli, I had done something wrong. But I was not sure what. I was aware, too, that for some people— especially theologians— such is the condition of Human Existence generally. Such that we are always doing something Wrong. Even when we believe we are doing something Right. Though what exactly we are doing Wrong we are never sure. And not only in regard to slurping muesli, either. But in regard to everything.

I was not convinced, however, that Tommy wanted to talk about theology at that moment. Or even about philosophy. What did he want to talk about, then?

The magazines, perhaps?

This seemed unlikely.

"I suppose," Tommy said, opening his eyes again and looking at me, "you must be wondering at this point why I invited you up here."

What was I to say? If I had wondered— and of course I had— was I wondering any longer?

Because, surely, I must at least have been making for better conversation...than did the goat.

And yet...did I want to brag about my conversational skills?

Or pre-empt the revelation?

Assuming there was one.

Tommy, meanwhile, had closed his eyes again. And was shaking his head slowly from side to side, as it rested in the palm of his hand.

Did this mean there would be no revelation? After all?

Nevertheless, I Intuited, right then and there, that this might indeed be the moment...to ask him the question I had wanted to ask, since my realization the previous evening. Namely: that the house beside which we had just pulled up, in the truck, was...empty.

"What happened, Tommy," I said very slowly, "to all your friends?"

There. The question was out. At last.

Tommy opened his eyes, and took his head out of the palm of his hand, and looked at me.

"What?" he said.

"Your friends," I said again. "The other Hippies. That I used to see you with at school. And your girl friend. Allie."

"Oh," Tommy said. "Them." And put his head on the palm of his hand. And closed his eyes again.

Now I was even more confused. But before I could say anything, or elaborate further, Tommy spoke.

"They fucked one another silly," he said. Without opening his eyes. "We all fucked one another silly. And then, when we were all fucked silly...they left. One by one. Sometimes two by two." He opened his eyes and looked at me. "People get jealous, man," he said. "Or they get bored. But I guess I've got a really high boredom threshold. Because I'm the last survivor. After all that silly fucking." His eyes seemed very tired.

"Ah," I said. It was all I could think of to say.

"But if you're worried that's why I asked you up here," Tommy added, "for still more silly fucking, don't be. Forget it."

"Ah," I said. Yet again. But then realized, suddenly, what he might be imputing. In regard to me? An aspiring Imitation, of the Idea of a Philosopher? "Oh, no," I added quickly. "I wasn't worried about that at all." It even occurred to me, as I said this that I ought to describe to him my exercises in fleshly mortification, so recently enacted.

"I'm comforted," Tommy said, before I could decide how to do this. "Really, man. I'm comforted. The problem, though, man, you see...is that this place really does bore me out of my skull."

"Ah," I said. Reduced, again, to the all-purpose phoneme.

"But if you're imagining we can liven things up by going out and tramping around in the grass and bush, getting soaking wet," Tommy said, "you can forget that, too. Because it's deer hunting season. And odds are, after ten minutes you'd be mistaken for a deer by some blind drunk hunter, even with a bright yellow coat on. And he wouldn't know the difference until he pulled out his knife to gut you."

"Oh," I said this time.

"And maybe not even then," Tommy said.

I was silent. This was all too much. Terrifying, even. What was Tommy trying to do? Rob me of all of my longings? And of any basis for ever getting them back again? All at once?

Such was the price. Of my spontaneity. In asking him about his friends.

I reminded myself, silently, that I must be more circumspect. In future.

Tommy looked at me. "It's a long way from Kant, isn't it, man," he said, as he pushed his chair from the table and stood up. "Oh yeah, man. I remember," he said. "The little talks we used to have. After classes. I remember. Well, I'll tell you something, man. This whole place is a long way from Kant." He gestured toward the window beside the stove, that was covered with plastic. "It's the dissonance, man," he said. "Let me tell you. Out there, beyond that window, about a hundred yards down the field, there's a swamp." He leaned across the table toward me. "It's huge. And getting bigger. With dead trees sticking up all over the place, and mosquitoes, and black brackish water that's held in by beaver dams. Chaos, man. From our point of view, it's just chaos. The only thing the locals use it for is hunting ducks. But me, I go in there and what I feel is that it wants to swallow me up." He clapped his hands. "Just like that. Gone. Poof. A little blurp of brackish water. And that's it. Gone."

Tommy had begun to pace, back and forth, on the other side of the table. I had wanted him, as soon as he mentioned the swamp, to stop. So we could get our coats on and pay a visit. Chaos or not. Except then I remembered what he had said. About the hunters...

"And in here," Tommy was saying meanwhile, as he paced, "in here are all those fucking categories that old Kant was talking about." He poked his right index finger against his forehead. "The ones that tell us what kind of world we can see. Except Kant, for all his comprehensiveness, wasn't comprehensive enough." He continued to poke his head. "There are more. More. Not just space and time, causality, modality, the timeless ones. But also the ones that are shaped by language. By history. Look at you, man," he said. "Look at me. Transcendental syntheses of apperception if I ever saw them." He giggled. "And how are we, with this baggage of European language and rationality, and the experience of growing up in cities, for Christ's sake, supposed to relate to THAT?" He waved his arm, rather violently I thought, in the direction of the covered window. "The only people who could understand That were the Indians, man. But they weren't thinking in German. Or in English. Their languages evolved with That. Over thousands of years, man. So they knew the sacred places. The places that stood out from the chaos. But we don't. Our own ancestors wiped them out. And we can't find them. But the Indians knew where to find them. They heard spirit voices in the wind. In the water. Do you know that?"

He was by this time leaning across the table again, staring at me. His eyes, behind the wire glasses, glittered.

"No," was all I could think of to answer.

"Well, they did," he said. And went back to pacing, on the other side of the table.

Leaving me to wonder, as I watched, whether he had talked in this way also to his fellow Hippies. Was it possible that this might also have had something to do, causally speaking, with their departure? Tommy was certainly not being very "laid back," the way the Authoritative Hippie Books said that True Imitations of the Idea of Hippies were supposed to be.

I did not, however, know how to tell him this.

Tommy, meanwhile, continued pacing. "But these old houses, man," he said. He waved his arms. "These old houses are like fortresses. Palisades. Against the great Other beyond the window. And watchtowers. To make sure the Other stays subjugated. Because that was what it was all about, you know, man, for the farmers who lived here. The pioneers. Subjugation." He turned and looked at me.

"Subjugation," I repeated.

"Subjugation," Tommy said. And started to pace again. "Of the land. Of their own bodies. Of the spirits. I used to think there was something vaguely romantic about the pioneer thing. Maybe even heroic. But now I think it was just the shits."

"Ah," I said. But this conversation— so called— was turning into a roller-coaster ride. It was making me dizzy. Even sitting down.

"The shits," Tommy repeated. "Listen, man," he said. Leaning forward with his hands on the table. "Do you know what those people had, that got them through day after day, year after year, of back-breaking work on places like this?"

I could only shrug. This seemed to be going far beyond— or below, or behind— the Imitation of the Idea of a Hippie Farm.

"Religion," said Tommy slowly. "They believed. They had faith. Maybe they didn't have any choice. Because they didn't see any escape. But they believed that if they worked really hard, and never deviated from what the Bible and the church told them to do, and maintained their faith..."— Tommy put a lot of emphasis on this word, "faith"— "then they'd go to heaven when this miserable slog, this vale of tears, this testing, was over. Then they'd be happy. Forever after. You understand that, man?"

"Yes," I said slowly. "I think."

"Anyway, man," said Tommy, still leaning across the table, "I've tried. Jesus Christ, I've tried. To hear the spirit voices, I mean. To break out. I even used to dress like an Indian. Breechcloth. Moccasins. The works." He grinned at me, somewhat maniacally I thought. "But it just doesn't click. All I hear is wind. Wind, wind, wind."

I was reminded, as he said this about the wind, of the passage from Ecclesiastes, in the Bible: All is vanity. And a chasing of wind.

But I did not know whether he would care to hear this either, just then. Lest it remind him of the Pioneers. With their Religion.

"Except that sometimes," Tommy went on, with his eyes still shining, "I do seem to hear laughter. In the wind. Mocking laughter. And I wonder whether it's Mother Nature herself. Laughing at me. Sometimes it feels like she just wants to swallow me up. Devour me. The winters. Oh, the sheer indifference of Mother Nature. Jesus, Jesus, Jesus."

With this, Tommy pushed himself away from the table and strode across the room to the counter. He leaned against it instead, and stared out the window. Or at it, because it was covered with plastic.

It occurred to me, at this moment as I watched him, that Tommy himself might profit, in his current frame of mind, from a re-enactment. Of the very scene in which we had shared on the staircase, the night before. But with the roles reversed. I could hold the lantern as he had, at the top of the stairs, so my head was hidden behind the glow of light. While he could huddle, as I had, on the stairs themselves, and await a voice, from behind the light. This would be not quite the same as hearing a voice from within the wind, as he had wanted to do. But it would be something. And perhaps even a powerful enough experience, in itself, to...

To what?

Because would I know what to say, as such a voice?

And in such a way as to renew Tommy's own faith, in his Imitation of the Idea of a Hippie Farm? Which Imitation was now beginning to look pretty tarnished. Even from my perspective.

I had to admit that I would not. Know what to say, I mean. Despite my access to Authoritative Hippie Books. Which I had not brought with me anyway. Lest I spoil the surprise.

But was this not precisely the sort of challenge to which Socrates would have risen? Socrates would surely have taken the terms of Tommy's disaffection with Mother Nature, and with the Wordless

Wind...and by probing questions would have arrived himself, and led all those present, to a higher stage of Perplexity, regarding the essence of Disaffection itself. How I missed his presence, which would have made such a difference! For I was not even sure where to start, with my questioning, so as to arrive at this. Although at the very least, I reasoned with some relief, there would now be little likelihood that such questioning would lead, as it had in the truck, to limpness on my part. On account of mention of Tommy's girl friend. Who seemed not to exist at all, at the Farm at least, any longer.

Except...

Except for that unresolved matter of her potential presence, as a Photographic Imitation of the Idea of Female Beauty. On the pages of the magazines. Upstairs.

I felt a twinge.

But even as I felt it, I had to wonder: did Tommy's disaffection with Mother Nature, who he seemed to fear would swallow him up, have anything to do with why he now resorted, for female company, to the motionless and silent Images that were ranged across the pages of the magazines?

But at this very moment, before either the twinge or this train of thought could go any further...Tommy turned from the window.

"Ah, fuck it," he said, as he did so. "Let's eat some Special Shortbreads."

## §13

I wish I could now provide my usual concise account, of the events that followed on this suggestion by Tommy, about the Special Shortbreads. Which, immediately, he procured from beneath the counter, and set before me on the table, in the form of a tin box labelled precisely this: Special Shortbreads. But if the photograph on the top of this tin depicted pale white cookies, what I saw when Tommy opened the box were neither white, nor cookies. They were instead dark brown and crumbly. Like the brownies that my mother used to bake from mixes.

"Here, man," Tommy said, even as I was contemplating this latest problem of skewed referentiality. "Try some Special Shortbreads."

I looked at him. His eyes were still shining somewhat as he leaned across the table.

"But Tommy," I could not help but say. "These don't look like Special Shortbreads. The kind on the box top, I mean."

"Oh, but they are man, they are," he said. Clearly untroubled by this lack of correspondence between the Image and the Object. Or between the Object and its Idea. Or between the Imitation...

I was getting confused. Again.

"Believe me, man," Tommy was saying anyway. "There's not a whole lot else to do out here on a rainy afternoon in November than eat Special Shortbreads." He proffered the box again. "They do wonders for your point of view."

I examined the Special-Shortbreads-That-Did-Not-Look-Like-Special-Shortbreads-But-That-Still-Were-According-To-Tommy. The problem of referentiality had become even more complex than usual. Especially given that nothing seemed to be Corresponding with the Idea which I had had of it. And least of all the Hippie Farm. Did this mean, then, that such Correspondences were not to be relied on at all? Ever? In spite of Socrates?

"Go on, man," Tommy said. "They won't bite."

It occurred to me, at this very moment, that these Special Shortbreads, which looked like brownies but weren't, might be Tommy's way of trying to induct me, at last, into the secrets of "Mood Expansion," such as he had practised at university. I had learned a little of this from the Authoritative Hippie Books. It consisted, I had read, either of "Smoking Up," or of "Dropping Acid." This had long confused me. For I had never understood how "Smoking Up" and "Dropping Acid," though directionally opposite, would both lead to "Mood Expansion." Nevertheless, I had also managed to infer that such "Expansion," whether directionally upward or directionally downward, did often lead to problems of referentiality. Was I about to find out how? Was I not already finding out how? For the Special Shortbreads looked not like the Special Shortbreads on the lid of the tin...but like brownies. Before I had even touched one.

"But Tommy," I finally managed to say, as I looked at the Special Shortbreads. So called. "What are they?"

"Whole-wheat flour," Tommy said. "Honey. Cocoa powder. Goat's milk. Baking powder. And..." He smiled at me, showing his teeth. "Renfrew Rocket."

"Renfrew...Rocket?" I said.

"I grow it," said Tommy. "On the hill up back. How do you think I pay the taxes on this place? And buy the food?"

"Renfrew Rocket?" I said again.

"It's a name, man. Just a name," Tommy said. "You want some others? Smoke. Dope. Mary-wanna. Cannabis sativa, to be precise. Except I don't smoke it any more because it's hard on the lungs. Go on. Try some. It's a great high."

I looked at the Brownies. Sure enough I could see, when I examined them closely, bits of what looked like dried leaves sticking out of them.

I sensed not only that I might be on the verge of being inducted into a True Imitation of the Idea of Hippie Ritual...but also of resolving longstanding Perplexity. Concerning "Smoking Up" and "Dropping Acid." A paradox. If there ever was one.

"Will this be like...dropping smoke?" I said to Tommy.

"Yeah sure, man," Tommy said. "Sure. Now go ahead and eat one, will you?"

I was disappointed, somewhat, that Tommy had not grasped the significance of the profound philosophical paradox that I had just resolved. Nor could I but wonder with trepidation: might this ritual— if this was what it could be called— affect my mental processes? Making them less precisely logical? Less rigourous?

And yet...was this ritual not at— or at least near— the very core of the Idea of True Hippieness? Had I not gained this impression from the Authoritative Hippie Books? And might it not— as ritual— thereby at least redeem, a little, Tommy's farm? As an Imitation of the Idea of a Hippie Farm?

I reached out and touched...whatever it was.

"Now," said Tommy. "Eat it."

I looked at him. He was leaning across the table, with an expression of what I can only call "child-like anticipation" in his face and eyes.

"Go on," Tommy said.

The Whatever-It-Was, when I tasted it, was dry and crumbly. But sweet. I chewed. It clung to the roof of my mouth, feeling sticky.

Tommy left the table, and came back with a glass of milk.

"Here, man," he said. "This'll help it to go down more easily."

I sipped the milk. I then took another bite. And another. And another...

I had eaten so little in the past two days, that once I had started I couldn't stop.

"Great, man," Tommy said. "Great." And ate a Brownie himself.

I was about mid-way through the third— or perhaps it was the fourth— Brownie when I began to notice a sort of change. That I can describe only in terms of the words "a melting." It began in my stomach, and percolated outward, like a warm wave. Tommy sat across the table. He had loosened his pony-tail, and his pale hair fell in strands around his face. He smiled. A great warmth engulfed me. I seemed to float, even though I was still seated at the table.

"Tommy," I managed to say. "What's happening?"

"Never been stoned before, man?" Tommy said. And his voice seemed to reverberate, the words getting thicker, like liquid.

This did not make sense to me. That words should be like liquid.

But neither did I want to admit to Tommy that I had never been "stoned" before. As he put it.

"Of course I have," I said. And the words congealed, like thick butter. Or a record player. Winding down.

"Well, just keep at it," Tommy said, the words reverberating as though the walls of the room were a trampoline, and they were bouncing off it. "There's lots more where that came from."

It was at this moment that not only the words, but the room itself seemed to blur, to begin to melt. Perhaps it was the flickering shadows, that were set in motion by the lamp. I watched these shadows, still eating Brownies. Then suddenly, there appeared in front of me, as though by magic, a bowl. Containing oats. And milk. And tiny shrivelled things. Like snails. I took one out. It was a raisin. Never before had I seen such a raisin. It seemed the uniquest thing in the world, with its shiny folds, and its film of goat's milk. This makes no sense now, that I should assign such significance to a meagre raisin, but it made sense then. I set the raisin on the table, the better to contemplate it. From above it resembled a tiny tank, alone on the great dark plane of the kitchen table. A shrivelled tank to be sure. But a tank no less. I realized a great potential in this, that resided in my very bowl. For an entire tank army. I plucked them out, the shrivelled raisins, and set them beside one another, in rows. They would attack across the plain, toward the lamp.

But as I moved them, they underwent a further change. So brown, so shrivelled, they looked like nomad horsemen. They lost their order. Attacking randomly. Fanning out across the steppe. I shouted commands, in a language I did not understand. But the shrivelled horsemen knew the words. All arriving, eventually, at the base of the lamp. They circled it. A great victory. I joined them. At the level of the table. Looking up at the flickering lamp. Its yellow glow. And never had I seen such a glow. The very walls behind it seemed to dance, in rhythm to its flame. I remembered it, too, from the night before, as Tommy himself had held it up before his face. Giving to his own features, or lack thereof, an otherworldly presence. I looked around. Tommy was seated across the table, watching me. I picked up the lamp, and held it in front of his face. This was reassuring. Somehow.

"Hey man," said Tommy's voice. Still thick like liquid, but also seeming to echo. "You should probably leave the lamp on the table. 'Cause the wood in these old places is really dry. If you stumbled, it could be one fuck of a mess."

His voice, emanating in this way from behind the lamp, again possessed great authority, as it had the night before.

I humbly returned the lamp to the table.

"Too bad it's still drizzling," Tommy said. "If it was nice we could go out and I could show you the place."

I looked at him.

The shadows seemed to flicker around us. Like in a cave.

Like in Socrates' cave, I realized. The one that Plato wrote about. In the *Republic.*

Even as Tommy said: "But actually, even if it was good weather, this time of year we'd be crazy to go out for a walk."

The shadows flickered. So that he seemed like an old sage. Wrapped in furs.

"Oh," I said. And my voice seemed itself to be coming from inside a cave. For it all was cave-like. Womb-like even.

"On account of the hunters, man," Tommy said, his voice seeming somehow clearer. "I told you. It's deer season now. As well as duck, grouse, goose and bear season."

"The...hunters?" I said. And my voice, compared to his, sounded like thick syrup, being poured. But I recalled the nomad raisins. Was Tommy now going to tell me that there were in fact nomad hunters, who inscribed upon the walls of caves such as the one we seemed to be seated in, the images of the deer they hunted? Might there already be such images, magical in their sheer power, on these walls?

I looked around. The shadows flickered.

"One of the real joys of country living, man," Tommy said as I was doing this. "The nicest time of year for walking in the woods is fall. But around here it's also the likeliest time of year for getting your head blown off. By some drunken asshole."

"Drunken...asshole?" I said. And suddenly stopped searching with my eyes for magical paintings of deer on the kitchen walls among the shadows.

"But that's okay," Tommy said. "The weather's too shitty for us to go outside anyway."

"Ah," I said. As I did so, I noticed that I had somehow stood up. The better to look, no doubt, for the magical paintings. Which, apparently, did not exist. I therefore sat down.

I did not, however, want to think about the hunters. The assholes. As Tommy called them. For I sensed that if I did, some sort of process might be set in motion, that would be difficult to stop once underway. I stared instead at the shadows, intently, and at their flickering, and at the lamp's flame, which made them flicker.

What did this, I forced myself to wonder, say about Socrates? And his claim, in the *Republic*, that far better was it to escape the cave, and its flickering shadows that were only illusions, in order to enter into the sunlight, of Truth? I looked toward the window, that was covered with plastic. Beyond it, the sky was grey. And beyond it too, there might lurk, in the woods, the hunters, with their shotguns...

It was at this moment that I remembered also what Tommy had said, about Prune-Eyed Squint. And his shotgun.

And as well what he had said, a little earlier, about "blind drunk hunters." Who wouldn't know the difference between a deer and a human— even a human in a bright yellow coat— until...

I began to shiver, somewhat. And not only about Squint-Pruned Joe, and the hunters with their gutting-knives.. But about whether— once again— Socrates' assessments were always right. I watched the shadows, the flickering walls, the orange flame. All illusions, according to Socrates. Illusions that I should leave behind, to venture forth... I looked toward the window. To venture forth into what? The drizzle? With the possibility of being targetted, at any moment, by a "blind drunk hunter"? Or an "asshole"? Or maybe even by Convenience Prune? Who had reminded me of Elmer Fudd. And who might, for all I knew, have jumped into his own pick-up truck the moment I was out his door. And then tailed us, all the way to Tommy's Farm. I suddenly sensed, beyond the window, legions of them, whole legions, of Elmer Fudds. Pruned-Faced Eyes. Convenience Joes. Lurking in the shadows. Blind drunk. But looking at me anyway. With their gutting knives between their teeth. And taking aim. With their weaving shotguns...

"Get under the table," I said to Tommy. I could not prevent my doing this. I was concerned. Not only about my own safety, but for his.

I pushed my chair back, slipped forward off of it, and slid beneath the table.

They seemed to be there. I could sense them. Beyond the window. Beyond the plastic...

Tommy's face appeared a few feet from mine. In shadow somewhat. And tilted sideways. Because he too was leaning under the table.

"What's the matter, man?" he said. "What's up?" Then he giggled slightly. "Or down, I mean," he said.

I was stunned, a little, that he did not understand. Since he had been the very one who had brought to my attention all of these menaces. The blind drunk hunters. Prune-Squaced Fint. The shotguns. Gutting knives. Elmer Fudd...

"The...the funters," I managed to say, aware even as I did so that the words were not coming out quite right. But I couldn't help this. It was clearly that problem of referentiality. Manifesting itself. Irresistibly. But I had to try to get the message across. "Felmer Stud," I said.

"Goon-Squaced Finience. Shutting fives." I pointed toward the window. My finger trembled. I couldn't help this either.

"Yeah, it's sometimes like this the first time, man," Tommy said. "Don't worry about it. It's just a bit of paranoia. It'll pass."

"Pass?" I managed to say.

Tommy put his hand on my shoulder.

"Yeah, man," he said. "Look. I didn't mean to make you frightened. Don't worry. The weather's so lousy there won't be any hunters out. I can understand though, what with the dope and all..." I felt the pressure of his hand on my shoulder. "Come on. Sit back up again. It's all cool. There's nothing to worrry about."

I let myself be led from underneath the table. The room still flickered.

"Here, man," Tommy said, and his voice was not so thick any longer. "Just sit down. I'll make us some coffee. How's that?"

I sat in the chair again.

Tommy went to the counter.

"The thing to do, man," he said, "when you're like this, is to focus on something. Try focusing on the flame of the lamp. I do that sometimes myself. It calms you down."

I tried to do as he asked. The yellow flame. Pale. Flickering from side to side. I tried to Recollect. What it was that had...

The pure flame.

The pure flame of truth.

I watched it. The purifying yellow light.

The light that Socrates had said the chained prisoners would have to go outside the cave to find, in the sunlight.

But he had lived in Greece.

Where there were no hunters.

With shotguns.

Whereas here, in this old farmhouse, the light was clearly to be found not outside the cave at all, where the sky was full of clouds and drizzle, and the forest might be full of hunters, but instead...in this simple flame.

Its uniqueness.

As before with the raisin.

This calmed me.

But as I became so calmed, in the presence of this discovery, as the tension drained from my body, leaving it warm and heavy...I became also aware of something else. For there must always be something else, of which one becomes aware. It is a condition of consciousness. In this case, the something else pertained to my body, which hunched around me, legs, arms, torso...and nether parts. It was from the nether parts that the appeal to awareness seemed to issue, transforming the sense of heaviness...into a sort of weight. Which soon, as my awareness shifted, became a pressure. I don't remember exactly when this happened. Only that it did. Except I still didn't know where the bathroom was. This made for a novel feeling, this build-up of solid waste— for that was precisely what I had to infer the pressure was— in my large intestine and colon. It began to fill my lower abdomen, pulling it downward, seeming to root it even, after a manner of speaking, to my chair.

Of course, I had felt this build-up before, it is a common feature of being attached to, or part of, or integrated with, a body. This is another problem with which philosophers have a great deal of trouble, the body generally, I mean, and not only the poop it contains, in its relationship to mind. But what made the build-up so different this time, was that I became so intensely aware of it, as it took place. The Authoritative Hippie Books had long advised me, to the effect that Substances such as the "Renfrew Rocket" are supposed to "sensitize" a person to music. Or perhaps to Nature. But there didn't seem to be any music, at Tommy's Farm. While Nature, besides being sopping wet, was separated from me by translucent plastic. And besides that, might be full of hunters. My "sensitization" then seemed to be taking place in something of a vacuum of stimuli. Which vacuum was being filled, irresistibly, by the pressure on my nether parts. Which expanded, as their own internal volume filled with poop. And as, according to the Tommy I had known in university, my mood should be doing also. Expanding. Though not with poop.

As this was taking place, I could not help wondering, whether in this respect I might be unique. In that I had never read, in the Authoritative Hippie Books or anywhere else, about this phenomenon. But I did not wonder very much, because mostly I participated in the feeling. It seemed to fill me. Much as, according to the Authoritative Hippie Books, True Imitations of the Idea of Hippies fill up with feelings of "Peace" and "Love," when they get "Stoned." But I, instead, experienced the feeling of being filled with Poop, or if not of being filled with Poop, quite, at least of filling up with Poop, slowly. I wondered why the Authors of the Authoritative Hippie Books had never written of this, it was such an amazing feeling. But I also wondered, though fleetingly, if perhaps my difference in this regard was just one more reflection of how different I was, from most seekers after the Idea of Hippieness. In that, while they filled up with Peace and Love, I filled up with Poop. Or, to paraphrase Socrates, with the Imitation of Poop's Idea. This disturbed me briefly, though not as much as I might have expected, because the experience itself was so compelling.

And for just this reason, I could not long reflect either upon the question of whether it was with a True or False Imitation of the Idea of Poop that I was filling up. Or whether in fact— as perplexed Socrates in regard to dirt, mud, and hair— Poop was such as to deserve its own transcendent and eternal Idea at all. As Love and Peace surely do. This was because whatever it was that was filling me up— an Imitation of Poop's Idea, or True Poop, pure and simple— was doing this so relentlessly. For a time, I was able simply to experience this feeling...even though according to Socrates such an experience would be deemed very low, mere aesthesis as distinct from thought. But Socrates, for all his vast experience, had surely never tried Renfrew Rocket. And least of all as Special Shortbreads. Had he ever experienced, then, what it was really like, to fill up with Poop? Perhaps if he had, I realized even as I was filling up, he might have been furnished with quite the ammunition, to use against Parmenides in regard to this question of whether dirt, mud, and hair— not to mention poop— had their own Ideas.

In the midst of all of this low aesthesis, in any case, the load suddenly, and without any warning, became too much to bear. That is to say: one moment, I was simply sitting there, at the table, feeling myself fill up with whatever it was, becoming more focused on my abdomen, and more bound, it seemed, to my chair. Then suddenly, it was as though I were about to burst. Just like that. This too must have been the Renfrew Rocket. Just like that.

"Tommy," I managed to say, in a kind of gasp. "Where's the bathroom?"

Tommy was sitting at the end of the table, with his elbows resting among the bowls and raisins, and with his cheeks in the palms of his hands. His hair fell in clumps around his face. He had also removed his glasses, and his eyes as they looked at me seemed bloodshot. Glazed even.

"What?" Tommy said. Thickly again, as though his voice were being filtered through water.

What was most amazing about this transformation, the moment in which my focus changed, was that now I had become aware that I was no longer filling but had filled with...whatever sort of Poop it was...I could not maintain awareness of anything else. I pulled my sphincter in, as best I could. But I was sure that I would not be able to hold out for long. Because in seconds, mere seconds, my trousers, and the chair, and even the floor perhaps, would be awash. With foul reeking plops and puddles. True Imitations. Of Poop's Idea.

"The bathroom," I whispered. "The bathroom. Where is it? I have to go."

"Oh, the bathroom," Tommy said. And seemed to chuckle quietly. "It's just an outhouse. There isn't an indoor bathroom, man." And he chuckled some more.

"The outhouse, then," I said. Pushing myself with both hands up from the table. This was difficult. I felt like a cripple, or even an expectant mother, about to give birth. I hobbled along the table. "The outhouse," I repeated. "Where is it?"

Tommy sighed, and stretched. "You mean you've got to take a shit or something?" he said, looking up at me with his bloodshot eyes.

"Yes," I said. Conceding this simplistic resolution to the Problem of Poop's Idea. Because I had no option. "Yes. I've got to take a shit. Please. Where's the outhouse?" The pressure was becoming unbearable.

"Well, why didn't you mention it before?" Tommy said, pushing himself to his feet.

I wanted to tell him it was the Renfrew Rocket. "The Dope," as he had called it. And surely not the Imitation of the Idea of Renfrew Rocket, either. Which I could not conceive as being any more Real than what I was already experiencing. But I didn't say any of this. Because so advanced had the problem become, I sensed that if I opened my mouth...my sphincter might open too, in a kind of involuntary synchronization. And out would come the whole stinking steaming mess, on Tommy's floor. So instead I merely nodded my head and smiled, as best I could. But this probably wasn't very well, because I had clenched my teeth tightly, also in synchronization with my sphincter.

Tommy walked toward the main door of the kitchen. Once there, he removed the yellow plastic raincoat from its peg. He tossed it to me.

"Here, man," he said, as he did so. "You'll be needing this."

I caught the raincoat with both hands, even as I employed both buttocks, to catch my sphincter. Tightly. My impulse, in fact, was simply to drop the raincoat, and bring my hands to my buttocks' aid. But I refrained, for the sake of what was left of propriety. Quickly, I put the raincoat on. Then I followed Tommy, hobbling, through the door and into a sort of shed— the darker room through which I had stumbled the previous evening on my way to the kitchen. The light was dim, and I stumbled, yet again, several times. Each time I stumbled, I was sure I was going to lose the load of Poop, right there. I even managed to get one hand onto my bum without Tommy's noticing, to keep it in.

Tommy stood in the open doorway, and pointed. The light beyond was pale grey.

"You see that little clump of trees over there?" he said.

I squinted. There was a small clump of evergreen trees about a hundred feet away and down a shallow slope to the right. Around it were misty fields with long brown grass, and beyond these what looked to be a forest of deciduous trees, bare and grey.

Thus did I receive my first view, unobstructed by darkness or plastic, of Tommy's Farm.

Once, I might have wanted to walk among these fields and trees. These...True Imitations of the Idea of...

But I could only gasp "Yes," and pull my sphincter more tightly, to keep the load from sliding out...

"The outhouse is just in there," Tommy said. "I should've shown you before. Except the occasion never came up." He chuckled again.

I tried to ignore his chuckle, and focus on the clump of trees. This was no time for Dialogue. Socrates' own adaptability notwithstanding. I pressed my hand against my bum.

"Thank you," I wheezed, and then pushed my way past him.

## §14

I dashed through the grass toward the clump of trees. My trouser legs got wet. The damp air, thick with mist and drizzle, surrounded me. Like water. This was apt, since the pressure of my lower parts propelled me forward, as a motor does a motorboat. I did not, however, press my hand to my sphincter, lest Tommy be watching. Except I also sensed that, in this regard, the present flight would likely resemble that other one. From the truck. To pretend to throw up. For would he not be on his way back already, through the woodshed, and into the house? To sit at the table, and rest his head on his hand? Just as he had done in the truck? Had he left the doorway? I didn't look. Nor could I afford to care. Because this time I was dealing with a load of Real Poop— or at least with the Truest of all True Imitations of Poop's Idea, I wasn't sure. But whatever it was, it had a greater degree of pressing Reality, than had my load of Unreal Vomit the day before.

As I reached the evergreen trees, then, I made another resolution. Though somewhat dimly. I would again suspend all inner colloquy concerning the Reality of Imitations, until I was emptied of whatever it was. I felt a great weight lift, the weight of possibly unresolvable Perplexity, even as the other weight remained implacable. Following the path, I parted branches that drooped with their own load of rain. And then I saw it, directly before me, in a clearing hedged on its far side with other trees and wreathed in mist. A small wooden building with a tilted roof, and made of grey boards slicked with rain. I rushed toward it. The door was of grey boards also, with a wooden handle, and I yanked it open. Inside was a sort of counter, a couple of feet in height and of solid boards, front and top. On the surface were two holes the size of pie plates. I realized what these were for. Though it surprised me, even in my state of distraction, that there should be two such holes instead of one. Did this mean, I wondered, as with fumbling fingers I loosened my trousers, that when this had been an Imitation of the Idea of a Hippie Farm, the Hippies had not only lived "communally"? They had pooped communally also?

Further speculation, however, on this subject or any other became impossible, the instant my trousers dropped. I lunged toward the right-hand hole. My fingers clenched the damp wood, and I settled my buttocks in the indentation, made smooth no doubt by many Hippie Bums. Or by Imitations of the Idea of Hippie Bums, I could not be sure. But the familiar gateway to Perplexity this time stayed closed. Even as another opened. Not to Perplexity. But to...Release. For once so settled in the outhouse hole, my sphincter let go its hold. And out poured its contents, all of them, like a geyser turned upside down. Or maybe, given the heat and steam, like a volcano. The sound reverberated upward, like distant artillery, through the other hole. But in the midst of these reverberations, I was myself convulsed, with the sheer Ecstasy of this release. Which was intensified, undoubtedly, by my being "expanded," in mood. Even as, colonically, I was "contracting," in the extremity of peristalsis. Clinging to the edge of the counter, I closed my eyes. Shivers rushed through my body, as salvo after salvo burst explosively. And with every salvo, there was a satisfying "plop," which I Intuited was the sound of each glob as it landed, on what I realized must be an enormous pile of earlier poop, produced by Tommy and by who could tell what other Imitations of the Idea of Hippies, below.

As the spasms subsided, and the bursts quelled to trickles, I began, in fact, to grasp, in the afterglow of ecstasy, the significance of all of this. For here I was, in the "outhouse" with all this Poop. And not just my Poop. But Tommy's Poop also, and— even more important— what was left of the Poop of his fellow Imitations of the Idea of Hippies. And surely even, down there somewhere, what was left of his girl friend's Poop. The Poop that is, of that Truest of all True Imitations of the Idea of a Hippie Girl. All mushed together. In what could only be— I realized with rekindled excitement— the Truest of All True Imitations of the Idea of Communal Hippie Poop.

This was extraordinary. For Tommy himself, after all, was still stuck in the farmhouse proper, alone. And with, from day to day, only the Special Shortbreads, and the little goat, and perhaps the magazines I had seen that morning, for company. Alongside his Recollections. While I was now enjoying the benefit of a different kind of company, on the part of all the Imitations of the Idea of Hippies Past, and even of Allie, Tommy's girl friend, in the form of their Poop, or of whatever it was that old Poop turned to, in the bottom of an outhouse. And was this not more Real, in terms of proximity to True Imitations of the Idea of Hippieness, than was Tommy's empty house? I felt a thrill of anticipation. In fact, my impulse was to stand, as soon as the last of my own Poop had trickled out, and take a good look down the hole. To see whether I could discern any distinctive Imitations.

But I did not do this, precisely because the last bit of Poop was still trickling slightly. I felt it turning quickly cool. So that if I had stood, it would have trickled down my leg. I resolved, then, to postpone my exploration of the hole and its mysterious contents, until I had found some toilet paper. I looked around in the gloom. For although I had left the outhouse door open in my rush for the hole— an indifference to privacy most unusual— the interior of the outhouse was still gloomy on account of the drizzle outside, and the dense drooping branches of the trees. But I did not see any toilet paper, even with the door wide open. Nor was there an electric light, that would aid my search. Had I perhaps knocked it down the hole, in my desperation? Not the light, but the toilet paper. As I was about to rise, though, and initiate this further search, I noticed, beside the other hole...a magazine.

Instantly, I felt a different kind of quiver. For could Tommy, even in the outhouse, in the presence of his girl friend's Poop— or the Imitation of its Idea, I had not resolved this— seek refuge in... I leaned toward the magazine. My noodle, which by this time was chilled from dangling down the hole, was sending its own sort of signals, that obliged me so to lean. Was I betraying Socrates? Yet again? Happily— though less so from my noodle's point of view, limited as this was— I did not need to answer this question. For the magazine, far from being of the sort which I had found beside the pile of rags that morning, proved to be...a catalogue. With coloured pictures, of the sort produced by department stores. A complexity of emotion, difficult to describe, engulfed me as I made this realization. Disappointment. Guilt, that I would have suspected Tommy of placing such a magazine in the outhouse, with his girl friend's Poop. Though he had, admittedly, already placed many of these beside the pile of rags, which presumably he had once shared with her. But also exasperation, that Tommy— as by this time a clearly Inept Imitation of the Idea of Hippieness— should have placed so clear a reminder of the Temptations of Consumer Society right beside me.

But then I noticed also, as I looked at the catalogue, that many of its pages were torn. Why might this be? I looked more closely. Television sets, washing machines, kitchen tables— or at least their Images, in Photographic Imitation— were torn apart, willy nilly. I felt a different thrill, of Excitement this time. For clearly Tommy, in his Hippie hostility to Consumer Society, was carrying out his own little war against it, here, in this very outhouse, by means of its Images. For did not the fact that so many pages were torn apart indicate that Tommy was using, on his own bum, not toilet paper that would provide a most un-ecological abuse of trees...but this catalogue, this archive of the very Commodities that as much as defined Consumer Society. Which all participants in the Idea of Real Hippieness must loathe— as I did— heartily.

Leaning across the hole, I picked up the Catalogue. Realizing, as I did, that I now held, in my very hands, the means of striking my own small blow for Hippieness, against Consumer Society. My fingers trembled as I flipped the ragged pages, their Photographic Imitations of so many Icons of that Society, torn as by a force of nature through their middles. The first complete page held Images of television sets. Of television sets! I gazed at them in the gloom. Each Represented Screen contained its own Image. A sailboat. A racing car. A handsome man and a beautiful woman, head and shoulders only, about to kiss. False Imitations, all of them. Images of images of images. Mystifications! Propaganda!

Was it any wonder, then, that Tommy used this Catalogue to wipe his bum? For even as a student of Kant, he was clearly sensible to this distinction, between the False and True Imitation. And Catalogues, emphatically, contained False Imitations! For they were designed to entice the reader, in the interests of Profit. Tommy's stock, as a True Imitation of the Idea of a Hippie, was on its way up again. And I decided that, whatever pleasure Tommy might get from wiping his bum with such False Imitations, I would get some, too. I tore off the page, and folded it, so that not the False Imitation of the sailboat, nor of the racing car...but of the Handsome Man looking into the eyes of the Beautiful Woman was front and centre. It occurred to me— fleetingly— that Tommy himself might have been saving this very Image— this calculated Image of Supposed Romance— for such a moment. But I was too far gone to stop. I quivered with anticipation. Leaning toward the wall, I slid my hand holding the False Imitation between board and buttock, twisting the paper to ensure that the instant of contact would make for maximum coverage. I pressed. The paper was sharp and crinkly. I appreciated, as I was doing this, that Tommy, used to these qualities, probably achieved the optimum wipe with a short quick slash, such as to gather up the Poop as it dripped or dangled, and whip it instantly away to the pile. But such simplicity was not my goal. I pressed some more, not with the plan of being better able to soak up Poop, but rather...

I looked at the paper. Brown smears streaked the faces, both the handsome and the beautiful...or rather the False Imitations of the Idea of the Handsome and the Beautiful. I almost swooned. The False Imitations seemed no longer to be looking into one another's eyes, but to be squinting through a screen of Poop. With a sigh I threw the paper into the hole. More pleasure. Then I tore out another page. This contained False Imitations of the Idea of Washing Machines. The non-absorbency of the first page had been such that there was Poop left over from the False Imitations of Ideas of the Beautiful and Handsome. In love. Supposedly. I tore out the page, folded it, then scrubbed again.

I used several more of the catalogue's pages. Some contained False Imitations of the Idea of Television Sets, some of Refrigerators, some of Furniture. Each time I looked at the False Imitation, after it was smeared with— might I dare to say it— a True Imitation of Poop's Idea— I felt a thrill of pleasure, of contact with Reality even, and then flung the False Imitation down the hole. But soon I realized something. Was I not in doing this polluting the residual Imitation of the Idea of Hippie Communality, that lay below? I stopped. Clearly, Tommy too had been using the catalogue to this same purpose. But he perhaps had shown more restraint than I. Leaning over, I looked down the other hole. I saw little. For already the light, such as it was, had begun to fade. And it was just that much darker, down the outhouse hole. All I saw, therefore, was a dark blur, spotted with paler blotches. These I assumed must be Consumer Society's False Imitations of the Idea of Icons, smeared with my own True Imitation of the Idea of Poop, scattered randomly. Still, I sensed its presence, the True Imitation of the Idea of Hippie Communality Through Poop. To which I was, at last, so proximate.

Yet there was also an irony to this presence. For here I was, looking down the outhouse hole, in order to find anything really Communal, about this Imitation of the Idea of a Hippie Farm. Where seekers after the Idea of Hippieness had been supposed to intermingle, in Imitation of the Ideas of Peace and Love. But where they had managed to stay intermingled, on a lasting basis, only through Imitation of the Idea of Rotting Poop. There must, I sensed, as I gazed down the hole, be something profound in this. Not least because it seemed to give me more in common with these Seekers than I had thought, a little while before. On account of my own experience, while "Stoned," of filling up not with feelings of Peace and Love— or with imitations of the Ideas Thereof— but with Poop! For I had imagined, on the basis of the Authoritative Hippie Books, that this must signal my own inadequacy. Yet it did not! For clearly, it had been but preparation for my own Co-Mingling, in True Imitation of the Idea of Hippie Communality, with their Poop. With which they had also filled. Perhaps while "Stoned"!

This was gratifying. As well as— I realized— important, philosophically speaking. Because it seemed to make for yet another inversion, concerning which sorts of Phenomena merited their own Ideas, of which to be Imitations. For surely, if there was one thing that Socrates would have rated even lower than dirt, mud, and hair, in his assessment of what merited an Idea and what did not...it would have been Rotting Poop. Yet here I was, using it as the very basis for an Idea of Participation in Hippie Communality. Much as, perhaps, Socrates himself had said that True Imitations participate, in their own Idea. A significant advance. But, I realized also, as I took a breath while leaning over the hole, a smelly one. An acrid odour filled my nostrils. Or not simply one acrid odour, but many, a layering of acrid odours that could only have come from the many different layers of Poop, in their stages of turning to compost. With my own being the layer of most recent vintage.

I braced myself and— as the odours engulfed me— leaned into the hole. But I still didn't see very much. Then I realized that if I stood up, or at least got off the hole on which I was sitting, an opening would be provided for the daylight, or the dusklight, to illuminate the pile, while I looked down the other hole. This I did. And sure enough, the pile took on more definition, though not very much, and most of it provided by my own contribution, which glistened like a sauce that had been poured upon the pile underneath, as on a chocolate sundae. And the bits of Catalogue, smeared with Poop, were like little wafers, the kind that are added to chocolate sundaes in better restaurants. This was diverting.

But so diverted was I, in this sheer aesthesis, that suddenly, I realized also that I had forgotten why I had wanted to peer down the hole in the first place.

Such, evidently, were the continuing effects of "mood expansion," via Renfrew Rocket. A blurring not only of referentiality, of the relationship of Words to Things, and of Phenomena to their True Ideas— though this was, for me, generally pretty blurred anyway. But also a blurring of memory, and even of the sense of causality. What was I to make of this?

Especially since I was still bending over, leaning into the hole, with my naked bum in the air. Not knowing why.

Yet in the midst of this confusion, I sensed that I had just been vouchsafed, perhaps, profound insight into the nature of the Human Condition.

Would Socrates have appreciated this insight?

Had he ever stood staring into an outhouse hole? With his naked bum in the air? Not knowing why?

I could not know this, either, since Plato— his only chronicler apart from Aristophanes who, of course, cannot be taken seriously— never said.

But even as I prepared to grapple, with both the implications of this Insight, and the further question of Textual Truth into which it opened...there was...a sound.

Behind me.

Such as might be made by a human being, in the act of clearing his, or her, throat.

I stiffened.

I had thought myself to be alone. In my Meditations.

And what was more: was I not still standing, with my trousers around my ankles, and my bum in the air, naked, as I looked down the outhouse hole?

Yet were I to straighten up, and turn around, would I not be exposing, not my bum any longer...but my noodle?

Perhaps I had imagined it, this sound. Or if I had not...perhaps whoever or whatever had made it was also wondering whether, at that moment, he or she or it had imagined, was imagining, seeing a naked bum, poised above the outhouse hole. Would it not, therefore, I reasoned— undoubtedly in a manner influenced by "mood expansion"— be most politic for me to remain...stock...still. So that assuming there was someone who had made the sound, he or she or it might imagine that what he or she or it was seeing...was a statue. Or a mirage. Which illusion would, however, be broken were I to move.

"Man?" said Tommy's voice suddenly, behind me. "Are you still...functioning?"

I closed my eyes. It was Tommy, then, who had cleared his throat. Tommy who had seen me, who was seeing me at that moment, bent over the outhouse hole. With my bum in the air. And Tommy, who was probably wondering why I was doing this. Would he be insulted if— and it was at this moment, due undoubtedly to pressure of circumstance, that I did remember why I had been staring down the outhouse hole— he realized I was doing so to look for evidence of True Imitation of the Idea of Hippie Communality? That could no longer be found at the house itself?

"Yes," I said. Without either standing up or turning around. "I'm functioning." My voice was muffled, on account of my addressing these words down the outhouse hole. Though there also was an interesting stereophonic effect, as the sound reverberated up again, through the other hole.

"Aren't you getting a little cold doing that?" said Tommy's voice.

I realized, through listening closely, that Tommy could not be standing directly behind me. But must be, instead, near the edge of the glade.

But I also realized, even as he said these words, that, as a matter of fact, yes. I was getting cold. My legs especially, and my bum, which were naked. Very cold. Why had I not noticed this before?

"Yes," I said. Though still without moving. "I'm getting cold."

"Then...um," said Tommy's voice, "have you thought about pulling up your pants and getting the fuck back to the house? I mean, even I'm getting cold standing here, man. And I'm fully dressed."

What could I say to this?

Slowly, I straightened up. My back was stiff. How long, then, had I been leaning there?

"I was getting worried about you, man," said Tommy's voice. "I thought you'd got lost in the rain. And it's going to be dark soon."

"I've been fine, Tommy," I said. Though still without turning around. "I've been right here all along." I was relieved to be able to reassure him, regarding something. I took this feeling of relief as a sort of cue, to bend over and start to pull up my trousers. As I did, I felt the skin of my legs. It was almost numb. This was an odd sensation. Even as I did not seem able to feel the skin of my legs from the inside, as being cold.

"I don't know if I can see this properly, man," said Tommy's voice. It seemed a little closer. "But your legs look almost blue."

"Blue?" I said, as I lifted my trousers from around my ankles. There seemed, however, to be no feeling below my knees.

"Man, how many of those Brownies did you eat?" said Tommy's voice. "Did you even realize your legs were getting cold?"

"No," I said. I finished doing up my trousers, then turned around. Tommy was a few feet away, a little dim because the sky was getting darker. He was wearing another yellow raincoat, that looked identical to the one he had given me.

"We'd better get back to the house," Tommy said. "So you can get warmed up." There seemed to be fatigue in his voice. "Come on."

"Wait!" I said. It had occurred to me, at that very moment, that we were about to leave this site where I had first encountered— albeit in the past tense— a True Imitation of the Idea of Hippie Communality. In the form of Mingled Imitations, of Poop's Idea. With which I, too, had mingled my own Imitation, successfully. Was I to leave this Site— this site of Real Discovery— without any sort of ceremony? As Tommy was urging me to do?

And yet, were I to explain this to him...would he not feel insulted? That I seemed to prefer this Imitation of the Idea of Hippie Communality Through Mingled Poop...to his own humble— but solitary— company?

"You go ahead," I said. "I...I want to commune with Nature. I'll be right along."

"Man," Tommy said. And his face seemed suddenly pinched. "You know, man... In the course of all the years I've lived here..." He paused and sighed. "Well, let me put it this way, man," he said. "There've been some pretty weird people pass through this place. But you..." He shook his head. "You've got to be just about the weirdest. Have it your own way, though. You want to commune with nature? Go right ahead. But don't get lost, man. And I also suggest you do it with your pants up. It's warmer." Then he turned, and walked toward the edge of the glade. When he got there, he looked back. "The path is this way, man," he said. "Okay?" He gestured with his hand, to the muddy ground. "And don't be too long, man," he added. "Otherwise, I'll have to come out and look for you again. And I really don't want to do that."

Then he disappeared between the evergreen trees, whose dripping branches now seemed almost black.

I was alone again, with only the sound of drizzle on the outhouse roof. This was what I noticed first, in the renewed silence of the glade. But I was inside the outhouse, and so was not getting wet. The door hung open, as it obviously had done since my arrival. I soon became aware though, while looking at the outhouse door of just how cold my legs were. And my bum. Tommy had been right about this, anyway: it had not been such a good Idea to conduct my meditation on the outhouse holes— and their contents— while bereft of trousers. It would then, would it not, be a wise Idea also for me to make my way to the house, as Tommy had. But I could not resist one more look down the holes. For what useful reflection they— and their contents— had prompted. What a feeling, even, of Sharing, at last, in some sort of Imitation of the Idea of Hippie Communality. I leaned over, first the right hole, in which had been deposited my own humble contribution. But I saw little, because— what with the early November evening as well as the drizzle— there was very little daylight left. I tried the left hole. It was just as dark.

Yet I did not want to leave this place without some gesture of appreciation, of how much it had meant to me in providing the Residues of Hippie Presence. Fortunately, by this time I had to pee again. I withdrew my noodle from its envelope of underwear, in which it had been regaining its proper warmth. I peed. First in the right hole. And then— stopping the flow for a moment so as to spare the wooden seat— the left. This was most fulfilling. A suitable conclusion, I decided, to my encounter with a True Imitation of the Idea of a Hippie Outhouse. As well as with a True Imitation of the Idea of Hippie Communality, Through Mingled Poop. I put my noodle away, deciding as I did that it was too bad Tommy's house wasn't more like the outhouse. For it was in the latter— and certainly not in the former— that I had got my only sense, since arriving at Tommy's Farm, of Hippie Presence.

I resolved, therefore, as I did up my fly, and turned away at last from those holes that had meant so much to me, to keep this in Mind.

Then I started along the path, through what little bit of daylight was left, toward the house.

## §15

When I got back to the kitchen, Tommy seemed more distressed with me than ever. This I didn't understand. But perhaps I'd been gone for too long.

"I've got to milk the goat," he said, as I came in. He was still wearing the yellow raincoat, and was leaning on the table, in much the same way as I had been leaning on the outhouse counter. Except the table was higher. And his trousers were up.

But he no more than glanced at me, and then went back to looking— perhaps even staring— at the flame of the lamp.

Did this mean he was trying, as he had urged me to do when I was "paranoid," to calm himself?

"Oh," I said, in answer. This was all I could think of, perhaps in part because I was also noticing the warmth of being back inside.

"Is that all you can say, man?" Tommy said, turning to look at me. "I mean, it's either 'Oh' this, or 'Ah' that. Or 'Quick, get up so I can take a shit.' Then once you're outside taking the shit, making me go find you because you've got your head down the outhouse hole. I mean, give me a break, man."

He then went back to staring at the lamp.

I was not sure what to say. Tommy clearly was experiencing difficulty with my company. Of which, perhaps, he'd expected more, since he now seemed to lack for precisely this. Company. Of any kind, except for that of the goat. Why, had he not said earlier that even the dog had run away? And the cat? Yet obviously, to judge by the contents of the outhouse, he'd had a fair amount of company of the people kind too, at one time. And they had even been Hippies. Or Imitations of the Idea of Hippies. But they too, apart from the Traces that remained in the outhouse, had vanished.

"I'm sorry, Tommy," I was able to say. But I felt that, if I was failing Tommy as a new form of company...then he, too, was failing me. In that he was proving such a poor example, insofar as my own project of learning how to Imitate, Truly, the Idea of a Hippie was concerned. Just as his farm, for the most part, was proving such a Poor Imitation of the Idea of a Hippie Farm.

I didn't want to say any more than this simple, "I'm sorry," though. I sensed that were I to do so, I might blurt out by way of excuse the reason I'd been peering down the outhouse hole. And my blurting this would then lead, in all likelihood, to the subject of the Missing Hippies. Or the Missing Imitations of the Idea of Hippies. Whatever they were. But in such a way as to embarrass Tommy further, about their absence. Because it had been their poop, all of their Poop, as a True Imitation of the Idea of Hippie Poop, that I'd been looking at. As a once-removed Imitation of the Idea of a Hippie Commune.

But even as I stood there in silence, a flash of Intuition suggested something. Might it help smooth things over with Tommy, if I explained to him the novelty— without mentioning these other, more complex matters— of simply looking down an outhouse hole?

"I've never looked down an outhouse hole before," I therefore said. "It was a new experience."

"What?" said Tommy, raising his head.

"When I was looking down the outhouse hole," I said. "I've never seen one before. It was just so..." I hesitated. "It was such a perfect circle," I said. I felt pleased about this description. For even Socrates would have appreciated the value of contemplating perfect Form. Especially if it was geometrical.

Tommy continued to look at me, even as I was feeling pleased. Then he said: "The occult harmonies of the universe filtered through the scale of an outhouse hole, eh, man? Well, I guess there is something to be said for that. Around here, anyway." He seemed to hesitate. Then he pushed himself away from the table. "Come on, man," he said, and picked up first the lamp, and then a plastic bucket that was on the floor beside him. "I suppose you might as well meet Camilla."

With that he walked past me, toward the door. The light went with him, so that as usual the room seemed to quiver. But the kitchen, as the lamp receded, looked almost as forbidding as the outside had been. Especially since the stove door seemed to be closed. So there wasn't even the flicker of a fire through the grate.

Quickly, then, I followed Tommy, unable in my necessary haste to give thought to this apparent concession on his part...to Socrates. And to the Theory of Transcendent Forms. He went out through the woodshed. Our boots thudded dully on the boards. Then we were through that doorway also, and into the drizzle and the early night. Tommy kept his hand above the lamp, I assumed to protect it from the wind and rain. Around us, there seemed to form another circle, of yellow light, beyond which there was only darkness. I sensed this darkness as we walked, perhaps as a further effect of the "Renfrew Rocket." It did not seem malevolent, but vast and indifferent and silent. I began, then, to get a sense of what Tommy had meant when he'd spoken of the silence of Mother Nature. This was not something of which the Authoritative Hippie Books had spoken at all. And neither had Socrates.

We turned left along a sort of path, that wound amid tall wet grass. The path was so narrow that the grass rubbed against my legs. On either side, it was brown and glistening, irregular tier upon tier of it, getting darker the farther away it was from our moving circle. Soon the wall of a building took shape along the edge of lamplight. The wall was of dark grey logs, laid horizontally on top of one another. Their rough surface glistened in the drizzle. The path led to a crooked door that was set in the wall, and made of wide grey boards. These also glistened, but in streaks, because some parts had not got wet.

"Here, man," Tommy said. "Can you hold the lamp so I can get the door undone?"

I took the lamp from his hands, feeling the warmth of its flame and putting my own hand above the open top, as he had done, to keep out the drizzle. Yet I could not but wonder whether this was why Tommy had asked me along to begin with: to hold the lamp. Such by this time were my suspicions of his motives. Why, was it not obvious also that he had asked me to visit his farm not out of interest in me— whose name he could not remember— but because he did need company? Of the human kind? I watched as he tried to open a rusty latch that seemed to be stuck. He was muttering under his breath. And the more he struggled, the more this hypothesis seemed to make sense. I had been recruited on this occasion as the lantern-bearer. Because he had known the latch was going to stick.

But even as I watched, it also occurred to me that the two of us, immobile in our yellow raincoats, would in the circle of the lamp's glow make excellent targets. Should any hunters still be around...and experiencing frustration from having not yet shot any animals. On account of the rain. Might they not, therefore, at this very moment, be conspiring to make amends, by shooting a couple of Imitations of the Idea of Hippies, or Freaks? Instead? And were this to happen...who would know? This made me shiver. I looked around. The darkness seemed no longer indifferent. Might eyes be watching us? Human eyes? I could see nothing beyond the pool of light, and the semi-circle of wet grass that curved behind us.

"Finally," Tommy said beside me. "That's a stubborn motherfucker when it gets wet, isn't it." He pulled on the latch, and the door swung outwards, creaking. Beyond it was what looked to be a jet-black hole.

Tommy had not, to the best of my Recollection, even used the word "motherfucker" since his reference to Goon-Squaced Finty, just after our departure from the store. And in conjunction with his reference to shotguns.

This did not seem auspicious, insofar as the hunters were concerned. Yet what was to be more greatly feared? The shotguns which might be trained on me, at that very moment? Or the black hole, that lay before me.

"Here, man," Tommy said, even as I was considering this latest set of superlative choices, that his Farm was providing. "You'd better give me the light back, because I know where I'm going in here. Thanks for holding it."

I returned the lamp gladly...though not without some small self-recrimination at this gladness. For was he not thereby rendered the better target, when standing at the centre of the circle of light? But I needn't have worried about him. Because once in possession of the lamp, he did not tarry. Instead he simply ducked his head...and entered the hole. I was reminded also, as he did this, of my suspicions the evening before, when I was sitting in the truck after our arrival. Concerning the existence of a house at all. And the possibility that Tommy might live in a burrow instead. For there was something burrow-like about this building, and its entranceway. Except that as he entered the burrow, the light went with him. What had been dark— namely the rectangular hole— turned light, and what had been light— namely outside where I was standing— turned dark. The metaphysical implications of all these changes were boggling...not least because the changes themselves seemed to revisit, in quick succession, the earlier stages of Tommy's own archetypal Identities. But I hadn't time to reflect on this. For I realized that with this latest shift of chromatic values...it was now I who stood— in silhouette no less— against the open doorway, which wa bathed in orange light. And I who thus became a clear target.

Quickly, I entered the hole. But this meant, of course, that i hunter wanted one last shot at my back, now was his chance. Ra than simply stoop, then, I twisted sideways and lunged throug doorway, as a precaution. My head rammed into somethin Stepping back, I saw a pile of squared bales of hay. Yet the very of this impact was welcome. For not only did it signal that I w both target range, and the drizzle which— despite the raincoat— had soaked my head. Amid so many repetitions, could I not but be reminded of earlier impacts also, in the course of this visit? Squaced Printy's plate-glass door for example, into which I had walked. Or the very mud of Tommy's Farm, into which I had fallen the night before, when I left the truck.

That this impact was soft, then, could surely only be auspicious...notwithstanding the initial appearance of the doorway. I brushed the hay from my face and looked around. And in doing so, had to wonder whether this was indeed what the repetitions had been leading to. A breakthrough, which superseded all of them. For this barn— as Tommy had called it— was profoundly different from any place I had thus far been on the Farm, even the outhouse. But it was also profoundly different from any place I had ever seen...except in the pages of the Authoritative Hippie Books! Parts of it were in deep shadow, as the lamplight flickered. But on either side of me rose piles of hay, some stacked in bales, and some lying loose in rounded heaps. Their smell was rich and heavy. A foot or so above me were low log beams, each one as wide as I was, with rough boards laid atop them to form a ceiling. The lower surfaces of the logs were chipped and scarred, from what looked like axe cuts. But along their rounded sides, the woodgrain seemed to run in a twisted spiral. The ceiling boards, and the logs that formed both the walls and rafters, were grey, though they were tinted orange by the light. The barn's interior looked about as big, in terms of floor space, as the farmhouse kitchen. But it reminded me most of the surface of the kitchen table. Except it seemed far older, ancient almost, like a part of the earth itself.

"Yeah, I like the barn too, man," Tommy said from a few feet away.

He must have seen me looking around.

I turned toward him. And as I did so, the Vision fell into place. For with the lamp in his hand, and with his wire-rimmed glasses and beard and pony-tail, he suddenly looked— against this background and despite the plastic raincoat— like that True Imitation of the Idea of a Country Hippie, which I had believed him to be. Completing the picture, so to speak. And this time...it was the right picture.

"It's...Beautiful," I said.

But before he could answer, there was a bleating which came from behind a pile of hay.

"Over this way, man," Tommy said, moving through the gloom with the light.

I followed, in a kind of stupor. The goat bleated again. Then I saw her as she stood up. She was white, with enormous ears, and a few dark spots on her back.

"Meet Camilla, man," said Tommy, as the goat moved toward him and nuzzled his hand with her nose. "She's a little over two years old." He rubbed the goat behind the ears.

This, truly, was the moment that I had been waiting for. The moment when, even in the absence of other Imitations of the Idea of Hippies— or at least in their withdrawal, to Co-Mingled Traces— Tommy himself seemed to manifest this Idea. To become, in effect, its Incarnation, in all its Purity.

Especially with the lamplight. The half-lit piles of hay. The immense log beams. The little goat.

All together.

A timeless Moment. Of Correspondence.

"But she wants to be milked," Tommy said, with typical understatement. Which in this case— given the intensity of experience I was undergoing— was almost stunning. Yet I clearly could not allow the extent of my epiphany to disrupt the proceedings, on whose very process the epiphany itself had relied. So I merely watched without protest, as— with admirable unself-consciousness— Tommy set the lamp on several wide grey boards that were nailed together. Then he pulled up a wooden bench, and coaxed the goat onto a low platform, which was also made of boards. Setting the bench beside the platform, he with a large fork lifted some hay from a nearby pile, and shook it into loose clumps in front of the goat.

Clouds of grey dust rose from these clumps, as Tommy went to the goat's side and sat down on the bench.

I realized, as I watched, that I was no longer afraid of hunters.

"This'll take a few minutes, man," Tommy said. "So you can just relax." He took a glass jar and a metal bucket from under the platform. Opening the jar, he removed a cloth, which he used to wipe two thick nipples that protruded from the goat's huge udder. Then, when he had put the cloth in the jar again, he set the bucket underneath the nipples. Resting his head on the goat's side, he began to pull these between his fingers. Instantly, white streams of milk squirted into the bucket, making plunking sounds.

This was extraordinary. For at last I was getting a glimpse-in-time of a True Imitation of the Idea of Hippieness. Such as the Authoritative Hippie Books, with similar photographs, had pointed to. But that seemed now to supersede, in the immediate Authority of its Imitation, even these. I almost swooned. And yet, in watching, I could not but Recollect both the outhouse...and the farmhouse that we had just left. In the former, I had indeed found traces of this Imitation...and especially of its subset, the True Imitation of the Idea of a Hippie Commune. But presented only residually, through mingled Poop. In the farmhouse, though, the situation was far, far worse. For apart from the Imitation of the Idea of a Hippie Stove in the kitchen...there were few such traces of any kind. Instead, its cold empty rooms and peeling wallpaper, even in the kitchen, suggested quite the opposite. Via the the cardboard boxes, for example, with their scattered rags. And the magazines. Especially the magazines. With their pages printed with full-colour False Imitations, of the Idea of Naked Girls.

Before me, meanwhile, the milk was spurting into the bucket, slowly filling it. Such Purity! Would Tommy let me pull the nipples, too? Perhaps not, because being inexperienced, I might pull too hard. Yet I was not disappointed. Instead, I touched the goat's head, petting it. Her hair was warm and sleek. I even put my hand to her nose, and she nuzzled it, as she had nuzzled Tommy's.

Tommy, I wanted to say to him as the goat's nose touched my hand. This is so different from the house. Why don't you simply live out here, with the goat? You could even bring the stove along. And your shelves. Then, when you wanted to go to bed, you could simply curl up in a pile of hay. Albeit no longer with a True Imitation of the Idea of a Hippie Girl. But at least you wouldn't have to crawl into a pile of rags. With a lot of False Imitations of the Idea of Naked Girls. That would exert who could tell what unwholesome influences on you...

So preoccupied was I with the Logic of these thoughts, however, as well as with the sheer pleasure of stroking the goat, that I neglected to notice something. It happened slowly. But once it began...it didn't stop. This was a gradual build-up of mucus, in my sinuses. Or perhaps I didn't want to notice this, lest it detract from the Purity of the moment. But then my throat began to tickle, and my eyes to itch and water, and my nose to fill, almost to dripping point. This was clearly on account of the hay. Not that which was scattered inertly throughout the barn, perhaps. But rather that which Tommy himself had just sprinkled onto the platform, raising dust. I had never liked to admit, either to myself or to anyone, that my hay fever might pose a problem, insofar as the goal of Imitating Truly the Idea of a Hippie was concerned. And this was, actually, one of the advantages I might have hoped would accrue, from the timing of this visit to Tommy's Farm. For in November, usually, there is no pollen in the air at all. And consequently, for me, no hay fever either. Except that what I had never anticipated— although I should have— was a barn full of hay. Which would be especially full in November, at the start of winter, when— as the Authoritative Hippie Books had told me— many months' worth of food must be stored. On a farm.

This was most embarrassing. Here I was, experiencing the one Real Moment when something of a True Imitation of the Idea of a Hippie Farm did seem to be unfolding around me, in the way I had hoped it would. And what was happening also? I was getting hay fever. My very own body was betraying me. Is this not why so many philosophers feel distrust, precisely in regard to this body? I began to sniffle. I could not control this. Nor did I have a kleenex. I wanted to blow my nose. I needed to. But I did not have a kleenex. So all I could do was sniffle with increasing frequency, and swallow mucus. I would have spat the mucus out. But I did not want to foul the little goat's area. And besides, did I want to draw Tommy's attention to this failing, on my part, to adapt precisely to his Imitation of the Idea of a Hippie Farm? Which had finally been feeling Truer with each passing moment? I did not. So I simply swallowed. But the more I swallowed, the more my throat itched. And the more my throat itched, the more I felt the need to make disgusting noises— more disgusting noises— to clear it.

But I didn't want to make disgusting noises there, in the little barn. It was all so Pure. And here I was, poised to wreck this Purity, with disgusting noises. And what was more: would these noises not be even more incriminating than had been my stomach sounds the night before? Insofar as my project to Imitate Truly the Idea not only of a Philosopher...but of a Hippie, or Freak, was concerned? Was Tommy struggling to hold back mucus as he milked the goat amid the piles of hay? He was not! He instead, and at last, was displaying precisely those attributes which I had long been sure belonged to a True Imitation of the Idea of a Hippie Farmer. Patience. Tranquillity. Simplicity. Such as these might have been defined by Socrates himself, through Dialogue. While I, no more than a few feet away, could increasingly think only of my itching eyes, and dripping throat, and the build-up of mucus in my nose. The irony was sickening. I might even have felt like weeping, had my eyes not been running anyway, and starting to puff and swell. The itching made me want to rub them. But I knew from experience that if I started, I would trigger a chain reaction. For they would then itch even more. And I would rub them more. So that the skin around them would turn almost purple. And balloon so I could barely see.

This had happened before. But always during the summer, on drives in the country with my parents. They had always given me an anti-histamine. And my father had closed the windows, and switched on the air conditioner. We had then driven back to the suburbs. So that I could go and lie in the basement.

But this time, there was neither anti-histamine, nor air conditioner, nor basement. There was instead as True an Imitation of the Idea of a Country Scene as I had ever encountered. Or even imagined. With Tommy in his work suit and faded cap, and even his rubber boots. And beside him the little goat, being patiently milked in the pool of yellow light. Amid piles of hay— True Imitations of the Idea of Country Things if there ever were such. And with Tommy proving, by his very silence, that as— at that moment— the Truest of All True Imitations of the Idea of a Country Hippie, he had as great a mastery over his mucus as, the night before, he had proved to have over his stomach sounds. As an Imitation of the Idea of a Philosopher.

Which mastery I had also lacked. I felt most inadequate. As well as desperate. I fought back the urge to hork, and continued to swallow mucus while sniffling quietly. But would I be able to keep this silence? The answer was not long in coming. For in the continued presence of these True Imitations of the Idea of Country Things— the particles of hay dust, I mean— I had to sneeze. I tried to suppress this. But I could not. Suddenly, the sneeze was upon me. And once I began, I couldn't stop. One sneeze. Another sneeze. Another. Another.

I heard Tommy's voice.

"Hey man," it said— for I could no longer see him, I was sneezing so hard— "What's the matter? Have you got hay fever?"

I couldn't answer. I could only sneeze. My nose ran. My eyes ran. I couldn't see. But I did wonder silently— as I did or did not do every one of these things— whether this might be a further effect also, of the "Renfrew Rocket." In that, like the need to go to the bathroom, the hay fever now seemed overwhelming. It was as though I were trapped, in a steadily contracting universe of snot, and mucus, and itching, and swelling, and sneezing. I tried to speak, to answer Tommy. But I could not.

"Hey man," said Tommy's voice. "Maybe you'd better get out of here. Just go outside and wait, okay? I'll be fast."

I was dimly aware, as he said this, of the profound new irony that was implicit, even in this familiar Hippie greeting, which I had first encountered in the Authoritative Hippie Books. "Hey man." Which throughout my visit, I realized, could have, even should have been interpreted, by me, as a warning. To wit: "Hay man!" Which I had not heeded. Having become too "hung up"— as the Hippie saying went— on the second part of this greeting. The "Man" part.

How extraordinary language can be! Premonitory, even. If we only Listen.

But I hadn't Listened. I realized I had better start. For Tommy was, at this point, obviously giving me good advice. To go outside. Yet I did not want to follow this advice.

Because to do so would be to admit defeat, at last, in my hopes of ever Imitating Truly the Idea of a Country Hippie. And to admit the victory of that vile betrayer of these hopes: my body. I therefore tried to stay. I shook my head, to let Tommy know my intention. But only throwing, as I did so, streams of snot in a wide arc all around me. I could feel them swirling forth, these streams of snot. But I ignored them...and reached out, instead, to touch the goat, so as to re-establish the connection I had felt before. But no sooner did my hand touch her fur than I was forced to double over with a bout of sneezing. It was as though my very lungs were now proclaiming, irrefutably, the failure of my ambition. And it was at this moment, too, that— with no other option— I ceased resisting. I began to hork. I blew snot out of one nostril, and then the other, pushing my index finger into each, the better to focus the stream. But not caring where it went. While with the knuckles of my other hand I rubbed my eyes.

Then I felt Tommy's hands on my back, a gentle pressure that propelled me toward— I had to assume— the door.

"Here, man," I heard him say. "Let's get out of here. Before you choke."

My only response could be to let him direct me. Because my own living flesh had by this time set its own priorities. The sneeze. The clutching at nostrils. The ejection of snot. The loud hork. Another sneeze. The series repeating itself. Again. And again.

I felt the colder air on my face, as Tommy pushed me through the open door. His hand slapped my back. I wheezed, and rubbed my eyes. They itched even more.

"Okay, man, okay, it'll be all right," Tommy was saying as he slapped my back. "Just take it easy. Get it out. Jesus Christ, why didn't you tell me you had an allergy? It's okay. Just get it out."

"Because..." I tried to say. But all that came out was another wheeze. Along with globs of drool. But I wanted to tell him that I hadn't known the barn would be full of hay. Or that he would use this hay, to feed the goat. Or that this usage would release clouds of stored-up pollen. Or that this pollen, once released, would— in the penultimate phase of this chain reaction— act as a trigger. For that further series of biochemical breakdowns, in "my" body, that would announce, decisively...my failure.

I could only sneeze. Bending above the sodden grass with my hands on my knees. Or rubbing my eyes. Or compressing my nostrils.

I was reminded, as I did this, of my deluded ruse the day before. When I had stood in identical position, and pretended to vomit. The better to keep Tommy from suspecting me, about his girl friend.

Another— and far worse— repetition. When I had thought they were over. And I had broken through...into something...else.

"Oh, Jesus," Tommy said above me. "Just let me get the lamp, okay? Or no. I'd better try and finish with Camilla. Because otherwise, she won't know what's going on. Just stay here a minute, man, okay? It'll just take a minute. Honest."

His arms went off my shoulders. I stood alone in the darkness, leaning forward, wheezing, rocking back and forth. I couldn't see. But I could feel the rain— the cold rain— on my head. It was not drizzle any more, but rain. This was as bad as falling into the mud had been. Or worse. At least in the mud I had still had some expectations. However few. But now, even these were gone. I was obliged to admit, as I stood there, that I would never make a True Imitation of the Idea of a Country Hippie. Never. And not only on account of problems with the lack of other such Imitations, at Tommy's Farm. Or the furtive presence, of locals with shotguns, and hunters with gutting knives. All of which were external to me. But on account of my body. The body I had been born with. Which continued— with its own blind momentum— the production of mucus. And tears. And sneezes. And sniffles. These just kept on, as though my body were indifferent, utterly indifferent, to the decisions— the concessions, even— that my Mind had made.

It then occurred to me, as I was leaning over, that my body certainly did have much in common, in this respect, with the rain and the mud and the darkness. All of which had seemed so indifferent to me since my arrival. And that Tommy, too— uniting them under the rubric of Mother Nature— had said were indifferent to him. Socrates had been right, then, about that split between the body and the Rational Soul, that he promoted in the *Phaedo*. Because it was obvious that "my" body, with its allergies, did not care a whit about my dreams of Imitating Truly the Idea of a Country Hippie. In fact, it was obvious that "my" body didn't "care" about anything. It just went about its business, the way the trees did, and the rain, and the sodden grass. This, then, was yet another epiphany for me, a very different one, as I stood there precisely amid the trees, the rain, and the sodden grass. In that I realized *I* could no more be a part of that body, which was responding in its own dumb way with sneezing, sniffling, and horking, than I was of the night and the trees and the rain. For even if my body itself reacted, mindlessly, to that part of Mother Nature called "hay," still it shared with Mother Nature a profound indifference. To my very Essence. Precisely as Mind.

"Socrates," I wheezed, unable to contain my excitement at this new understanding. The revelation burst from my lips, mixing as it did with the streams of mucus that were pouring from my nose. "Socrates," I cried. "You were right. Transcendence. The body must be transcended. Transcended. TRANSCENDED."

I believe that in the midst of this outburst, I began to walk, or to stagger, the prisoner of revelation. "Transcendence," I was saying. Between the sneezes. "Transcendence." I stopped and blew my nose into the grass. "Transcendence. The Pure Light of Consciousness. Transcendence."

"Hey, man. Man?" I heard Tommy's voice saying, in the distance. "Where are you?"

I turned around. My eyes were by this time so swollen I could barely see. But I was able to make out, through the thin slits left between puffed-up skin, a yellow glow. I stumbled toward this. "Transcendence," I wheezed, as best I could. In order to share with him the sheer power of this revelation. And also to let him know that I had not disappeared. "Transcendence," I repeated. "Transcendence."

The glow got brighter.

"Man?" said Tommy's voice. And suddenly it was right beside me. I felt his hand on my shoulder. But I could not see him very well. Only the yellow glow.

"We'd better go back to the house now, man," Tommy said. "I'm not sure I can take much more."

I let him lead me. Yet again. I also lapsed into silence. For, given his comment, that he was not sure he could "take much more," perhaps he would be unprepared for the sheer intensity of my revelation. Concerning the body. And its indifference to higher strivings.

## §16

I was once more supine, on the pile of rags. Tommy had placed me there, and then had left. First, to go back downstairs with the lamp, to find another candle. And then, when he had lit this, to go back to the barn. In order, he said, to finish with Camilla.

I lay there sniffling. My eyes were slits. The ceiling was a flickering blur, in the candlelight. I could barely move.

Nevertheless, from within a zone of Thought that was perfectly clear, I grasped that I had achieved...Transcendence. It was a Transcendence, yes, that seemed to have little to do with my long-time goal, of Imitating Truly the Idea of a Country Hippie. Yet it was also a Transcendence wedded profoundly to my other goal: of Imitating Truly the Idea of a Philosopher. For I felt I had at last understood, as Socrates did, the sheer indifference of the fleshly body to this latter, exalted calling. Even as my body, in this very indifference, had revealed to me the sheer impossibility of my ever Imitating, Truly, the Idea of a Country Hippie. This, for me, was a decisive moment. When I Transcended also, at last, the flawed intermingling of two goals that were— for me— incompatible. Leaving the Other behind. In favour of the One.

I experienced, then, as I lay on my back in the pile of rags, and in spite of the sniffling and horking and itching in my eyes, a feeling of profound peace. Of success even, that far outweighed my disappointment. For I was, admittedly, still disappointed a little, at the failure of this intermingling. Which had taken place even at the moment of my discovering— improbably, given all that had gone before— clear evidence that the Idea of Hippieness was indeed being Imitated Truly. At Tommy's Farm. And clear evidence, too, that Tommy himself could— under certain conditions— be precisely that Truest of All True Imitations, of the Idea of a Country Hippie. That I had long imagined him to be.

Such irony! And such paradox! For had Tommy himself not as much as said, in the kitchen that morning, that this entire project— of Imitating the Idea of a Country Hippie, or Freak— for him retained little interest? Yet was he not, at that very moment, still out in the barn with the goat? And Imitating, in the Truest of All True Ways, just that Idea? Was he aware at all, of the extent of his inconsistency? Or had living with it every day simply numbed him? Granted, that his Farm's Imitation of the Idea of a Hippie Farm had seemed initially to shrink to the scale of a cold dark house, and a rain-soaked landscape that was— according to him— infested with hunters. And granted also, that any Imitation of the Idea of a Hippie Commune seemed still to reside only in the piles of communal poop at the bottom of the outhouse hole. But what I had seen in the barn superseded all of this. So that in watching Tommy with the goat— before I had been stricken with hay fever— I had grasped that it was in these simplest of surroundings...that I was seeing him revealed. As what he was supposed to Be.

Yet there was more. Much more. For did Tommy not demonstrate also, as he went about this Imitation, a mastery— impossible for me— of both stomach sounds and mucus that surely even Socrates, in his deepest Perplexity, would envy? A mastery, that is, which through Transcendence of bodily weakness appertained precisely to the Imitation not of the Idea of a Country Hippie...but of the Idea of a Philosopher! Here, then, was evidence of that Higher Intermingling of these two Goals of which I— not to mention the intermingled poop in the outhouse hole— was incapable. Indeed, was it not the mastery of mucus which enabled him to Imitate, in the barn, the Idea of a Country Hippie with such success? Nor was this the only such evidence that Tommy had given. Had he not also, in first milking the goat, then bringing me to the house in my time of need, and finally returning to the goat, shown something else? Namely: that truly Kantian commitment to Duty, which I had first noticed in the truck! And which also suggested— albeit in a Kantian way— his continued Imitation of the Idea of a Philosopher! So that in this "much more" lay Tommy's Synthesis— embryonic and provisional, perhaps— of precisely those two projects which were beyond my capacity. Namely: True Imitation of *both* the Idea of a Hippie Farmer, and the Idea of a Philosopher. At the same time.

But clearly, this Synthesis was within Tommy's grasp only under certain conditions. Which, to go on evidence gleaned before I fell victim to my treacherous body, were: in the barn, and with the goat. For only there, and in that labour, had been displayed the Purity which I could identify with a True Imitation of the Idea of a Hippie Farm. Even as Tommy, in Imitation of the Idea of a Philosopher, had been carrying out his Duty and maintaining his Mastery, over both mucus and stomach sounds. All of which seemed to imply, then, that as long as Tommy stayed in the barn with the goat, he was capable of this Synthesis. As I could never be. Whereas, by contrast, when he was in the house, he had seemed— even in the course of Hippie Ritual— to be laden down. And not just with his own Cares. But with the inherited Cares of all those generations of faith-bound Farmers. Who had, he said, built the house as a fortress. A palisade. A watchtower.

It became clear to me, then, in this process of sustained Reflection, that Tommy still deserved to be the object of my admiration. But not only of my admiration. Of my help! Toward achieving with greater consistency that goal which Transcendence was enabling me to understand was within his powers, even as it lay beyond mine. Namely: the Ultimate Dialectical Synthesis, between the Being of a True Imitation of the Idea of a Country Hippie, which I had seen him achieve in the barn...and the Becoming of a True Imitation of the Idea of a Philosopher. For he still, I feared, had a distance to go in regard to the latter. And not only on account of his preference for Kant over Socrates. But also, and perhaps especially— I Recollected with further Insight— on account of his sad entanglement with those False Imitations, of the Idea of Beautiful Naked Girls, that still lay beside the pile of rags.

Or...I assumed they still lay there.

I hadn't looked, because I had been so ill when Tommy brought me back to the room.

Except that now, with the clarity of Thought which Transcendence of bodily limits had granted me...I began to sense just how significant the presence of these False Imitations might be. For might they not inhibit Tommy's reaching with consistency that Dialectical Synthesis of which he was capable? And which he deserved? Because they themselves discouraged Transcendence of base desires? Of bodily need? Even though they might— theoretically— serve as Aids to Contemplation, of mathematically perfect Female Form. Or of Imitations Thereof. Yet had I not— that very morning— myself experienced the potential treachery, of such Contemplation?

I was, I realized, back to my original dilemma, which had been interrupted by the call to breakfast. But since which so much had happened, that could only enrich both my Understanding of the situation, and— on account of Transcendence— my Logical Capacity to deal with it! For was the response of my own vile body to these False Imitations any more paradigmatic...than had been the unruliness of both my stomach sounds and my mucus? What if Tommy had mastered— in a way that I could not, and as successfully as he had mastered both his stomach sounds and mucus— the baser inclinations of his own body during such Contemplation? And what if he did employ these False Imitations, as aids not only toward Contemplating Mathematically Perfect Female Form...but also toward Mortification of fleshly desire? This would change the picture— so to speak— completely. For it would imply that, even as he Imitated Truly the Idea of a Hippie Farmer in the barn with Camilla...he was Imitating on-the-way-to-Truly the Idea of a Philosopher in the house, with the magazines!

The clarity of my Reasoning on this matter was truly remarkable. And such had been its intensity that I was now even lying on my side. The freshly sniffled snot trickled down my throat. And my eyes itched. Yet these discomforts only further spurred the relentlessness of my Thought, in the interest of Tommy's Potential. I looked around, through my slitty eyes. Did he, then, keep the strands of barbed wire, or at least the rods made from local birch, somewhere nearby? With which he subdued his noodle? Or— who could tell?— his entire anatomy, including his stomach sounds and mucus. Every morning. Standing naked in the presence of these False Imitations. Flagellating himself— or at least his potentially rebellious Flesh— into complete cooperation.

The next step, clearly, would be to Investigate. In order to confirm, if I could, this hypothesis. For if I did find strands of barbed wire, or birch rods bundled together, or perhaps even flecks of dried blood strewn across the floor...then would this not be evidence— circumstantial, but almost conclusive— that Tommy did employ the False Imitations toward Mortifying Fleshly Desire? And that in consequence they did contribute, on an ongoing basis, toward his own True Imitation of the Idea of a Philosopher...

But even as I dragged my body into sitting position on the pile of rags, so as to search the room for barbed wire, or for bundles of birch rods...I had to wonder about their role...in his Imitation of the Idea of a Country Hippie. Not the barbed wire or the birch rods directly, I mean. But the False Imitations. For the goal was to aid, was it not, Tommy's capacity to Harmonize— Dialectically, and in a way closed to me— his Imitation of these two Ideas: of a Philosopher and of a Country Hippie. And how— even if he did lacerate his noodle, or for that matter his entire body, with barbed wire or birch rods every morning— would this contribute to such Harmonization? The answer to this question suggested itself with the Clarity of Transcendent Intuition! Why, clearly by rendering him the more impervious, to the Temptations of Consumer Society! Which themselves were as inimical to the one Idea, as to the other.

But did he? Lacerate his noodle, I mean. Of this I was not yet sure. Had he, perhaps, in his Wisdom, another way of using these False Imitations, toward Higher Synthesis? The complexity of this question was such that I felt, momentarily, the pull of weakness. Physically speaking. My head ached. Snot dripped from my nose, and trickled into my mouth. My eyes still itched, and were so puffed up I could barely see. I could have used some kleenex. Since I was swallowing snot, in great amounts. This was most uncomfortable. But I could not blow snot onto the bedroom floor as I had been able outside to blow it into the grass. And neither, I knew, did Tommy, as a True Imitation of the Idea of a Country Hippie, sink to the use even of such small Temptations of Consumer Society as kleenexes. Not even in the outhouse. So instead, as the latest expedient, I pulled out my shirt-tail, and blew the snot— first from one nostril and then the other— into the plaid pattern of its fabric.

But having done this, I realized I must proceed with my Investigation. However much my miserable body wanted to collapse on the pile of rags, and even sleep. To persevere was, I resolved, the least I could do both in the cause of Transcendent Logic...and for Tommy himself. I pulled, therefore, on the swollen folds around my eyes, so that I might return for the sake of this mission to the world of the senses. The lids stuck together, as well as itched. While the expanded glands underneath my eyeballs had by this time so enlarged that they were— to the touch— like rubber balls. Although I knew from Experience that they probably looked more like sagging breasts.

I persisted, though, so that gradually my eyelids came unstuck. And having thus established a narrow band of visibility, I peered toward that area of floor, near the head of the sack, where Recollection told me the False Imitations should still be lying. In their pile. I had not the slightest intention of examining them myself, and of thereby risking that spell of their bewitchment, to which I had almost succumbed in the morning. No. It was mere reassurance I sought, that they had not been a dream perhaps, a figment of Imagination in the process of waking from sleep. In the flickering candlelight, though, I saw the blanket, just as I Recollected having left it that morning. Leaning forward, I raised it. And saw them. Or at least their edges.

So they were Real. Physically speaking. Yet did not their continued presence mean, then, that even if Tommy had himself Recollected having left them beside the sack...he had not retrieved them? I dropped the blanket. Lest I be tempted. But did this not imply also— the undisturbed presence of the pile, I mean— that he did not feel embarrassment, that I might see it? And could this not in turn hint— at least potentially— that he did not use these False Imitations toward unworthy goals: namely entanglement in bodily pleasure? But instead did employ them toward higher goals, namely Transcendence of Bodily Desire, enacted through denial of the vile Temptations of Consumer Society! Thus Synthesizing, in this very room, the Being and Becoming of those diverse Imitations of Diverse Ideas, Philosopher and Hippie, that for me were inaccessible!

Once again, I was much impressed with my Logic. And yet...I had still not found any evidence— the barbed wire, birch rods, flecks of dried blood— that this was how the magazines were used. And I had set myself the goal, to find such evidence. I made therefore to drag my aching body to my, or its feet. But even as I did so, I was overcome by the urge to sneeze. Perhaps in moving I had stirred up dust. My usual indifference to which had probably been translated— as had happened before— into allergy by my weakened frame. I could not suppress this urge. I sneezed. And sneezed again. And again. And again. By this time I was bent over double. But so much sneezing seemed also to trigger another deluge of mucus, from whatever pores· or sacs or crannies produce such gunk, inside the nostrils.

I reeled, in response to this latest assault by my despicable body. Nevertheless I knew that— for Tommy's sake— I had to surmount these perils. Drawing myself into a semblance of verticality, I shuffled closer to the centre of the room. But I did not see, in my field of vision such as it was, any evidence either of barbed wire or local birch rods. Only the same old cardboard boxes, flickering in the candlelight, and disgorging old clothes like ragged corpses.

I shuddered slightly, at this simile. Which had risen unbidden to my Mind.

Yet would it not make sense, I reasoned, as I strove to recover the equanimity of Transcendent Thought and banish such an image, that if Tommy made use of barbed wire, or of local birch rods for his morning flagellations, he would not store them far away from the magazines, in some rarely used part of the room?

No. He would probably store them near the magazines, as well as near the pile of rags where he slept. For convenience.

Turning, therefore, I made my way, unsteadily, back to the pile of rags. But before I got there, I was beset with another fit of sneezing, as well as of snot pouring from my nose. I employed my shirt-tail. This was getting soggy. As well as making the tip of my nose sore. But having once again blown and rubbed, I stood above the pile of rags and surveyed it. The shadow cast by my body in the candlelight prevented my inspecting it fully, however. So I stepped aside.

And such, by this time, was my body's debilitation, that in conducting this simple manoeuvre...I tripped. Perhaps on a shoelace. I fell headlong. And was forced to roll quickly, so as to avoid the wall. Thus landing sideways, on the pile of rags. In such a way as to raise more dust. I breathed this dust. And began to sneeze. My eyes ran. As did my nose. Copiously. With some desperation, I looked around me. For a means of relieving this latest deluge.

And then, through a screen of tears and mucus...I saw it. Pushed between the pile of rags and the wall. In such a way as, evidently, to have been exposed by my disruption of the rags, when I tumbled into them.

It looked...like a crumpled kleenex.

A...kleenex?

Even in my state of debility...I realized instantly that this seemed incongruous.

For there was not even toilet paper in the outhouse.

Why, then, would there be...a kleenex? In the pile of rags.

Nevertheless, I viewed this kleenex with profound relief. For was it not what I needed? To staunch the flow of snot and mucus from my nostrils?

I reached for it, this little miracle of a kleenex, which seemed to have appeared to me, to have been placed before me, at the perfect moment.

But then, as I touched it, the very instant that my fingers came into contact with its stiff crumpled surface...I realized.

This was a kleenex which had been subjected to no innocent use.

A kleenex which had been subjected to no use whatever that was in keeping with a True Imitation of the Idea of a Philosopher. Such as Socrates.

Nor even a kleenex which had been subjected to a use that was in keeping with a True Imitation of the Idea of a Country Hippie. As had been revealed to me. By the Authoritative Hippie Books.

I withdrew my fingers. Quickly.

No.

This kleenex...

And instantly, I realized the folly of my hope, that Tommy was employing the False Imitations of the Idea of Naked Girls toward Mortification of his Fleshly Desires. And the folly, too, of my hope that his encounters with these False Imitations was accompanied, admirably, with Flagellations. And the folly, still further, of my hope that these False Imitations were contributing, in any way, to Tommy's Imitation of the Idea either of a Philosopher...or of a Country Hippie. Never mind both at once.

For Tommy evidently was, in the presence of these False Imitations, surrendering to their bewitchments. As among the most tempting of all Temptations, of Consumer Society. And in so surrendering, emptying himself— and who could tell how often— of his Essential Maleness. That— I knew from sad Experience— provided in its dried out Form the stiff crumpled texture of the kleenex that I had touched.

The waste of it all!

Vigorously, I wiped my hand on the pile of rags, to cleanse it of this pollution. For this was a pollution, of that there could be no doubt. Had Socrates himself not stressed the need for Chasteness, in a True Imitation of the Idea of a Philosopher? In order that his Intuition might stay Clear and Pure? And in order that his grasp of Ideas, of which visible things are mere Imitations, might be honed?

Why, no wonder Tommy seemed so imperfect an Imitation of the Idea of a Philosopher! And no wonder he seemed also such an inconsistent Imitation of the Idea of a Country Hippie! For in evacuating himself— perhaps habitually— of the True Mystical Essence of Masculine Substance that Resides in Semen...he was clearly scrambling Everything up!

I rose to my knees. My nose still ran, and lifting up my shirt-tail, I blew into it. My Mind was reeling, from this discovery. For what else could it be...but irrefutable Evidence of what Tommy was doing, many mornings and perhaps many evenings too, as he lay alone in this filthy room, in this cold dank house...with the False Imitations. I shook my head.

Poor Tommy.

No wonder he had so pessimistic a view, when he was in this house.

No wonder he seemed so little like a True Imitation of the Idea of a Country Hippie.

And no wonder it took his getting out of here, and going to the barn to be with the little goat, for any semblance of this True Imitation to be revived.

But that it did revive I had little doubt. I had seen it do so. With my own senses. Insofar of course as these provide accurate evidence. Of anything.

Nevertheless, this sort of evidence was, at that moment, all I had to go on. And it seemed to point, irrefutably, to the seriousness of the situation. Which was so far gone that even Tommy himself seemed powerless, to release himself. What sort of hold, then, did this dark cold house have on him? Was he its prisoner? Did it in fact contain ghosts— angry ghosts— of the many generations of farmers who had lived in it, and worked in it, and probably even died in it? Hungry for the Resurrection that was promised them by their Faith? But angry and bitter that they had worked so hard. All their lives.

I swallowed— snot as well as saliva— and looked around me. I would, I knew, be taking a tremendous gamble, with the angry ghosts. Assuming they existed. And yet— I realized in this further instant of Transcendent Insight— this was a gamble I would need to take. And who could tell? Perhaps, in releasing Tommy, I would also be releasing them. For had they not also— or at least the better part of them— built the barn? And worked in it? So that they too might want to be freed to go back to it? For this was what I realized I had to do. Provide terms of release, for Tommy certainly, and maybe even for the ghosts themselves, from the hold of the house, and of the False Imitations that it contained! In order that he would be freed, to bring to fulfilment that

Synthesis of True Imitations, that Higher State of Being, of which I was myself incapable. But regarding which I could at least serve as helper.

And it was at this moment that I Understood, too, that Tommy himself, through the name he had been calling me by, had indeed been Calling me, in a deeper way! One even more profound than that which had seemed to emanate from behind the lamp the night before. For had I not realized, as I stood in the mud outside the truck, shivering and soaking wet, that the name "Man" owed as much to the legacy of Kant, as to that of Hippieness? And that as such it signalled Tommy's will to— if not his achievement of— Synthesis. So that in assigning this name *to* me, had he not been investing *in* me— perhaps unconsciously— his hope that I would help him translate this naming into a Synthesis both more enduring, and more comprehensive. For him.

I knew then, according to the sheer power of Transcendent Intuition, exactly what I had been Called to do.

What Tommy had been expressing the desire I do...every time he addressed me as "Man"!

For it was I who could— who would— provide to him the Transforming Light!

A heavy burden. But one that I was prepared to shoulder.

For his sake.

Turning, I knelt beside the pile of rags and extended my hand. I felt them there, beneath their own rag, in their cold hard pile. The False Imitations. I fought down the urge to sneeze. And also— in my own weakness— to touch them. To uncover them. To look at them...

To look for pictures...of Allie.

For I Recollected also, in this moment of touch, precisely what I had been doing, when interrupted by Tommy. With his summons to breakfast.

But did it matter now, whether the magazines held pictures of Allie specifically or not? Given how Tommy used them?

Only insofar, perhaps, as she had seemed to me...the Truest of All

True Imitations, of the Idea of a Hippie Girl. Just as Tommy himself had seemed the Truest of All True Imitations, of a Hippie. The difference being, however, that I now had evidence Tommy could still, under the right conditions and with help, be such an Imitation. Whereas with Allie...

What could I possibly learn then, from the magazines, about her? Even if they contained...her picture?

Only that she had Fallen! From being the Truest of All True Imitations of the Idea of a Hippie Girl. To being no more than a vehicle, via the surfaces of her own vile and naked body, for Consumer Society to deploy its False Imitations. Its Temptations!

Did I want to know this?

For what could I do to help...a frozen Image?

Or for that matter any of the frozen Images, in the magazines. Even if all of them were — like those of Allie— depictions of the bodily surfaces, naked, of Former Imitations of the Idea of Hippie Girls? What could I do? Even if all of them had Fallen?

Nothing! Whereas with Tommy, who was even then out in the barn with the little goat, there was Hope!

Through this Reasoning, then, I fought back the urge to look. As— it was clear from the crumpled kleenex— Tommy himself had not been able to do. And perhaps never would do, so long as this house continued to exercise its hold on him. Through the puffed-up slits that defined my field of vision, I noticed again, in the candlelight, the shambles of Tommy's room. The peeling wallpaper. The cardboard boxes. The scattered rags. All of which seemed now to fit, with the magazines. As well as with the use Tommy made of them.

I had rescued Tommy once, from the "Bad Vibes."

I could— I told myself silently— rescue him again.

But I could not hesitate. Lest the False Imitations, in their insidious and silent allure, begin to dissuade me. Sapping my resolve. As well as—

who could tell— eventually the very Essence of my own Masculinity. As they had already sapped Tommy's.

Accordingly, I set to work. With great Resolve.

Flipping back the rag that covered the pile of False Imitations, I refused to regard them. Instead, keeping my eyes raised to heaven, I felt for, then seized, then picked up the topmost magazine. Its glossy coldness. Bringing it round in front of me— but still without looking at it— I tore off its cover. Then, clenching my teeth I crumpled this, and threw it onto the floor.

My nose was running. I blew it out. Not troubling to use my shirt any longer.

I tore out the second page. And crumpled it. And threw it onto the floor.

The third page. The fourth. The fifth.

As I was doing this, however, I realized how much this process recalled my visit to the outhouse. The crumpling up of False Images. Of Temptations of Consumer Society. Those others— the kind that were contained in the Catalogue— Tommy clearly had been able to master, as he had been able to master so much else. Yet they just as clearly retained a hold, when they took this special shape. Namely: the False Imitation of the Idea of Female Beauty.

I sighed. And tore out another page.

By the time I had finished with the first magazine, I could see through my swollen eyelids that I had made quite a pile. All crumpled. I proceeded to the next magazine. Still— and with what I cannot but view as remarkable Self-Discipline— avoiding looking at any pictures. Or pages. Each one of which I tore out, with great resolution. Stopping only to evacuate my nostrils, directly onto the wooden floor. But I knew I had also to hurry. Lest Tommy come back, from his encounter with the little goat, and then attempt to mount the stairs, to check on my well-being.

The second magazine. The third. The fourth.

I would succeed. For the second time in two days. In rescuing Tommy. But it now seemed that the initial rescue, too, in Squoon-Cased Jinty-Fied's store, was a rehearsal for this one. As well as a warning. So that I also resolved, as I tore and crumpled the pages, that I would not make the mistake this time of looking back. Which had come so close, in the store, of vitiating the entire Rescue by trapping me. And as in that case it had been Joon-Squaced Finty at whom I looked...so this time it would be— I knew— my relenting and looking— even once— at a magazine. For pictures...of...Allie...

At once I felt my firm resolve weaken. I felt the tingles. The limpness. Saw the long blonde hair. The painting by Botticelli. All before me. But in Imagination. While I might be holding, in my very hands...

I closed my eyes.

Furiously, I tore out a page. Crumpled it. Tore out another. Crumpled it. And another. And another. Throwing each as I crumpled it onto the pile of crumpled pages. That I could see through the slits that served as eyes was rising steadily, in front of me.

I blew my nose onto the floor and sniffled. My throat itched.

The longing...that I felt for Allie...

Or for pictures of Allie...

However False the Imitation...

For a moment, I believe I almost swooned.

The long blonde hair...

The...

I tore the pages.

Crumpled them.

Threw them onto the floor.

I could not turn back.

Not least because if Tommy came into the room and saw...

Would he understand?

At the very least, on account of my need to explain, the momentum would be lost. And perhaps, even, the possibility.

For *would* he understand?

Or if he did understand...agree?

On account of his own...weakness?

My hand grasped the last magazine.

The last.

I picked it up.

Held it before me.

Without looking at it.

Even though it might contain also...my last opportunity.

To look for pictures of Allie.

And even, perhaps, *at* pictures of Allie...

This was it.

The decisive moment.

Would I flag? In my Resolution?

Would I not, in doing so, fail Tommy? Profoundly?

And would I not also— perhaps even more importantly— fail the cause of Higher Synthesis, between the True Imitation of the Idea of a Country Hippie, and the True Imitation of the Idea of a Philosopher? Of which I— on account of the weakness of my own vile body— seemed incapable. But of which Tommy— "With a little help from his friends" as the saying in the Authoritative Hippie Books went— might just be capable?

I was convinced.

I ripped the magazine down the middle. Tore apart the pages. Crumpled them. Threw them down.

This was it.

I walked to where I could see, through my slitty eyes, the candle's flicker.

I knelt beside it, and pried the candle itself off the floor.

Holding it up, I walked slowly clockwise, around the pile of False Imitations.

"I hereby liberate Tommy," I said, "from slavery to Illusion." I swept my free hand slowly from left to right as I walked. Taking in the entire room.

Then, when I had reached the starting point of my circumnaviga-tion around the pile...I once more knelt. And this time held the candle to the crumpled pages.

Lit one.

Then, moving to the left, another.

And another...

It did not take long for the entire pile to become a roaring pyre, of False Imitations.

I watched the flames, until they had merged into one immense Light. Of cleansing Truth. And also until I was sure they would be unstoppable. By Tommy. Should he not, upon seeing them, grasp my Logic. Instantly.

The room shone white.

The fire moved across the floor.

Toward the boxes. The piles of rags. The walls, with their peeling paper.

I turned and— this time with no last look— rushed down the stairs.

To retrieve my suitcase.

And my bedroom slippers.